THE TUSCAN ORPHAN

SIOBHAN DAIKO

Boldwood

First published in Great Britain in 2023 by Boldwood Books Ltd.

Copyright © Siobhan Daiko, 2023

Cover Design by Lizzie Gardiner

Cover Photography: Shutterstock

A CIP catalogue record for this book is available from the British Library.

Paperback ISBN 978-1-83751-873-9

Large Print ISBN 978-1-83751-869-2

Hardback ISBN 978-1-83751-868-5

Ebook ISBN 978-1-83751-866-1

Kindle ISBN 978-1-83751-867-8

Audio CD ISBN 978-1-83751-874-6

MP3 CD ISBN 978-1-83751-871-5

Digital audio download ISBN 978-1-83751-865-4

Boldwood Books Ltd
23 Bowerdean Street
London SW6 3TN
www.boldwoodbooks.com

In memory of World War II nurses, whose bravery and dedication to duty inspired this book.

PROLOGUE
MIMI, TUSCANY, AUTUMN 1944

'*Non avere paura*,' a voice whispers. Don't be scared. '*Stai all'ospedale*.' You're in the hospital. '*Prendiamo cura di te*.' We're looking after you.

I blink my eyes open. My head feels heavy, and my mind is woozy. There's a lady sitting on a chair right beside me. '*Ciao, tesoro*.' Hi, darling. '*Come ti chiami*?' What's your name?

'Mimi.' I attempt a smile.

The woman is a nurse, I realise, and she smiles right back at me. '*Mi chiamo Carrie*,' she says.

I'm tired, so I fall into the strangest dream.

I was huddling with my friends in the back of a truck, my heart booming. We'd left the convent where the nuns were looking after us only a short time ago, all of us terrified because German soldiers had locked us up in the cellar until two men had come to rescue us.

It had been the most horrible time of my life. Not as bad as when I'd had to leave Mammina and Babbo behind in Florence a year before, when I was only four – that had made me cry for days and days – but horrible all the same. We could hear the soldiers' loud voices coming from the dining room above us. The nuns were praying and we were crying and then we heard big explosions and we could smell burning. Our eyes stung.

Someone began to shoot at the cellar door, and we cried out in fear. A tall man ran forward and Sister Immacolata called out his name. Vito. She picked me up and ran towards him. He took me from her and kissed her on both cheeks.

'Our prayers brought you to us,' she said.

Mother Superior spoke next. 'I presume you killed those Germans. May their souls rest in peace.'

'Indeed.' Vito shifted me onto his hip. 'We'd best go back upstairs and work out a plan.'

We met another man in the hallway, and Vito asked him to check on the German vehicle outside.

I wriggled in Vito's arms and stared at him.

'*Ciao*,' he said before introducing himself.

I felt shy and buried my face in his chest.

'So,' he said to Sister Immacolata. 'Who are these children and why are they with you?'

'They're Tuscan. From Florence. Their parents are Jewish and went into hiding from the SS after the Wehrmacht occupied the area. The church arranged for us to take the *bambini* into our care. I don't suppose they ever imagined the front could possibly move up here.'

'Ah.' Vito frowned.

His friend ran back into the hall, a set of keys jangling in his hand. 'These were still in the truck's ignition.'

'Excellent.' Vito turned to him and suggested that he go to Bologna. 'I'll meet you there as soon as I can,' he added.

'Don't you need my help?' the friend asked.

'There isn't enough room in that truck with the nuns and

children. And it would draw too much attention if you marched alongside us.'

'Where are you heading?'

'Florence,' he said.

My heart leapt. We were going home.

Sister Immacolata touched his arm. 'Are you sure this is a good idea? There's a big battle going on in the area between San Ruffillo and the road south.'

'Germans are attacking from the north. We'll soon be at the rear of the Allied lines.'

After Vito and his friend helped us all climb aboard the truck, his friend shook his hand and wished him luck.

Vito got behind the steering wheel and started the engine. The truck set off up a winding, narrow dirt road, its massive tyres churning up chunks of mud.

I grasped hold of Sister Immacolata's arm.

Something had landed on the road.

The truck juddered to a stop.

A bomb exploded with a loud bang. It covered us in dust and bits of rock.

My whole body began shaking.

'Get out,' Vito yelled. 'We need to take cover.'

German soldiers were coming down the road towards us. My heart thudded as loud as a drum.

Vito helped the nuns from the truck, then he picked me up and ran towards some trees. 'Follow me,' he shouted.

And then, without warning, he stopped running.

More soldiers were coming from the opposite direction.

Bullets whistled past my ears.

Explosions made me cry out in fear again.

A sharp pain pierced my forehead.

I opened my mouth and gave a scream.

1

AIN EL TURK, ALGERIA, SEPTEMBER 1943

A warm breeze, redolent with the fragrance of jasmine flowers, blew a strand of hair into Carrie's eyes. She tucked the errant blonde curl under her cap, her chest fluttering with anticipation.

The truck on which she was travelling had pulled up in front of the hospital staging area. She adjusted the olive-green cuffs of her uniform jacket, proudly glancing at the insignia worn on her epaulettes. The single yellow bar indicated she was a second lieutenant, like all newly recruited American Army nurses. The gold-coloured US pin worn on both of her collars, and the golden caduceus with a red N on each lapel, shone brightly in the African sunshine as she climbed down from the back of the four-tonne vehicle, about to start the biggest adventure of her life.

She bumped arms with Louise, the fellow nurse she'd met on board the USS *Edmund B. Alexander*. The ocean liner, which had been converted into a troop ship, had brought them to Oran from New York, zigzagging across the Atlantic, completely blacked out to avoid U-boat attacks. It was only after they'd sailed that they'd gotten the low-down on their destination: a troop convalescent facility in Algeria.

'Well, we're finally "over yonder",' Carrie said to Louise as they went to find their luggage.

Louise's laugh tinkled. 'You mean "over there", eh, Tex?'

Louise had given Carrie the nickname from the outset and Carrie, not wanting to use the pejorative term 'hillbilly', called her new friend 'Kenny' in return. Chubby, with chestnut-brown hair and hazel-coloured eyes, Louise hailed from Kentucky. She smoked a corncob pipe and had taught Carrie to play cribbage. They were both worried about how they'd cope so far away from home. During the crossing, they'd gone up on deck every night to gaze at the stars and escape the stuffy heat of their quarters below. There, they'd shared family tales and stories of their youth, promising they would look out for each other come what may.

Carrie gazed at the tented campsite up ahead, which was set on a bluff overlooking the azure Mediterranean Sea. They'd been told they'd be there only temporarily prior to being transferred inland. She pulled in and then slowly released a deep breath. Had she done the right thing?

She'd only just turned twenty-four when she'd enlisted a couple of months ago. Fresh out of nursing school, like many others, she'd rushed to answer Uncle Sam's call to join the Army Nurse Corps. She'd soon realised she had no clue what she was letting herself in for. The daily drills. Hup, two, three, four, left face, about face; lectures twice a day; foxholes dug into the dry earth beneath the hot Texas sun; obstacle courses, crawling in the dirt under barbed wire with live ammunition being fired overhead; the session in the gas chamber wearing impregnated clothing and a mask. Gritting her teeth, she'd soldiered on, excited about the prospect of serving overseas.

She set her jaw, picked up her kitbag and slung it over her

shoulder. Smiling, she linked arms with Louise. 'Let's go report for duty,' she said.

* * *

A week later, Carrie was strolling past the big red cross painted on the ground at the back of the General Hospital, erstwhile known as the Grand Hotel in Bou Hanifa. The building rose out of the desert like an art deco mirage and had been a hot water spa resort before its requisition by the US military. Palm trees swayed in the warm breeze and bare brown hills formed a backdrop to the scene.

Under her white nurse's cap, sweat prickled Carrie's hairline, and she rubbed her hands down the skirt of her seersucker ward dress. Shame she was no longer stationed by the ocean; at the staging camp, she and Louise had enjoyed swimming off the beach.

She stopped in her tracks. A tall man was approaching. A captain, judging by his insignia. She raised her arm and saluted.

'At ease, Lieutenant.' A smile gleamed in his light blue eyes. 'Have you just arrived?' He removed his hat and wiped his brow. Dark red hair cut short, Army-style, framed his freckled cheeks.

'Yes, I'm Carrie Adams. I've been stationed here to learn the ropes.' She tore her gaze from his attractive face.

'Bill Ainsworth, surgeon.' His accent sounded Midwestern. 'We need more nurses. We've been hard-pressed to handle the casualties sent here for further treatment from Sicily. Not to mention German and Italian POWs requiring surgery.'

'I'd like to specialise in surgical care,' she said. It had been a long-held ambition.

'Well, you've sure come to the right place.' He gave a wry laugh.

She laughed with him. 'I'd better shake a leg, sir. My shift is about to start.'

'No doubt we'll cross paths again.'

She wanted to say, I hope so, but that would have sounded dumb. Instead, she simply nodded and saluted once more.

After returning her gesture, he turned and set off in the direction of the tented accommodation area.

A sigh escaped her. Chances were the good-looking doctor had a wife back home in the States. As for her, she'd been too busy of late for a heartthrob and didn't expect the situation to change. There was a war on, wasn't there?

Her attention was drawn to the imposing white buildings up ahead. The main three-storey block housed the hospital, but a domed structure to the right bore the inscription 'Les Thermes'. She couldn't speak French but guessed the thermal baths were inside and wondered if the medical staff were allowed to use them.

She made her way up the wide front steps and reported to 1st Lieutenant Betty Thompson, nurse anaesthetist. Frizzy red hair poked out from under the older woman's cap. She gave Carrie a warm smile.

'Follow me, Lieutenant. We'll scrub up and then you can make a start.'

* * *

Carrie lifted her eyes from the letter she'd just received from Mom and Daddy. A small brown mouse had come into the tent. She stamped her foot to scare it away, but it simply stayed put and stared at her. Since disembarking in Algeria two months ago, she'd learnt that creatures in this country seemed to move at a snail's pace. Because of the daytime heat, she guessed. Whenever a fly landed on her arm, it wouldn't move until she'd brushed it off.

She returned her focus to her letter and carried on reading the latest news from home. Food, gas and clothing were still being rationed. The radio provided her parents with updates on the fighting overseas. They missed her, hoped she was safe and not too lonesome for them.

She folded the pages of the letter and tucked them back into the envelope. How she longed for her family. She remembered her eager-beaver attitude when she'd first arrived. She'd been so busy, she'd barely had time to think, let alone be homesick. Her work involved preparing the operating rooms for patients, setting up the equipment and making sure everything was sterile. She also helped the surgical teams into their masks, gloves and gowns. Her favourite job was when she was called upon to work with the physicians during surgery and pass them instruments. Often, she'd worked with Captain Ainsworth. Their eyes would meet over their masks as she passed him scissors, wound retractors, or forceps. Each time, a thrill would tingle through her and her pulse raced.

When not in the hospital, she liked to stroll around the village with Louise, making purchases to brighten up their barren tent. She'd bought a tufted rug made of natural-coloured wool that she'd placed beside her cot, together with an orange camel-skin hassock embossed in gold and a hand-woven blanket which went on her footlocker. A big copper tray with a hammered design, an artisan bowl, a jug and a wooden inlaid box completed the décor.

In the evenings, she went to parties and dances given by some of the nearby units. Men whirled her around the floor, cutting in constantly. She'd never been as popular in her life but reminded herself it was because there were so few girls and all the guys had been away from home for such a long time. Her head spun from dancing and listening to non-stop flattery, but there was only one person she longed to dance with. Bill. And dance with him she did. When they were both exhausted from jitterbugging, they would sit it out and talk. Being with him made her feel less lonesome for her folks.

She learnt he was born in December 1912 in Scranton, a small town in Pennsylvania, the third child and oldest son of a doctor and stay-at-home mom. Bill had played quarterback in high school and Georgetown University. After graduation, he'd taken the necessary science classes to apply to medical school and had gone on to study at Jefferson Medical College, from where he'd graduated in 1939. He'd done a year of internship followed by a year of residency in surgery before he'd been called to active duty. He was shipped overseas in November 1942, part of the Western Task Force whose mission it was to take Morocco from the Vichy French. He hadn't enjoyed Casablanca; there hadn't been enough for him to do. At the end of March, he was moved to Rabat where again he'd sat around reading surgical textbooks, doing calisthenics and going on marches. Finally, in early May, as a 'mobile surgeon' he was flown to Oran and from there transferred to the General Hospital, where he'd hit the deck running.

Carrie, in turn, recounted that she'd studied at the Texas Woman's University nursing school, having grown up in Dallas, the eldest daughter of schoolteacher parents. Her younger sister, Helen, taught grade school. Carrie shared with Bill that she enjoyed hiking, swimming and playing tennis. She'd hugged herself with joy when he'd revealed that he was single. Apparently, he, like her, had been too caught up with study to have time for a steady sweetheart.

She glared at the mouse and puffed out a quick breath. Rumours had been flying around of late that the General was soon to be closed as hospitals were being set up in Italy for convalescence instead. She recalled how, after the Allies had conquered Sicily, they'd launched attacks on the Italian mainland. An internal revolt had overthrown Mussolini, and the new Italian government had signed an armistice with the Allies. Everyone thought they would make haste to Rome and conquer the rest of the country in no time at all.

But the Germans had other ideas. Their reaction to the news of the Italian capitulation was to rapidly occupy the entire peninsula, disarm the leaderless Italian army, and smash any units who resisted.

On 9 September, the US 5th Army under General Mark W. Clark landed near Salerno, 150 miles up the western coast from the toe of the boot. Since Italy had capitulated, Clark expected only light opposition, seemingly. Perhaps a few coastal defence units who hadn't gotten the memo, but nothing serious.

Bill had a radio and listened to the BBC bulletins from London. He told Carrie that American troops had run into searing fire from the moment they'd hit the shore. Expecting Italians, Clark had met Germans. The adversary was a veteran, battle-tested unit – the 16th Panzer Division – who dug into strongpoints along the beach, with artillery emplaced on the high ground. Clark's shaken army had managed to land, but the unexpected resistance penned it into a shallow, vulnerable semicircle along the coast and, before too long, German attacks had crumpled the American beachhead.

But then the US had reached for the hammer and laid on their heavy metal. With assistance from their British allies, they'd poured down a rain of death on Jerry. On the first of October, the Britishers went on to occupy Naples without opposition, leaving the city to be garrisoned by the Americans, who'd set up a hospital there. Carrie chewed at her lip. Was that to be her next posting? She hoped she wouldn't be separated from Bill. He'd come to mean everything to her.

Her heart throbbed as she thought about him. That night, a dance had been organised on the roof of the hospital. She'd go for a bath in the spa before getting ready. One of the perks of staying here was that the blue-tiled *Thermes* had been made available for the staff. She planned to doll herself up so Bill would be proud of her. Maybe he'd even ask her to officially be 'his girl'.

She clasped her hands in prayer and pressed them to her lips. *Please, Lord, let it be so.*

* * *

'Dagnabbit, there's a peeping Tom mouse staring at me!' Louise exclaimed as she was putting on her white V-necked evening dress.

Carrie laughed. 'I've decided to call him Mickey.' The thought had just occurred to her. 'Ain't he cute?'

She smoothed the silk of the emerald-coloured gown she'd made for herself while at college and checked that the pencil-thin straps were securely placed.

Louise shooed the rodent out through the tent flap. 'If we leave him alone in here, he'll eat all my candy.'

Carrie giggled. Her roommate had the sweetest tooth she'd ever encountered. All Louise's parcels from home contained homemade cream toffees from her mom.

'He stayed put while I went for my bath. Anyway, I think mice prefer cheese to candy,' Carrie said, reaching for her lipstick tube. 'But you could be right.'

'So, are you fixin' to dance every dance with the dreamy Captain Ainsworth?' Louise said, changing the subject.

'That's if he'll ask me.'

'Oh, he'll ask you for sure. He's sweet on ya, Tex.'

A blush warmed Carrie's cheeks. 'I like him too.'

She went to stand in front of the mirror and applied a dash of red to her lips. She'd pinned her blonde hair up in a victory roll earlier and had applied mascara to emphasise her green eyes.

'You two are made for each other.' Louise sighed.

Carrie glanced at her friend. All the men liked Kenny, from what she could gather. But Louise appeared to be playing it cool and didn't flirt with any of them.

'Let's go,' Carrie said. 'The night is young but it won't get any younger if we stick around here.'

She fetched her wool bolero – the desert nights were cold as a frosted frog – then linked arms with her friend. Soon they'd climbed the stairs to the terrace at the top of the hospital. It was the only part of the building which had kept its pre-war function and provided an oasis of tranquillity for the hard-working doctors and nurses.

Brass brazier fire pits warmed the air as Carrie made her way to where Bill was standing by the bar. An Army combo was playing 'Boogie Woogie Bugle Boy' and the music was so catchy that she found herself dancing a jive with Bill almost as soon as she'd said, 'Howdy.'

Dance followed dance – all fast. Eventually, they took a break and went to drink a Tom Collins, sitting on cane armchairs at the edge of the roof garden. The fresh scent of blue irises, flowering in pots lining the terrace, wafted towards them. Carrie glanced up at the bright moonlit sky. 'It's so beautiful,' she said.

Bill took her hand, lifted it to his lips. 'Not as beautiful as you.'

'Or you,' she said, blushing.

'Will you be my girl, Carrie?' He gazed deep into her eyes. 'I love you so much.'

Happiness radiated through her. 'I love you too, Bill. Of course I'll be your girl.'

The music switched to a slow number, 'Cheek to Cheek'.

'Let's dance,' he said. 'I want to hold you.'

She fell into his arms, relishing the feel of him against her.

'I'm in heaven,' Bill whispered.

She lifted her face and he kissed her. His lips so tender and loving she could dissolve. He held her close and her body melded to his, desire igniting between them.

Without warning, the combo stopped playing.

An expectant silence came over the terrace.

Major Wood, in charge of the hospital, tapped the microphone.

'Sorry to break up the party,' he announced. 'But we've received our redeployment orders. Tomorrow we'll start packing our equipment. Then we'll leave for Oran. Can't tell you where we'll be going next.'

Carrie grabbed Bill's hand. 'Will it be Italy?'

'More than likely. Although it could be France.'

'Hope it's Italy,' she said wistfully. 'I've always dreamed of seeing Rome.'

'You're so sweet.' He kissed her on the lips. 'I love you with all of my heart. No matter what happens.'

His words brought home to her the uncertainty of their future. A shiver of fear chilled her. She wrapped her arms around his waist, and he held her as if he never wanted to let her go.

2

It was a week before Christmas, and in the medical facility near Naples where she was now stationed, Carrie was gazing up at a mural painted on the ceiling of the operating room. Depicting the square-jawed Mussolini riding on horseback, dressed like a Roman emperor, the painting was peppered with bullet holes made by the Germans prior to their retreat. Before the war, the buildings had housed an exhibition promoting Italy's colonies, with exhibit halls for each of the subjugated territories. The mobile surgical service had been set up in the 'Albania' building, its partially bombed roof patched with plexiglass and gobs of asphalt. A recovery ward had been established in a chamber decorated with images ironically praising the prowess of Italian soldiers. But she and Louise were both auxiliary surgical nurses; it fell to others to give post-operative care to American casualties.

While Carrie scrubbed the operating table, she thought about the events of the past month. After sending her Bou Hanifa purchases back to the States and helping to pack up the General Hospital equipment – she'd heard it had been secured into more than three thousand crates – she'd travelled with Louise and the others to Oran, where they'd awaited further orders. She'd had to say goodbye to Bill soon afterwards. He and his team were being sent on ahead to Naples via a cargo plane. She'd ached for him so much during those weeks of separation, which had been made even worse by the arrival of the cold, wet Algerian winter. It had rained cats and dogs; her tent had dripped with water, and there was mud everywhere. She'd been so sad and lonesome spending her first Thanksgiving away from home. Louise, too, had been homesick and Carrie had sat in a miserable heap with her, eating overcooked turkey, then reading and rereading letters from their loved ones.

Finally, they'd embarked on the hospital ship, USAHS *Shamrock*, making a three-day crossing in the middle of a convoy. The sea had been calm and they'd spent the time playing bridge and taking Italian lessons. As they drew nearer to the coast, Carrie went up on deck. Salerno appeared on the horizon and she remembered Bill telling her about the landings on the beaches and the terrible bloodshed. Her heart wept for those poor, brave troops who'd given their lives for their country.

Soon, the *Shamrock* was steaming past Capri and Carrie's spirits had lifted. White pathways wound up to the summit of the rugged island, turquoise water lapping at the base of its dramatic cliffs. When the Bay of Naples came into view, with its volcano, Vesuvius, towering in the background, it was late afternoon and raining heavily. But that didn't stop Carrie from remaining on deck to take in the sights. The volcano seemed to be smouldering its welcome, sending out sporadic red spurts and glowing like the tip of a huge cigar. Would Bill be on the dock to greet her? She couldn't wait to fall into his arms.

The harbour was overflowing with half-sunken ships. Rowboats approached, weaving their way between the floating hulks. Carrie's eyes widened; the boats turned out to be amphibious produce shops. She and the other nurses tied money onto the ends of ropes and lowered them down to the vendors so they could purchase some fruit: apples, walnuts and oranges. They'd been paid in Allied Military Currency lire before they'd left Oran.

It was dark by the time they'd been transferred by barge to the docks. Carrie scanned the pier for Bill, but he was nowhere to be seen. Disappointed, she disembarked with her fellow nurses.

Of course he wouldn't have been there; he'd have been too busy working.

Open trucks were there to take them to their new base in Bagnoli, a seafront suburb.

Carrie gave a shudder as they'd made their way through Naples, shocked by how destitute the city looked under the streetlights. A grey and grubby wasteland of rubble. Jagged stones and twisted chunks of masonry. Her chest ached with sadness; *Napoli* truly had been bombed to bits.

Half an hour later, they'd arrived at their destination, and Carrie had jumped off the truck into Bill's waiting arms. After they'd kissed for the longest time, he said, 'Jerry is slaughtering our guys up in the mountains. We've been dealing with a huge number of casualties.'

Tiredness crinkled the corners of his light blue eyes. He'd been having a difficult time, for sure.

Bill showed her around the officers' billet: a tourist attraction, Terme di Agnano, just up the road from the exhibition centre. Like Bou Hanifa, it was a hot water spa which dated from the Roman era. Italy's wealthy once enjoyed health treatments there and the art nouveau buildings where she'd been housed reminded her of the Algerian posting.

After she'd dropped off her haversack in the quarters she was sharing with Louise, Carrie sat with Bill in the recreation room and they'd shared stories about their everyday lives while separated.

Bill spoke of the progress of the war and revealed that US troops were making repeated attempts to dislodge the enemy from their entrenched positions, attacking across cold, swift, deep mountain streams in the face of devastating fire. The loss of life had been immense. He'd hugged her tight then, and his sorrow mingled with her own at the terrible plight of their men.

With a sigh, Carrie carried on preparing the operation room for the next procedure. Since arriving ten days ago, she'd only had one day off. Yesterday, she'd gone with Bill and another surgeon in his unit, blond-haired Captain Max Jones, to visit Pompeii. While strolling around the ruins, she'd marvelled at the excellent state of preservation of the site, which had been excavated from the mass of ash and pumice under which it had lain buried from the time of a catastrophic eruption of Mount Vesuvius in the first century AD.

Pompeii had clearly been a wealthy town, judging by the fine public buildings and luxurious private homes with lavish decorations. Frescoes of Roman gods and goddesses adorned the walls and brightly coloured mosaics, looking as if they'd only been laid yesterday, graced the floors. Carrie had blushed furiously when they'd entered what had obviously once been a brothel. Sculptural reliefs of big phalluses decorated the portal. Inside, colourful murals displayed erotic scenes of attractive tanned men and beautifully pale women in a variety of sexual acts. Some of the women were riding the men, others were being taken from behind.

Carrie had glanced away, her face aflame. 'It doesn't seem a very nice place to work,' she'd said primly. 'The rooms are small and must have been dark and uncomfortable.'

Back out on the main street, she'd peered up at the still active volcano looming above them, belching black smoke into the sky. The last big eruption had taken place in 1926, Bill had said. She'd prayed to God Vesuvius wasn't due for another.

She was at the door of the operating room now, ready to help Bill and Max into their surgical gowns. She assisted while they performed all manner of difficult procedures. Her first amputation had filled her with sorrow, but she'd steeled herself for worse to come. Some of the boys were so badly shot up it was hard to believe they could have survived transfer by ambulance to the hospital. A fella came in the day before with a piece of shell still in his brain, a bullet lodged deep in his belly, and his left hand blown completely off. All the cases were like that. Not just one injury, but several. It was horrific. War was horrific. Carrie hoped against hope the fighting would end soon and that this war would be the last of them.

* * *

Christmas came and Carrie and the others received parcels from home: candy, cookies, warm socks and sweaters. But Carrie didn't feel Christmassy – not without Momma, Daddy and Helen. She missed them with an ache that saddened her.

She went to Midnight Mass with Bill in Bagnoli – they were both Catholics – and was surprised the locals didn't kneel to pray but simply stood. They sang 'O Come, All Ye Faithful' in Latin, the women in black headscarves and the few men dressed in shabby suits. Carrie practised speaking the halting Italian she'd learned thus far, warmed by their friendly responses. They told her they hated the Nazis and fascists – *i nazifascisti* – and that they prayed continually for the Allies, and for peace to come soon.

On Christmas Day, only the most urgent operations went

ahead so Carrie and Louise both had time off. Louise had bought candles and poinsettias from the women who did their laundry, and Carrie helped her decorate the tables in the officers' mess. They'd cut stars from used plasma cans and made decorations to adorn the fir tree one of the corpsmen had found for them.

Bill got off duty in time for lunch: delicious turkey and ham with all the trimmings. They even had fruit cake and red wine. Carrie smiled as she watched him eat. 'I think I'll burst,' he said, rubbing his belly. 'I'm stuffed.'

Later, she went for a walk with him in the surrounding parkland. 'I miss home so much,' she said, a sob catching in her throat. 'I can't stop thinking about my family.'

Bill wrapped his arms around her, and she snuggled into him. 'Hey, babe. You've got me. This goddamn war won't go on much longer.'

She lifted her face to receive his kiss. Such a sweet, tender, loving kiss. Her insides melted.

'I love you so much, Bill.'

'Love you too, darling.'

Without warning, he dropped to one knee.

Her heart set up a frantic beat. 'Bill?'

'Will you do me the honour of being my wife, Carrie?'

She pulled him to his feet. 'Yes, oh, yes.'

She might explode with happiness. His proposal had taken away the pain of her homesickness, for sure.

'I haven't got a ring for you yet.' He reached into his top pocket, extracted a small box. 'But I managed to find this in town last week. It's your Christmas gift.'

Tears of joy stung her eyes. 'Thank you.'

She carefully opened the lid to reveal a stunning shell cameo pendant, depicting what looked to be a Roman goddess carved in profile, fixed on a gold chain.

'She's Venus.' Bill took the chain from the box and fastened it around her neck. He kissed her behind the ear. 'She reminds me of you, babe.'

'I love it,' she said. 'I got you something too.'

She pulled his gift from her pocket and handed it to him.

He unwrapped it and a smile spread across his handsome face. 'Wow!' he exclaimed.

She'd caught him admiring the small figurine of a sleeping shepherd boy, carved in wood, in the window of a gift store outside Pompeii. They'd gone for a coffee before hitching a ride back to base. She'd made the excuse that she needed to find a drugstore and had slipped outside for ten minutes.

'He's called Benino,' she said. 'Apparently he's dreaming that he's at the nativity of the Christ child.'

'Wow!' Bill exclaimed again. 'Thanks.'

They kissed again, passionate kisses that begged for more. Carrie had never experienced such longing for anyone and, from the way he was reacting to her, she guessed Bill felt the same. She wanted to give herself to him. But when and how?

Suddenly, rain started to pour across the gardens.

'Dang,' she cussed. 'We'll be soaked.'

Bill removed his jacket and slung it over her shoulders. He put his arm around her and they ran back inside.

* * *

After a week of rain – Carrie wondered where the phrase 'Sunny Italy' had come from – on New Year's Day the sun came out. Two weeks later, she and Bill were strolling hand in hand in the park, taking advantage of a chance to be on their own.

Bill looked her in the eye. 'Rumour has it the Allies are about to launch an amphibious invasion.'

'You mean like the one at Salerno?'

'Yup. Further up the coast from here, by all accounts.' He squeezed her fingers. 'I expect us surgeons will be sent in behind the troops. Then we'll march on Rome.'

Cold dread squeezed Carrie's chest. She didn't want to be separated from him. 'What about the nurses?'

He held her close. 'I hope you'll stay in Naples, darling. It will be much safer for you.'

'When Rome is liberated, it would be nice if we could get married there,' she said, wistfully. She touched her fingers to the diamond solitaire ring he'd given her shortly after Christmas. Infection control regulations meant she had to wear it with the cameo pendant on the gold chain around her neck.

'Sounds like a great plan.' He kissed her on the lips.

She opened her mouth for him, and then they were kissing passionately. Her heart was pounding so much that her lips trembled.

'I want us to make love before you go, Bill,' she said without preamble.

He held her gaze. 'Are you sure?'

'Yes, I am. Louise and I have different shifts. You could come to my room.'

She decided not to let slip that she and her roommate had already discussed the arrangement. Nor that Louise had recently fallen in love too and had a similar agreement: she'd started to invite her heartthrob to their quarters while Carrie was working.

'If that's what you want, sweetheart.' He kissed her again, deeply.

'I do. And soon.' If she didn't give herself to him before he left for the front, she might regret it for the rest of her life. *No, Bill won't die. God won't let that happen to him.* She laced her fingers through his. 'We'd better head back to work, honey, or they'll be sending out a search party for us.'

* * *

The night prior to the departure of the mobile surgical unit, Carrie was waiting for Bill in her quarters. It had once been a maid's room, she'd discovered, and was at the top of the building. She kind of liked its small size and cosiness. If she thought she'd have been staying there longer, she'd have gotten knickknacks to make it homey like she'd done with her tent in Algeria.

A knock sounded at the door and she went to open it. Now the moment had arrived, nerves were fluttering in her stomach. But when Bill's handsome face came into view, she knew she'd made the right decision.

He took her in his arms and undressed her with reverence. 'You're so beautiful, Carrie. I can't believe you are mine.'

'And you, Bill. I keep counting my blessings that I met you.'

They fell onto the bed, kissing. Need sparked between them. Carrie hadn't registered that he'd undressed until she felt his warm skin on hers. He sheathed himself and took her gently. So slowly she barely felt a twinge, any discomfort soon evaporating in waves of intense pleasure. She locked eyes with him and called out his name.

Afterwards, they lay in each other's arms, kissing and whispering, 'I love you,' making promises about a future together that Carrie prayed they would keep.

'Stay safe, darling,' she begged. 'I don't know what I would do if you got killed.'

His mouth twisted grimly. 'I'll do my best.'

They kissed again, their tears mingling.

Bill's breathing slowed and soon he was asleep, one arm wrapped around her.

Carrie tried to stay awake. She didn't want to miss a single moment with him. But exhaustion overcame her and soon she fell into dreams. Dreams where they were making out on a grassy hillside, Vesuvius glowing in the background. Dreams that were filled with love and hope. Dreams that were only interrupted just before dawn when Bill kissed her awake.

'It's an hour till daybreak,' he said. 'I have to go.'

She kissed him, held him tight, and was soon crying out his name once more.

'I'll miss you,' she said as he pulled on his clothes.

'Don't worry, babe.' He held her face in his strong hands and kissed her again. 'I'll be back before you know it.'

And then he was gone.

Louise returned from her shift, tearful, having just said goodbye to her beau, Theo, who'd also left for the front. Carrie opened her arms to her friend, and they hugged each other.

'If they need surgical nurses, I'm gonna volunteer,' Louise said.

Carrie pressed her lips together. 'Me too. I want to be close to my man.'

She dressed and went to the officers' mess for breakfast. But she hardly touched the scrambled eggs on her plate. She took a sip of coffee and steeled herself to face the day ahead.

Work was slow as there was a lull in the fighting. Rumours abounded about an imminent renewed assault on Jerry's Gustav Line.

'Do you know where Bill's team has been sent?' Carrie asked 1st Lieutenant Betty Thompson as they prepped the operating room.

'It's a place called Anzio, on the coast about thirty miles south of Rome.' She shot Carrie a quick glance. 'They need surgical nurses. I'm going to volunteer.'

Carrie couldn't stop smiling. 'Count me in, ma'am. If I'm needed, I feel I should go.'

'Are you sure? We'll be right at the front.'

'I've never been surer of anything in my life.'

3

Perched on a chair in the wardroom of the British hospital ship *St Julian*, Carrie munched on the Snickers bar Louise had given her to settle her stomach. She, Louise, Betty and five other nurses had boarded the vessel early that morning, but rough weather had prevented the ship from setting sail. Painted white, with big red crosses on her hull and funnel, the *St Julian* remained at anchor in the Gulf of Naples, pitching and rolling on the choppy water.

Carrie heaved a sigh. A week had gone by since Bill and his surgical team had left for Anzio. A week of missing him. A week of worrying about his safety. And now, to make matters worse, she was fighting seasickness.

Taking another bite of her candy bar, she tried to hold onto the thought that she'd soon be reunited with him. But the night was dark, with heavy cloud obscuring the moon, and the *St Julian* was brilliantly lit like all the hospital ships. There would be no escort and she'd discovered that recently, three boats like theirs had been bombed.

Would she even make it to Anzio?

Finally, the wind must have abated, for the ship's engines had begun to rumble beneath her feet. She would be with Bill tomorrow, she comforted herself. All would be well.

'Time to hit the hay,' Betty announced.

In the cabin she was sharing with Louise, Betty and Marge – a veteran of the Salerno campaign – Carrie climbed up to the nearest top bunk with her fatigues and lifebelt on, canteen and helmet close at hand. She said her prayers and tried to fall asleep. But the thrum of the ship's engines, not to mention its tossing and pitching, kept her awake for hours.

* * *

Early the following day, excitement tickling in her stomach, Carrie was standing next to Louise and the other nurses on the foredeck, waiting to be transported ashore. Ahead lay the Anzio beachhead, the ground churned up and muddy. A range of hills on the horizon was partially obscured by a billowing smokescreen.

Carrie squinted her eyes and her blood froze.

Aeroplanes were dropping from the clouds.

High-pitched engines screamed.

The bitter taste of fear coated her tongue and she grabbed hold of Louise's arm.

German planes, black crosses on their sides and swastikas on their tails, streaked across the sky, bright red flashes winking from their wings. Egg-shaped pellets spilled from their bellies. Bombs!

Boom! Boom! Boom!

'Dagnabbit,' Louise exclaimed.

More bombs rained down like hellfire. Acrid smoke stung Carrie's eyes. Shells landed in the sea, sending up trumpeting waterspouts. Anti-aircraft fire almost drowned out the loud thudding of her heart. 'I'm scared, Kenny,' she said to Louise.

'Me too, Tex.' Louise took Carrie's hand and held it tight.

Carrie stared ahead. The beach and pier opposite were lined with stretchers carrying the wounded. How would they survive this maelstrom? But, within minutes, landing craft had started to transfer them to the ship. A shell fell at the stern, sending up another enormous geyser. Carrie tasted saltwater on her lips.

She waited anxiously with her friends until the last of the litters had been hoisted, one by one, up the side of the *St Julian*'s hull.

'Let's go,' Betty said as the nurses' luggage was stowed on an LST landing craft. 'We can't hang about here all day.'

Nests of rope ladders flapped in the wind. Carrie took her courage into both hands and climbed down, her legs shaking with every step. When she reached the landing craft, it was rocking so much that she fell to her knees. Louise pulled her to her feet.

'I've got ya, Tex.' Louise put her arms around her, and the two of them held onto each other for dear life.

The barge-like boat was tossing on the rough sea like a discarded matchstick as it made its way past the wreckage of a sunken vessel and headed for the beach. Carrie fought to hold down the breakfast she'd managed to consume earlier. Queasiness rose from her stomach to her chest and throat. Then relief flooded through her. The LST had bumped against the shore. She swallowed hard; she'd been told beforehand that she'd have to wade the final few yards.

She rolled up her pants and followed the others down the gangplank. Water reached up to her thighs and silt filled her rainboots. She gritted her teeth and held her knapsack above her head, fighting to keep her balance while she struggled through the rippling waves.

Drenched to the bone and shivering in the cold, she climbed onto the six-by-six truck that was waiting for them, an open-top vehicle. The truck set off, its three sets of wheels bouncing along a rough dirt road pitted with shell holes.

She huddled with Louise and the other nurses on hard benches. The going was slow. Soldiers waved at them, rifles on their backs.

Without warning, a shell whistled overhead.

Oh, my God, it had landed barely ten yards ahead of them, blasting a huge crater in the track and showering them with a hail of debris. Carrie's blood froze as she brushed herself down while, next to her, Louise whimpered.

Bill had arrived in Anzio several days ago, his mobile surgical unit attached to the field and evacuation hospitals set up in the medical installation. But the enemy wouldn't bomb hospitals, she reassured herself. The Geneva Convention prevented such action. He would be safe enough, wouldn't he?

A city of pyramidal tents came into view, stretching as far as the eye could see.

The six-by-six rumbled to a stop.

'You got here,' a familiar voice echoed.

Carrie jumped off the truck. 'Bill!' And then, remembering protocol, she saluted.

'At ease, Lieutenant,' he said curtly.

He planted his legs wide, and she took a step back. She wanted to hug him, but the stern expression on his handsome face stopped her.

Was he mad at her?

'Your bivouacs have been put up already, I heard.' He took Carrie's knapsack from her and slung it over his shoulder. He peered at her wet pants with weary eyes. 'You can get changed after we've dug your foxholes.'

He picked up the shovel that was lying by his feet.

Carrie's chest tightened. 'Thanks, but a foxhole? Whatever for?'

'Better to be safe than sorry, darling.'

* * *

After Bill and Theo had organised a couple of corpsmen to help them dig two long trenches down the sides of the tent that Carrie and Louise would be sharing with Betty and Marge – who'd gone to collect their duty rosters – they put two litters inside each and covered them with boards, leaving only an opening big enough to crawl into.

'We can't dig very deep or we'll hit the water table. This area is a former marsh,' Bill said grimly. 'But you should be protected from shrapnel and flying bits of flak.'

Shrapnel and flying flak? It couldn't be that bad or the Army wouldn't have sent them here, Carrie told herself. Bill was just being over-cautious.

He exhaled a loud sigh. 'I need to get a move on. My shift is about to start.'

'Mine too,' Theo added.

Carrie went to Bill and wrapped her arms around his waist. She lifted her head and he kissed her. A tender loving kiss that spoke more than words ever could. In the periphery of her vision, she caught Louise and Theo kissing as well.

'When will I see you, honey?' Carrie asked Bill forlornly.

'Later. I promise.'

And with that, he was gone.

* * *

Betty and Marge arrived momentarily with their schedules. Carrie hoped hers would coincide with Bill's like it had in Naples. But she was starting to recognise that Anzio was a whole different ball game. Bill hadn't smiled once. What had she gotten herself into?

The newly arrived nurses were expected to start work immediately, Carrie discovered. She and her companions had been assigned to the 56th EVAC. There were two other evacuation hospitals, the 95th and the 93rd. Two platoons of the 33rd Field hospital brought the total bed strength to 1,750. All surgery was forward surgery, Betty explained. The field hospital units weren't required to take non-transportable cases from the clearing stations, because the evacuation hospitals were as close to the front as the clearing stations themselves. Each hospital took all types of wounds, limited only by its own bed capacity. The mobile surgical teams operated in all the beachhead units, including the British installations two miles north of Anzio on the road to Rome.

Carrie frowned. Bill had rushed off before she could ask him where he'd be today. Once again, she hoped they'd be working together like in Naples.

After a quick lunch in the mess tent, maps in hand, she and Louise were led down a muddy tent-lined track.

'This is ours,' Marge said to Louise, gesturing to a big olive-green marquee, huge red crosses on its sides.

Carrie followed Betty to another big tent further down the line.

The nurse in charge greeted them. 'Good to see you, gals.'

Carrie's mouth fell open. There were six operating tables. *Six!*

Each boasted two surgeons, a nurse, a nurse anaesthetist, and a corpsman.

Betty nudged her. 'Simultaneous surgery is the name of the game here, Lieutenant. Shake a leg. We're needed.'

The surgical tent was minimal: supplies within easy reach, no poles to obstruct the work, a plank floor, and a small portable stove.

As the afternoon wore on, and procedure followed procedure, Carrie and Betty assisting surgeons they'd never met before, it fully dawned on Carrie how different Anzio was to Naples. The pace at which the wounded were arriving took her breath away. Stomachs shot to pieces. Chests blasted open. Bullet-ridden abdomens. The horrific list went on and on.

At last, their shift came to an end. Again, map in hand, Betty led the way, this time to the latrines. It occurred to Carrie that, if she had to use the toilets at night, she would have to negotiate tent pegs in the dark. As for showers, she discovered there weren't any. 'No hot water, I'm afraid,' Betty huffed. 'We'll just have to take sponge baths.'

Back in their tent, Carrie found Louise and Marge collapsed on their cots, fast asleep. Deciding to take a nap too, she removed her muddy shoes and stretched out. But despite her exhaustion, sleep eluded her.

A nerve ticked by her mouth. She jammed her quaking hands into her armpits. When would she see Bill?

How she longed for him to hold her in his arms.

The ache in her heart was almost unbearable.

* * *

She didn't meet him again until after dinner that day. He was waiting for her outside the mess tent. In the meantime, she'd learned that he'd been deployed at the 95th EVAC. If only they'd been assigned to the same hospital.

God's will, she told herself. *Thy will be done.* At least they could still spend time together when they were off duty. It was better than nothing.

'I'm sorry if I was a little curt with you earlier, sweetheart,' he said, stroking a finger down her cheek. 'It's just that the situation is real bad here. When I found out that you were arriving, I couldn't stop worrying about you.'

He kissed her then, gently pulling her against him. His mouth was so warm and wonderful she wanted the kiss to go on for ever.

'Let's go find a quiet place to talk.' He looked her in the eye. 'You need to know what's going on.'

Holding hands, they headed towards the edge of the medical facility. Bill squeezed her fingers. 'That's our library tent. We can go in there.'

They pulled out chairs at a table in the corner. The musty smell of old books felt comforting somehow.

'Please, Bill. Tell me what's wrong.' She reached for his hand again.

'Well, "Operation Shingle", as this action is known, was planned to be a quick amphibious assault. The Allies succeeded at first. The joint American Fifth and British Eighth Army forces went ashore here with virtually no resistance from the Germans.'

'What happened?'

'Things began to falter. Instead of pushing inland to force a German retreat, the Allied Command stalled. They chose to hunker down to secure the beachhead and wait for reinforcements.'

'Oh?' She tilted her head.

'A big mistake. With all our battalions convened and going nowhere, our troops sat on the beach like a giant flock of sitting ducks waiting to be culled. Masses of German troops moved down from the mountains and are now surrounding the area with their Panzer tanks. Kraut guns are pointing at us, Carrie, and they fire from every possible direction.'

'But we'll win, won't we?' Her voice trembled. 'I mean, the Allies will break through eventually.'

'Of that I have no doubt. But it will be a long, hard battle. With a lot of bloodshed.'

'Thank God we're out of harm's way in the hospitals. We're well marked with our big red crosses, aren't we?'

Bill's brow creased. 'Problem is, the area secured by the Allies is too small for them to put the medical installations out of range of the German guns, and it's been equally impossible in this over-crowded wedge of purgatory to situate us a safe distance from legitimate military targets.'

'What military targets?' The question quivered on her lips.

'Ammunition dumps, fuel depots, anti-aircraft batteries, the motor pool. All located at the edges of some part of this hospital area.' He gave a sigh. 'When we got here, we were warned to take cover whenever there was bombing or shelling. Obviously not when we were in theatre, but during our off-duty times. We didn't take the warning seriously. We thought it was just an exaggeration.'

'And?' She met his gaze.

'Let me just say we soon learned what we needed to do. Believe me, Carrie. You must do the same. Promise me you'll sleep in your foxhole. Jerry often attacks at night.'

'I promise,' she murmured, her heart beating fearfully. 'Promise me you'll be careful too, Bill. We've got to get through this so we can be married in Rome.'

He chuckled. 'You're a breath of fresh air, babe.' He rose to his feet and lifted her up so her body was resting against his.

Their kiss was interrupted by the PA system blurting, 'Attention, please! Red alert.'

'At least they said "please",' Carrie couldn't resist saying.

'Ha!' Bill's mouth twisted. 'It's an air raid, I'm afraid.' He dragged her towards the tent flap. 'We need to head for the nearest foxhole.'

4

The next evening, Carrie was making her way 'home' when the ubiquitous 'Attention, please! Red alert' rang out from the PA system. Another false alarm? The night before, she'd stood with Bill and a group of corpsmen and nurses in a damp foxhole for the longest time. Cold and shivering, her feet squelching in the mud, they'd waited and waited. But nothing had happened. At last, the all-clear had sounded and Bill had escorted her back to her tent.

A sudden rumble reverberated. Carrie stopped dead in her tracks. Aeroplanes were flying overhead, dropping flares which lit up the beachhead with an eerie green light. A whistling sound shrilled, growing ever louder. Deafening explosions boomed. Icy sweat beaded her forehead. She quickened her pace; she had to find a foxhole.

It had rained earlier, and the ground was so slippery she almost lost her footing. The odour of burning diesel and cordite filled her nostrils. *Oh, God, Jerry's hit a fuel depot.* Her stomach twisted into knots.

Allied artillery began firing shells into the sky, leaving traces like massive cascading ribbons ripped into pieces.

The German planes swooped down again. Another load of bombs whistled, then more explosions. *Boom! Boom! Boom!* Long red and orange fingers of flame shot upwards, followed by a giant mushroom cloud of black smoke.

Dear Lord, they've bombed an ammunition dump.

She ran as if the hounds of hell were at her heels, her ears ringing with the sharp sound of shrapnel tearing its way through canvas. Blaring Jeep horns and wailing ambulance sirens joined the cacophony of booming explosions and whistling bombs. Her heart thumped an agonising beat, and her breaths came in hoarse, excruciating, choking gasps.

She arrived at her tent to find it empty. Louise and Marge must have left for their rounds. Betty had gone to borrow a book, Carrie remembered. She crawled into the foxhole nearest her cot and laid herself down on the litter inside. Cold, damp air surrounded her. The boards only inches above her head gave her a terrifying feeling of claustrophobia.

Where was Bill? They'd arranged to meet after supper, so he should be off duty by now. Had he been out in the open when the bombs had started falling? How she prayed he'd made it to a foxhole. Silent tears trickled down her cheeks.

She lay in the foxhole for what seemed like hours, her frantic thoughts chasing each other in a never-ending spiral. Finally, silence fell, a silence only broken by a familiar sound.

'Carrie?' Bill's concerned voice came from above. 'Are you in there?'

Smiling with relief, she squirmed her way out of the hole, and he lifted her into his arms. 'I was so scared.' Her voice shook. 'Scared you'd be killed.'

He peppered kisses down the side of her face. 'Oh, babe. Thank God *you* are safe. I was out of my mind with worry.'

* * *

A week or so later, Carrie was lying on her cot, trying to get some sleep. The days since she'd arrived at Anzio had passed in a blur of feverish activity.

After her initial experience of being bombed, she'd made the decision to tough it out. She'd volunteered to be here because she wanted to be close to Bill. She would suffer the consequences with her head held high. She wouldn't give in to her terror, wouldn't worry about the future, wouldn't let the air raids shatter her equilibrium.

She preferred to be on duty when shelling occurred, preferred to keep busy despite the danger. Just yesterday, she'd been assisting in the operating tent when a shell ripped through the canvas. She'd fought the urge to run for a foxhole and had helped lower the litter cases to the floor instead. She'd placed a helmet on top of a patient's head to give him some protection while he was undergoing an amputation.

Although two corpsmen had been hit by flying shrapnel, Carrie had kept on working until the end of her shift. It was only when all the operations had been successfully completed that she allowed herself to tremble with fright.

The weather was so cold and damp, she and the other nurses had resorted to wearing long underwear under their fatigues. She worked with the incessant, ominous undertone of guns booming while she assisted the surgeons as they dealt with such cases as complicated fractures, shell fragments lodged deep in body tissue, bullet wounds to the head.

She tossed and turned on her cot now, thinking about how

the other day a man was stretchered in whose lower jaw had been completely blown away. They'd done their best for him, and he'd survived the procedure. Whether he'd survived transfer to the General Hospital in Naples, though, was something she'd never know. And, if he did, how would he cope with such a life-changing injury?

Sometimes, she regretted not having put herself forward for post-operative care. She would have liked more one-to-one contact with her patients. But she was needed where she was.

Even when a 'lights out' was ordered, the surgical teams carried on. The boys were so shot up they would die otherwise. Hour after hour, she worked with the surgeons, other nurses, and corpsmen, driving herself without rest until she was relieved by the next team.

Carrie gave a sigh as she thought about Bill. How she longed to be with him. He was working just as hard, if not harder than her, over at the 95th. When their off-duty time coincided, they were too exhausted to do anything other than hunker down in their tents and try to sleep. They had to make do with stolen kisses, 'I love you' whispered fleetingly, and tearful 'goodbye till we can meet again' moments. If only they still worked together, Carrie couldn't help lamenting. She squeezed her eyes shut and said a prayer for him.

As if on schedule, the pounding *boom-boom* of heavy artillery, the sharp *pop* of the 50-mm, the *rat-tat* and the *ack-ack* started up. Carrie rolled off her cot and into the foxhole. Sometimes Jerry was warded off, but more often not. Swoosh went his 'eggs'. The earth quaked as dirt sifted onto her. And she waited for what would happen next.

She didn't need to wait long. Anzio Annie, an enormous 220-mm howitzer gun the Nazis had moved out of its niche in the mountains, commenced her nightly visit. Carrie put her fingers

in her ears as a sound reminding her of the roar of an express
train passed overhead. Aiming for the Allies' ammunition
depots, gasoline dumps, ships in the harbour, troop concentrations, supply dumps, and harbour installations, Annie's shells
blasted holes big enough to swallow a Jeep. Bill had told Carrie
that the Fifth Army itself operated two 200-mm guns, with super-
charged ammunition, that could easily reach Annie, but the
effort was hampered by lack of knowledge of her exact position.
It was all too horrible for words.

* * *

Two days later, she was waiting for Bill outside the library tent.
She'd just had a late lunch and had arranged to spend some time
with him before her night duty started. For once, the timing of
their shifts had coincided. She couldn't wait to tell him that her
tentmates were all at work. A warm feeling spread through her at
the thought she could be alone with him like she hadn't been
since Naples.

He came into view and her heart leapt. Despite the dark
circles of tiredness under his light blue eyes, he was as handsome
as ever. Handsome and hers. She ran into his arms.

A noise like an enormous angry hornet reverberated. They
sprang apart. A Luftwaffe aeroplane was flying low. Probably
heading to bomb the port. Carrie steeled herself for the
explosions.

Bill pulled her against him protectively. 'We'd better run for a
foxhole.'

Before they could do anything, a British Spitfire appeared, its
machine guns blazing *ack-ack-ack-ack-ack* as it chased the
German plane across the sky.

The enemy aircraft lifted its nose. Was it trying to gain altitude? But its engine stalled. Carrie gasped. Bombs spilled from its belly. Massive explosions ricocheted in quick succession. Her blood froze.

'Holy Mary, Mother of God!' Bill exclaimed. 'That bastard has bombed the 95th!'

Carrie grabbed his hand. 'We've gotta help.'

They ran as fast as their legs could carry them.

Everywhere, people were running, screaming, and yelling.

Carrie and Bill joined the rescue efforts and began to scour the wreckage, searching for any survivors. She lifted a fallen tent pole and drew in a sharp breath. A young nurse, eyes staring sightlessly into eternity, was lying under the shredded canvas. Blood reddened her uniform, and an enormous hole gaped in her chest. Carrie couldn't stop herself from crying out.

'Are you okay?' Bill asked.

'I'll cope.' Her voice choked on a sob. 'I'm needed here.'

Fuelled by adrenaline, they helped pull out victim after victim. They found dead and wounded all over the place. Everyone was busy giving first aid to those who required it.

When the final ambulance had driven off, taking the casualties to the other hospitals, Bill picked up a piece of shrapnel and showed it to her.

'They were anti-personnel bombs. On landing, they eject explosive bomblets that are designed to kill individuals and destroy vehicles.' He gave a shudder. 'Our people didn't stand a chance.'

* * *

For the rest of the afternoon and through the night, Carrie worked side by side with Bill, who'd offered to help the surgical team at the 56th who were dealing with the survivors. In the morning, she sat with him in the mess tent. Her breakfast lay untouched on her plate as he recounted what he'd been told by Theo and fellow surgeon Max, who'd been on duty but were mercifully unharmed.

'Two bombs landed in our operating room HQ. Several wards were hit. Colonel Sauer got wounded in the leg and shoulder. Major Truman in the knee. Captain Luce in the chest. Captain Korda in the thorax and arm. Al Shroeder died at his desk. First Lieutenant Sigman, our Head Nurse, and First Lieutenant Sheetz, our Assistant Head Nurse, were both killed outright while they were giving plasma to patients.' Bill's voice shook. 'Twenty-seven ward tents have been destroyed. Our equipment is gone. All our X-Ray Technicians, except one, are casualties. Oh, and our pharmacist has also been killed. Best figures I can obtain talk about twenty killed, and fifty to sixty wounded.'

'Oh, honey.' She reached for his hand. 'I'm so sorry.'

'The stories I heard are soul-destroying. A fella visiting his wounded brother fell across him to protect him and was killed. A boy from New Mexico had his head blown off while hanging clothes out to dry. Chaplain Luskett was struck in the face. One of my patients with a fractured skull received another fracture to it while being X-rayed and didn't survive.'

Carrie kept to herself the thought that Bill might have died if he'd been on duty. It brought home to her now more than ever how precarious their lives were.

A rumbling sound interrupted her thoughts, and she raised her gaze.

Hundreds of Allied Flying Fortresses and Liberators were soaring over the beachhead on their way to bomb the enemy lines. Wordlessly, Carrie and Bill followed them with their eyes until they'd dropped their loads, turned around, and headed back to their base.

The catastrophes of war weren't supposed to strike hospitals, but when they occurred, the non-combatants needed to handle the situation with the coolness of a frontline veteran. Carrie just hoped she had the strength.

* * *

The next day, the commander of the medical installations in the Mediterranean theatre decided that the 95th Evacuation Hospital had lost too many key personnel to function effectively. He replaced the unit with the 15th EVAC, formerly stationed at Cassino. The 15th arrived at Anzio on 10 February, just in time to witness the bombing of the 33rd Field, when long-range enemy fire killed two nurses and a corpsman.

On 16 February, six German divisions with superior forces (100,000 more troops than the Allies at Anzio) attacked the beachhead, preceded by propaganda sheets scattered by artillery shells. The German radio commentator – Axis Sally, as she was known – promised that the Wehrmacht would push the Allied troops into the sea and turn Anzio into another Dunkirk. At night, there were times when the enemy was so close, Carrie could hear the chatter of their machine guns.

Carrie worried along with everyone else. But then the Allied Command sent massed American bombers to pound the German lines. She watched and cheered with her friends when, once again, hundreds of planes flew in formation above them. British warships in the harbour began to shell the enemy positions. By 20 February, Jerry's attempt to push the Allied forces into the sea had been repulsed.

The losses on both sides were so great they precluded any subsequent large-scale offensive push by either. Wehrmacht forces still held firm control of the hills, however, and they went on to punish the beachhead as fiercely as ever.

She listened to Axis Sally play popular records like Bing Crosby crooning 'People Will Say We're in Love', and Frank Sinatra singing 'You'll Never Know'. She bristled when the broadcaster told the Allied forces that they constituted 'the largest self-supporting prisoner-of-war camp in the world'.

During the remainder of the month and on through the next, there was no let-up. On 17 March, the British 141st Field Ambulance suffered three direct hits, with fourteen killed and many wounded. On the 22nd, it was the US 15th EVAC's turn as it was blanketed by 88-mm shells that killed five personnel and wounded many others.

Carrie learned that the combat troops called the hospital area 'hell's half acre' and that they felt safer in foxholes at the front. When the proposal came through suggesting the nurses should be evacuated to Naples, she and the others refused point-blank. It would send the wrong message to their brave soldiers.

If only the hospitals could be moved. But there was no safe place for them to go. They could not even go underground, but they could be partially dug in. With the arrival of spring the rains had become less frequent, and the ground had dried up enough to permit excavation of tent sites to a depth of three or four feet. Two ward tents were pitched in the EVACs end to end, with earth revetments around the walls. Steel stakes and chicken wire helped hold the facings in place. Sandbag baffles inside divided the double tents into four compartments of ten cots each. Patients and personnel were thus secure against anything but a direct hit. Operating tents were given the additional protection of a two-inch plank roof covered with more sandbags.

Carrie soldiered on. Enemy air raids averaged four per day. Dogfights high in the sky were common. On one night there were ten air raid alerts; on another, eight. Having to get out of bed and into foxholes so frequently meant that she and the others were always on the edge of physical and mental exhaustion. She couldn't remember the last time she'd slept more than four hours in a row.

Battle exhaustion cases poured in – a pitiful parade – among them, soldiers with gangrene, trench foot, malaria, FUO (fever of undetermined origin), and jaundice. They were given a new antibiotic, penicillin, and it saved many lives.

The one sweetener to her otherwise bitter existence was the fact that Bill's surgical unit had been redeployed to the 56th. Although their shifts rarely coincided, when they did, the joy of working with him made all the longing while they were apart worthwhile. The thrill of her eyes meeting his above their masks. The sense of accomplishment when she handed him the correct surgical instruments. The pleasure of hearing him say, 'You did a great job, Lieutenant.'

They managed to spend time alone together whenever they could, taking advantage of the occasional absence of their tent-mates to make love when they were off duty. Louise and Theo were in the same boat, and Carrie knew there were several couples at the beachhead who did likewise. Everyone felt they had to seize the moment for no one knew if it would be their last.

On the night of 29 March, Carrie was lying on her cot, listening to her tentmates snoring louder than a bunch of jack-hammers. Would she ever get any sleep? She was so tired, her entire body ached.

'Attention, please! Red alert,' resounded from the PA system.

With a groan, she rolled off her cot and into the foxhole.

Louise climbed down next to her. 'Dagnabbit, Tex. I was dreamin' I was home with my folks.'

'Thank God that Bill and Theo are off duty,' Carrie said. 'They'll be safe in their foxholes.'

Her words were interrupted by the pervasive whistle of bombs falling, followed by three massive explosions. The earth literally shook.

'Those were too close for my liking,' Louise muttered, already squirming out of their trench.

Carrie's skin prickled with sudden fear. 'I think they hit one of our wards.'

She pulled on her boots and ran.

But it wasn't the hospital that had been hit, she realised with sickening clarity as she rounded the corner. It was the surgical team officers' tent area.

'Dear Lord,' she cried out.

Before her, an enormous crater had opened. Everything had been flattened to the ground.

She looked from left to right. Where was Bill?

Theo and Max were climbing out of a foxhole.

Bill was nowhere to be seen.

Carrie's veins turned to ice.

Louise ran to Theo, and then came back to Carrie. 'Bill went to check on a patient, Theo said.'

Everything happened in slow motion, it seemed.

The pounding of her heart boomed in her ears. Voices echoed as if coming from the end of a long tunnel. What were they saying? She couldn't understand a single word.

Louise wrapped her arms around her. 'Bill didn't make it, darlin'.'

'What? No!' Carrie struggled from her friend's hold.

She'd almost arrived at the edge of the crater when Theo pulled her away. 'He wouldn't want you to see him like this, Carrie.'

'But he needs me.'

'He needs you to be strong, honey,' Louise said.

Carrie shook her head. 'Bill would have heeded the warning and found a foxhole.'

She took a step forward. A prone figure, covered by a blanket, lay on the other side of the crater. She stared at the exposed arm.

A wristwatch glinted in the moonlight.

Bill's Bulova.

And she screamed.

5

Louise led Carrie away from Bill and sat with her in their tent while she cried hot tears of grief.

'He was one of the good guys,' Louise said, stroking her shaking shoulders. 'I can't imagine how you must be feeling.'

'We were fixin' to get married in Rome,' Carrie sobbed.

'I'm here for ya, Tex. We all are. We'll help you get through this.'

Betty and Marge added their voices of concern and support to Louise's, but Carrie hardly heard them for the silent screams echoing in her head. She rocked and clutched at herself. How would she ever live without Bill?

The next twenty-four hours, she cried so much she wondered how she could have any tears left. Bill's life had been taken from him. He had been taken from her. Their future together had been taken from them both. She couldn't stop touching the engagement ring and the cameo pendant he'd given her. She'd never love anyone like she loved him.

The night before Bill's funeral, Father Anthony came to visit.

'I'm angry with God for taking Bill,' she said, the words trembling on her lips.

The kindly, middle-aged priest took her hand. 'I don't believe for one second that the Lord wanted this to happen. The tragedies that occur in this world are not God's will. Why do you think we pray, "thy will be done on earth as it is in heaven"? God gave us free will at the time of creation and that freedom limited His control over us while we are here.'

She nodded, her pain too raw to give voice to her thoughts. The Nazis were evil incarnate. Were they the result of God allowing people to have free will? She breathed out a heart-wrenching sigh.

Father Anthony prayed the rosary with her, blessed her, and when he went back to his rounds, Carrie fell back on her cot. She stared at the canvas roof of the bivouac and a fresh load of tears welled up.

Footfalls sounded as Betty approached. 'I've brought you a coffee, honey.' Betty's hand shook as she handed her the drink.

Carrie thanked her, taking in the dark circles of tiredness beneath the 1st lieutenant's eyes. A pang of guilt caught in her chest. She should have been working today.

'I'm sorry to have left y'all high and dry.'

Betty patted her arm. 'You're entitled to sick leave, sweetie.'

The sudden whoosh of 88-mm shells came from above. 'Get in your foxhole,' Betty barked, as she dived into her own trench.

Carrie's entire body turned to lead. A thought flickered through her mind: that only in death could there be release and peace. If a German bomb killed her, so be it. She believed in the afterlife. There, she would find Bill and they'd spend eternity together.

'Didn't you hear my order, Lieutenant?' Betty yelled. 'Get in your foxhole now!'

'Yes, ma'am.'

* * *

Bill's funeral passed in a blur of tears. Not just Carrie's, but also those of his surgical teammates and friends in the hospital. He was buried in the temporary cemetery on the beachhead, laid to rest in the cold earth. After the war, his folks would be able to ask for him to be repatriated, if they wanted.

Carrie went through the rituals like an automaton, determined not to break down in front of her peers. She was a lieutenant in the Army. She had to be strong. It was as if this was happening to someone else, not her. She felt as if she was in the midst of a terrible nightmare. How she longed to wake up and find it had all been a horrible dream.

After Father Anthony had sprinkled Bill's coffin with holy water and committed him to his grave, Carrie decided it would be best to return to work. She was needed. The hospitals were receiving a thousand patients a day and evacuating the same number, the wounded staying only long enough for their condition to be stabilised before they were transferred to a noncombat area to recuperate. The surgical teams were working around the clock.

But, when she was asked to pass a pair of scissors to Theo, her hand trembled so much that she dropped them.

Betty led her out of the operating tent. 'You came back to work too soon, Lieutenant.'

'I want to help.' Carrie looked her firmly in the eye. 'If I stay on my own any more, I'll die.'

'You can assist with the post-op patients. The ward nurses are run off their feet. They'll welcome you with open arms.'

* * *

And so it was that Carrie found herself doing the job she'd trained for when she was nursing back in Dallas. She tended to the wounded: blood reddening the gauze at their throats; others who already displayed the pallor of death, but breathed intermittently until they died while she whispered what words of comfort she could. On and on she worked, down the massive tent, helping soldiers; giving injections and oxygen, changing bloody bandages as they sprawled in all manner of prone positions. All so utterly exhausted that the noise of battle or even her presence passed unnoticed.

Why? Why is this happening? she asked herself again and again. Numbness and a forlorn sense of futility invaded her soul. The suffering seemed so senseless, so needless. But she had to do her job. *The show must go on.*

Enemy shells and bombs continued to strike the hospital. On 3 April, a medic, Private Harvin Estes, was killed when an 88-mm shell hit the mess tent. Two days later, Corpsman Pete Betley had both legs blown off during heavy shelling. In one week, the 56th EVAC had been shelled or bombed three times.

The shells were worse than the bombs. Carrie never knew when to expect them, and there was no time to take cover. By now, many of her fellow medical officers, nurses, and ward men were fearful and shaky. They were suffering from insomnia and several used sedatives to try to get some rest. Carrie didn't know how she'd have managed without the Nembutal she took when off duty. Not only did it help her sleep, but it also dulled the pain of her grief.

On the morning of 6 April, she got out of bed and combed her hair. How coarse and dusty it felt beneath her fingertips. She thought about having a sponge bath, but decided against it, the effort to fill her helmet with cold water and bring it back to the tent putting her off. She reached for a clean ward dress. The weather had warmed up recently, so she no longer wore the heavy gear she'd worn in the weeks after arriving at Anzio. Women from the nearby town of Nettuno did the medical personnel's laundry in adjacent streams, carrying it back to them in big baskets on top of their heads. Carrie gazed at the darning to the front of her garment, where a shrapnel hole had been made while it was hanging out to dry. How kind the local woman had been to mend it.

'Hey, Tex.' Carrie glanced up at Louise, who'd just returned from night duty. 'They've only gone and rigged up a shower for us.' Her voice bubbled with barely suppressed delight.

Carrie took a step back. 'But won't it be freezing?'

'Nah. They've used GI cans and solar heat. Come on! It'll be great.'

Carrie picked up a bottle of shampoo, a bar of soap and a towel and followed Louise to an area behind the mess tent, enclosed by a tarp.

Inside, galvanised pressed steel containers had been fitted with nozzles.

'Keep your underwear on,' Louise said, pointing to the corpsmen who'd grouped around to ogle.

Carrie shrugged. She didn't care if anyone saw her bare body. The only man she cared about was no longer there. She stripped down to her panties and bra.

As warm water cascaded over her head and down her shoulders, she scrubbed herself clean then lathered her hair, standing defiantly under the running water, staring at the peeping men until they turned away.

* * *

'Happy days are here again for the 56th Evacuation Hospital,' Axis Sally announced over the airways later. With a strong German accent, the woman went on to dedicate the programme to Carrie's unit, saying that they were leaving Anzio. Carrie thought it was a sick joke. She said as much to her tentmates, and they agreed with her.

But, the next day, Colonel Blesse called everyone together and asked anyone who wanted to quit the beachhead to raise their hands. No one did. Then he said that the 56th would be relieved by the 38th EVAC within seventy-two hours. They were all shipping out.

Carrie was stunned. Stunned and tearful at the same time. Ten days after Bill had been taken from her, she was under orders to leave him behind. If only he'd lived, he'd be leaving Anzio with her. Pain caught at the back of her throat, and she had difficulty swallowing it down.

Three days later, she climbed onto a six-by-six truck to make the two-mile journey to the seaport. Now known as 'Purple Heart Highway', the track was being shelled even as she and the others were driven along it. She remembered the first time she'd driven down this track, her excitement at the thought of seeing Bill, and she had to hold back a sob.

They were a tired, weary, unkempt, and haggard bunch as they boarded the barges that would carry them from the battered port. All the buildings had been reduced to rubble.

As if on schedule, Anzio Annie began kicking up trumpeting spouts of water in the harbour. Carrie climbed the Jacob's ladder up the side of a waiting LST landing ship in record time. It was Easter Sunday, a day of mixed blessings for sure.

The craft's engines vibrated beneath her feet, and the beleaguered beachhead faded into the distance. Her dreams had been irreparably broken there. *She* had been broken. And nothing would ever put her back together again.

6

The grief came in waves. Carrie would listen to a song Bill loved and pain would engulf her. He was gone. She'd never see his handsome face. Never hear his melodic voice. Never touch his beautiful body. It hurt so bad she had to keep finding places where she could be alone, so no one could hear the raw sobs rip from her breast.

Not even the delights of the new hospital complex that had been opened at Nocelleto, north of Naples, could comfort her. The medics had planted flowers and shrubs, and the fruit trees were in full bloom. For the next month, they had few patients and a lot of time on their hands. Carrie tried to enjoy the outdoor movies and baseball games, but the thought of how much Bill would have enjoyed them too dampened her sprits. Visits to the opera in Naples, the Isle of Capri, and the scenic beauty of the Amalfi Drive were made and Carrie went along. But her feet dragged and she couldn't bring herself to join in with the delight of her friends. And USO visited, including stars like Marlene Dietrich, Irving Berlin, Danny Thomas, and the Andrews Sisters. But, yet again, her enjoyment was marred by thoughts of Bill.

One morning in mid-May, Lieutenant General Mark W. Clark attended the 56th EVAC's formal review and presented eighteen Bronze Star Medals to staff and personnel for heroic achievements at Anzio. The hospital also received a Commendation. It was a memorable occasion, and Carrie tried to be happy, but all she could think about was how Bill should have been given an award as well.

The Allied forces finally pushed beyond the Gustav Line after intense fighting, especially at Monte Cassino. As the front moved and the Anzio beachhead troops met those from inland, it left the hospital far behind the front, and it was time to move on.

At the end of May, Carrie and the rest of the 56th were riding on two-and-a-half-tonne trucks to Fondi, about halfway from Naples to Rome. The journey took them through devastated villages and over narrow, dusty roads. The new location occupied a weedy patch of land, squeezed between Highway 7 and a war-torn orange grove. It couldn't be worse, Carrie thought as she climbed down from the truck. Engineers with bulldozers came and levelled the area so they could pitch their tents.

What struck Carrie most about her time in Fondi was the despair and abject poverty of the local people. During the past five months, while war had ravaged their town, they'd taken refuge in the hills and now that they were returning to their homes, it was evident they were suffering from starvation. Carrie helped one of the cooks to divide their leftovers equally among the families who regularly lined the fences, begging for food.

Again the front was moving and Carrie expected that the 56th would soon receive orders to follow the troops. When news came that the US Fifth Army forces had entered Rome on 4 June, it wasn't long before she was boarding a six-by-six once more. She felt sorry for the destitute population they were leaving behind. And her heart wept as the convoy motored past wrecked equipment, signs of severe tank battles, decaying bodies of enemy soldiers and horses, and ruined farms and houses.

When they arrived in Rome, one of the first Axis capital cities to fall to the Allies, Carrie steeled herself. This was where she and Bill had planned to be married. She needed to use every bit of strength at her disposal not to curl herself up into a ball and weep.

They were posted to an actual hospital building, the Buon Pastore Institute, a many-spired edifice, which they shared with the 94th EVAC. The place had been occupied by Jerry, who'd withdrawn in haste and had left behind meals half-eaten, medical supplies, and even two dead soldiers in the morgue.

After settling down, the 56th personnel had but one wish: to obtain passes to go out and about in the Eternal City. Carrie visited the Vatican and stood in the Sistine Chapel with Louise, Theo, and Max, gazing up in awe at Michelangelo's creation. God reaching out to Adam, their fingers almost touching. Was that the moment when the Creator gave humans free will?

Once more, the hospital was losing contact with the rapidly moving front, so it was back to packing and awaiting orders for the next move. At the end of June, the first trucks made their appearance and they all set off. The motor convoy followed Highway One over gentle rolling plains to Civitavecchia. There, Carrie's spirits lifted a little on learning that Anzio Annie had been captured and was being dismantled for shipment to the Zone of Interior for use by the Allies.

There was a lot of traffic, but they eventually reached their destination, a site near Riotorto, only a few miles southeast of the harbour city of Piombino.

The 56th was almost immediately swamped with casualties, most of them arriving at night and reminding Carrie of her busy days at Anzio. She immersed herself in work; it kept her mind occupied. Bill was never far from her thoughts. She missed him every second of every night and every day.

In early August, the hospital moved to Tuscany.

Their new home was Peccioli, a village surrounded by vineyards and apple orchards, a mile below the Arno River. One of her first patients was a local farmer, Signor Giacometti, who had driven his oxen over a landmine. Carrie was given the task of nursing him while he recovered from the amputation of his left foot. When his wife and family visited, she practised speaking Italian with them, glad she was no longer working in the operating rooms. She preferred the one-to-one contact with her patients.

After Signor Giacometti had been discharged, she was invited to eat at his home with his wife and almost-grown children. She'd had to disguise her shock at the primitive conditions in which they lived. They had no running water, no electricity, no telephone. The cattle were stabled on the ground floor. The toilet occupied an outdoor shack and the smell when she used it made her retch. But the family made the best of things, already organising the sons to take over their father's tasks. He would receive a prosthetic in due course, and Carrie was confident he would soon return to working his land. After she'd thanked them for dinner, she pulled out her purse and bought from them fresh eggs and a chicken, which she took back to the hospital. She shared her purchases among her friends to supplement their monotonous C food and K rations – canned meat, cheese spread, biscuits and packet bouillon – and, before too long, others were buying fresh food from local farmers too; the 56th's dietician started to organise supplies for the patients as well.

Life became full of little surprises. The personnel received a beer ration for the first time, and with it toasted the invasion of Southern France, the liberation of Paris, and General Eisenhower's prediction that the war in Europe would be over by the end of the year. One morning, Lieutenant General Mark W. Clark visited to award Purple Hearts to the wounded black American 'Buffalo Soldiers'. Joe Louis, the heavyweight boxing champion, came to entertain a large crowd of patients and personnel. There was also time for recreation, dances, sightseeing trips to Pisa and Siena, and even some shopping for souvenirs. Carrie made purchases of brightly coloured ceramics and attempted to have fun with her friends. But she was starting to feel annoyed by Bill's surgical teammate, Max, who showed up by her side far too often. Was he sweet on her? She hoped not.

The utter futility, destruction and waste of the war was brought home to her yet again when, one day, while she was making her way to the ward tent, she was startled by an explosion in the field opposite. Terrifying screams echoed. An ambulance siren shrilled and she went to deal with the outcome. Her pulse raced. An Italian boy of about ten had been stretchered in, together with seven other children. A German rifle grenade, with which the child had been playing, had gone off. The boy didn't make it, but Carrie helped take care of the other kids, who'd suffered shrapnel injuries. They cried for their mammas, who came to sit with them while they recovered. The incident played itself over and over in Carrie's head, sickening her and increasing her longing for peace to come.

The days went by and then news arrived that the British Eighth Army had secured Florence. Passes would be furnished to all hospital personnel who wanted to visit the Tuscan city, the cradle of the Renaissance. Carrie and her friends leapt at the chance.

* * *

A week or so later, Carrie was in the newly liberated town, sipping a coffee in Caffè Gilli, the oldest coffee shop in Florence. Her cup had the date 1733 on it and Carrie savoured the taste of the cappuccino on her tongue. It was a relatively new drink to her, but she'd learned that the Italians had been enjoying it for centuries. She'd recently discovered that the Italians drank coffee made with barley or ground acorns during the war, but life had already started returning to relative normality again. Either that or the coffee shop had gotten the beans on the black market.

The history of this country never failed to amaze her. She took another sip, thinking about the sites she, Louise and the ever-present Max had visited that morning. She'd wanted to view the masterpieces in the Uffizi Gallery, in particular Botticelli's *Birth of Venus*, depicting the goddess standing on a giant scallop shell, as pure and as perfect as a pearl. But the building, by reason of its height, had suffered much from when Jerry had blown up most of the bridges over the Arno.

Carrie recalled her excitement when first given the opportunity to visit Florence and see its priceless treasures. How disappointed she'd been to learn that the Uffizi galleries and those of the Pitti Palace were still bare of their principal works of art. They'd been taken for safekeeping to different depositories at various castles, monasteries, and villas in the countryside, apparently, and it wouldn't be until the war was fully over that they could be returned. She was thankful, though, that they'd been saved and hoped she'd get the chance to view them eventually.

Instead, they'd climbed to the top of the Santa Maria del Fiore cathedral dome, to gaze at the city below and feast their eyes on the cityscape: the centuries-old buildings with terracotta-tiled roofs painted in tantalising shades of ochre. Carrie's attention had been drawn to the towering mountains in the distance. The landscape of Italy was glorious. But not glorious enough to take away her homesickness for Texas. How she pined for the tree-lined creeks and rolling hills of home.

'What are you thinking about?' Max asked from where he was sitting next to her.

'Just how awe-inspiring Florence is.' She breathed a sigh. 'Shame Jerry blew up all those bridges, though.'

She'd been truly shocked by the damage she'd seen in the area around the Arno. They'd walked as far as they could go across the Ponte Vecchio, the only bridge left standing. The Wehrmacht had occupied the city for a year, but when the Allies were closing in, the Nazis detonated charges on all the other bridges before they began their retreat. Carrie had gazed at the fronts of buildings ripped open to the world, piles of rubble everywhere, and her heart had filled with its customary pain at the devastation caused by war.

Max reached for her hand now, but she whipped it away. 'Don't,' she said.

'Sorry.' He gave her a wink.

She could tell he wasn't sorry at all. How dare he? She hadn't sent him any signals that she was, or ever could be, interested in him.

'Excuse me.' She got up to go to the restroom.

She walked past two young Italian men, drinking the bitter black coffee she'd once tried but couldn't stomach.

'*Oi, Professore*,' the fella nearest to her called out. '*Guarda la bella signorina americana.*' Look at the beautiful American miss.

Carrie glared at him. She folded her arms and said, '*Capisco l'italiano.*' I understand Italian.

It was then that she noticed the men were armed. Tommy guns on lanyards over their shoulders. Who the heck were they? Not soldiers. They'd be in uniform. Instead, they were dressed in scruffy everyday clothes and wore red kerchiefs around their necks.

The man who'd been referred to as *Professore* jumped to his feet and bowed. 'I apologise for the rudeness of my comrade,' he said in perfect English.

'Apology accepted.'

What else could she say? The so-called professor's dark brown eyes burned with a kindness that belied his fierce appearance. Wild almost-black hair framed a face that could have been chiselled from marble by Michelangelo. A face that reminded her of the statue of David she'd viewed that morning in the Piazza della Signoria. She gave him a quick nod and proceeded to the bathroom.

By the time she made her way back to her friends, the 'professor' and his sidekick were gone. She pulled out a chair and sat as far away from Max as she could. 'Did you see those Italians at the back earlier?' she asked Louise and Theo.

'Resistance fighters,' Theo said. 'They were an underground movement until the Germans started their retreat. It was then that they came out on the streets to fight openly. From all accounts they're still doing battle with the last remnants of the fascists near here.'

'Ah,' Carrie said, intrigued. She'd heard about the Resistance. The partisans had helped to liberate Naples. But she'd never expected to come across any in Florence. 'The man I spoke to was called "*Professore*" by his buddy, but he seemed too young to be a professor. I'd have put him at my age or younger.'

'They all have aliases,' Max chipped in. 'Why are you so interested?'

Carrie stiffened at his insinuation. 'I'm interested in Italy, that's all. The people we've met have been so welcoming. I'm truly distraught at what has happened to them and their country.'

She left it at that, picked up her purse, and called for the check.

Bill would have loved Florence, she thought as she walked with the others towards the station, where transport was waiting to return them to the hospital. He'd have loved the view from the cathedral dome. He'd have lamented with her the sad fate of the bridges. And he'd have been fascinated to meet the partisans. She bit back a sob. War was unfair, unjust, unkind. If only things could have been different.

7

In his hideout high on a mountain north of Florence, Vito sat by the smoky campfire in an abandoned, half-ruined farmhouse while he cleaned his Tommy gun.

'*Oi, Professore,*' his best friend, Ezio, called out. 'What do you reckon your chances are with that American girl?' Ezio had been joking about their encounter ever since they'd met her. It was the first time he'd seen a woman apparently impervious to Vito's charms, he maintained.

Vito chuckled. Ezio seemed to think he was some kind of latter-day Rudolph Valentino, the archetypal Italian 'Latin Lover' who'd made it big in Hollywood. Vito carried on rubbing oil onto the pivot points and sliding surfaces of his weapon, unable to deny that the pretty blonde had attracted his attention; he'd been intrigued by the way her beautiful green eyes had burned with indignation before he'd apologised for Ezio's crass remark.

She'd been wearing the dress uniform of a nurse. Only a couple of days ago, an American hospital had set up its tented wards in Scarperia, about a ten-kilometre trek to the south from where Vito and Ezio had established a temporary base. But chances were she wasn't with that unit. He'd probably never see her again, which was a pity as he'd have liked to have practised speaking English with her. Anything else would have been out of the question; he'd only recently turned twenty and she would almost certainly consider him too young.

Vito exhaled slowly. His friends often told him he was good-looking, but he believed his looks to be more of a curse than a blessing. When he'd started studying English literature at the University of Florence barely a year ago, the girls wouldn't leave him alone, sending him notes in class and flirting with him shamelessly when all he'd wanted to do was focus on his studies.

He groaned to himself, remembering how devastated he'd been when Mussolini had established his Republican Army, soon after Hitler had arranged for his paratroopers to spring him from where he'd been imprisoned in a high-altitude hotel. The dictator now presided over a puppet state under German control. All young Italian men had been drafted, and Vito – who'd been ardently anti-fascist since he knew the meaning of the word – had immediately joined the Tuscan Resistance. He'd have done so anyway – not just to avoid conscription. When the Wehrmacht had occupied Florence, he'd fought with the urban guerrillas, *i gappisti*, but now the city was in the hands of the Allies, he'd gone up into the mountains with Ezio. They were on their way to join a group of partisans tasked with harassing the Germans while they were retreating.

Except now they'd stopped retreating and were fighting back. Hitler was determined to hold onto Bologna, a key transportation hub. He'd ordered his troops to resist the Allies on the Gothic Line, a series of fortifications which stretched across the northern Apennines from the Mediterranean to the Adriatic. The American Fifth Army were attacking from the west, the British Eighth from the east. And both armies were battling the

Wehrmacht forces in the central zone where Vito and Ezio had been ordered to operate.

Vito reassembled his gun, eager to make a start. He and Ezio were soon to meet up with the 36th Garibaldi Brigade and assist them in taking Monte Battaglia – an eight-hour hike north – from the Wehrmacht. The highest mountain for kilometres, Monte Battaglia boasted bare rocky slopes with a one-in-two gradient running up to a pinnacle crowned by an ancient, ruined fortress built over a thousand years ago. Whoever held the height controlled the area. It hadn't earned the title of Battle Mountain for nothing. If the partisans captured it, they would prove their value to the Allies and be allowed to fight on with them – at least, that's what Vito hoped.

His shoulders tightened as he thought about his sister, Anna, a nun in the Convent of San Ruffillo near Monte Battaglia. There she'd been protected from the troubles of the world – the cloisters were in an isolated hamlet – but now the Allied front had moved, she was far too close to the war for his liking. He fervently prayed there'd be a chance to make sure she was safe and sound, but first he needed to complete the task at hand.

'Time to get some shut-eye,' he said. 'We should leave at nightfall.'

He rolled himself up in his bedroll and closed his eyes; he'd become adept at sleeping anywhere at any time. Within minutes, he'd dropped off.

* * *

Vito woke in the late afternoon, ate a quick meal of roasted chestnuts and salami, then suggested to Ezio they depart.

Their route took them past Firenzuola and, as they passed through, Vito couldn't help bemoaning the sorry state of the ancient medieval town. Allied bombing had reduced three-quarters of the buildings to rubble and he couldn't fathom why. It wasn't as if any Germans had been stationed there. A mistake of war, no doubt. He heaved a heavy sigh and marched on.

Rain began to fall and the chill of autumn made him shiver despite the strenuous walk. Soon, he and Ezio had reached the Santerno Valley, which was still firmly in enemy hands. The Wehrmacht had blown up all the bridges as far as Castel del Rio on the Tuscan-Bolognese border, except for the humpbacked sixteenth-century Ponte Alidosi, which they'd deemed too narrow to bother with. Vito gave another sigh. By all accounts, the Fifth Army was making exceptionally slow progress in taking the valley, only gaining a couple of kilometres a day while the battle-hardened German troops, positioned on crests to the east and west of the river, brought their fearsome guns into play.

Vito and Ezio were due to meet the three hundred or so 36th Garibaldi Brigade partisans on a ridge to the south of Battle Mountain. They crept over the ancient bridge and trekked across country by torchlight under pelting rain to reach the rendezvous point at dawn.

'The Monte Battaglia fortress has been left unguarded by the enemy,' Bianconini, the black-bearded Garibaldi commander, informed Vito after greeting him. 'Someone needs to brief the approaching *'mericani*. You speak English, I've heard.'

Vito accepted the mission and asked Ezio to go with him. Problem was, how would they get close enough to the Americans without getting shot in the process? Vito hit upon the idea of calling out 'We are friends' with every footstep, which they proceeded to do. They didn't need to go far.

'Halt!' a voice shouted. 'Identify yourselves!'

Vito stepped forward. 'We're partisans and have information for your leader.'

A young captain approached. 'What information?'

Vito quickly explained. 'There's no time to lose,' he added.

The slopes of Monte Battaglia were mostly used as pasture-land by local farmers and tree cover was practically non-existent. Vito, Ezio, and the thousand or so soldiers of the 88th Division, 2nd Battalion, 350th Infantry Regiment of the American Fifth Army – also known as the Blue Devils – scaled the heights without further ado. Stones scattered beneath their feet, and a steady, cold drizzle fell from a thick blanket of gunmetal-grey cloud.

On the summit, they were met by the Garibaldi partisans. Vito took some restorative breaths and gazed at the view. The crests of the Apennine mountains stretched as far as his eye could see. The Santerno and Senio river valleys below nestled between a pretty patchwork of green rolling hills. In the distance lay Bologna and the Po River, the Allies' objective. Consolidating their position on Monte Battaglia would be vital. Vito prayed to God they'd be successful.

'Dig yourselves in,' the American captain commanded.

But it was impossible to do so. There was no loose earth, just rocky ground. Vito's skin prickled. He and his comrades were dangerously exposed. Like proverbial sitting ducks. He could only hope the Germans had given up and resumed their retreat.

The sudden rattle of machine gun fire came from below. Thousands of Wehrmacht troops were climbing up the northern slope, their helmets glinting in the pale morning light.

Vito was an urban guerrilla, used to fighting in small actions, so this was entirely beyond his level of expertise. He took cover behind a mound of rubble and started shooting amid a tempest of gunfire and screams.

Heavy guns and mortar barrages boomed. The stones beneath their feet had worsened the impact of German artillery, increasing the fragmentation effect of the shells. Bitter fire fights followed. Enemy flamethrowers set the stones ablaze. They charged with bayonets and hurled grenades. But the partisans and Blue Devils, battling side by side, gave as good as they got and, by the afternoon, had managed to push the Wehrmacht soldiers back down the mountain. It was only a brief respite. The enemy counter-attacked beneath the pouring rain.

Vito found himself firing through a hail of bullets. He collapsed to the wet ground and crawled forward, aiming at a Wehrmacht soldier less than a metre in front of him. His bullet caught the man in the throat. Blood and sinew spewed from the German's neck. Vito gritted his teeth and carried on shooting. Kill or be killed. *Whack-whack-whack.*

Men had fallen and were writhing in pain. Partisans, Americans and Germans. The earth turned red. Medical aid station personnel appeared on the scene to evacuate casualties, teams of litter-bearers courageously transporting the wounded through the terrifying artillery barrages, the noise so deafening Vito could barely hear himself think.

He and the others fought on. Eventually, at nightfall, the German guns fell silent. Their attack seemed to have come to an end.

'We know this terrain better than the *'mericani*,' Bianconini said as he sat with Vito and Ezio that night, while they smoked and discussed what to do next. 'Let's hope they realise that and allow us to fight on with them.'

But no such luck. 'Thank you, but we can handle things from here on in,' the young US captain said when they asked. 'Make a pile of your weapons before you leave.'

'*Porco cane*,' Bianconini swore under his breath.

'We need our guns,' Vito muttered.

'Don't worry. We have plenty more stashed nearby.' He pushed himself to his feet. 'Let's go!'

* * *

'Why do you think the Americans wanted to be rid of us?' Vito asked Bianconini later in a derelict barn on the ridge the partisans had occupied a couple of days ago.

They were surrounded by thirty or so of Bianconini's men, while they sat by a crackling fire cutting hunks off salami sausages and drinking grappa.

Bianconini swigged from a bottle, then passed it to Vito. 'They know we're communists.'

'Ah,' Vito said. 'I've heard of the Red Scare.' The brutal Bolshevik revolution in Russia had a lot to answer for. Vito hadn't joined the party; he'd yet to decide where his political affiliations lay. All he was interested in was freeing Italy from the Nazi-fascists.

Bianconini's men began to sing the partisan anthem, 'Fischia il Vento', and Vito joined in.

> *The wind ceases and the storm grows calm.*
> *The proud partisan returns home.*
> *Blowing in the wind is his red flag.*
> *Victorious, at last we are free.*

He fervently hoped the words of the song would soon come true. He was fed up with war, fed up with having to put his life on hold, fed up with living like an animal in the wild. The goal of going back to the University of Florence, to pick up his studies where he'd left off, had kept him focused through all the bloodshed this past year. That and returning to live with his parents.

(He'd moved out not to put them in danger when he'd become an urban guerrilla.) Now that he'd handed in his gun to the Americans, he had the perfect excuse to go home. But that would be giving up. And he must make sure Anna was safe. Afterwards, he'd go to Bologna. That's where Bianconini and the rest of the partisans were headed. They would gather there with Resistance fighters from all over to await the Allies' arrival.

Vito yawned as tiredness washed over him. He'd been awake for over twenty-four hours. What a god-awful day it had been. Clinging to the hope that tomorrow would fare better, he closed his eyes and promptly fell asleep.

* * *

The next morning, following a quick breakfast of barley coffee and stale bread, Vito and Ezio went with Bianconini to a cave at the back of the barn. There, they rearmed themselves with British Sten guns and hand grenades.

'Good luck, comrade,' Bianconini said, clapping Vito on the shoulder. 'I hope you find your sister safe and well.'

'*Grazie*.' Vito thanked him. 'I'll see you in Bologna.'

Vito and his friend set off under yet more rain, sliding down a steep track that had become a cascading river of mud.

Without warning, explosions boomed from the summit of Monte Battaglia.

'Take cover, Ezio,' Vito barked.

The Wehrmacht must have returned to counter-attack the American position. Vito's pulse raced. He needed to take Anna and the nuns to safety. But where? The valley below was in German hands. Above San Ruffillo, all hell was breaking loose. Maybe she'd be better off simply staying where she was? He had to check, though, to make sure she was all right.

Slowly, keeping to the treeline, Vito led Ezio towards the convent. When they were about a hundred metres or so from San Ruffillo, Vito went on ahead to reconnoitre, and quickly returned to fill him in.

'There's a German six-by-six truck parked out front,' he whispered. 'I crept around the side of the building and looked through the windows. About ten of those bastards are in the dining room, helping themselves to the nuns' breakfast.'

'Did you see any of the sisters?'

Vito pushed his unkempt hair out of his eyes. 'No. Let's go back there and take a look together.'

Which is what they did. Part of the convent's thick outer stone walls formed the ancient fortifications of the deserted village. The cloisters were built around an open courtyard at the front.

After ascertaining that the Germans were still in the dining room, Vito edged his way round to the other side of the structure with Ezio. The echo of female voices came through the ventilation shafts to the cellar beneath. The nuns were praying to God to release them. But their prayers mingled with the high-pitched whimpers of children. Vito sucked in a sharp breath.

'The enemy is holding the nuns captive and there are kids with them. We need to act fast,' he muttered.

Thank God the Germans were complacent; they hadn't posted any sentries. But all it would take was for one of them to finish his breakfast and come outside for Vito and Ezio to be discovered.

Vito and Ezio positioned themselves at the window to the dining room, and on the count of three, in a frenzy of movement, Ezio smashed the glass with the butt of his gun. They both lobbed grenades between the shards.

Explosions boomed. Screams followed by silence. Searing

black smoke belched through what remained of the shattered glass.

While Ezio climbed inside to finish off the Germans, Vito ran around to the big oak front door. He tightened his finger on the trigger of his Sten and let rip a series of loud whacking shots.

He gained entrance and went to locate the cellar. He tried several doors and finally found one leading to a flight of steep stone steps. A padlocked steel grille blocked the way forward, but he could see the group of about twelve nuns and half a dozen small children cowering behind it.

'Anna!' he shouted, discerning his sister's figure in the group. 'You must all stand clear. I'm going to shoot out the lock!'

Whack-whack-whack.

Anna ran to him, a little girl in her arms. He took the child from her, then kissed Anna on both cheeks.

'Are you okay?'

'Our prayers brought you to us.' Her voice shook, and her eyes were wide with fear.

The mother superior, an elderly nun with a beaky nose, bustled up.

'I presume you killed those Germans,' she said. 'May their souls rest in peace.'

'Indeed.' Vito shifted the weight of the little girl onto one hip. 'We'd best go back upstairs and work out a plan.'

They met Ezio in the hallway, and Vito asked him to check on the German vehicle.

The little girl squirmed in Vito's arms. She was as cute as a button, her dark brown hair in ringlets, and she was regarding him solemnly with enormous, amber-coloured eyes.

'*Ciao,*' he said to her. 'My name is Vito, but my friends call me *Professore.*'

Shyly, she buried her face in his chest.

'So, Anna,' he said, addressing his sister. 'Who are these children and why are they with you?'

'They're Tuscan. From Florence. Their parents are Jewish and went into hiding from the SS after the Wehrmacht occupied the area. The church arranged for us to take the *bambini* into our care. I don't suppose they ever imagined the front could possibly move up here.'

'Ah.' Vito frowned.

Vito was about to ask the little girl her name, but at that moment Ezio erupted back into the hall, a set of keys jangling in his hand. 'These were still in the truck's ignition,' he said.

'Excellent.' Vito couldn't resist a smile.

He suggested to Ezio that he catch up with Bianconini and his men and make haste for Bologna. 'I'll meet you there as soon as I can,' he added.

Ezio met his eye. 'Don't you need my help?'

'There isn't enough room in that truck with the nuns and children. And it would draw too much attention if you marched alongside us.'

'Where are you heading?'

Good question. He had yet to work out the answer.

'Florence,' he said vaguely, and left it at that.

Anna touched her hand to his arm. 'Are you sure this is a good idea? There's a big battle going on in the area between San Ruffillo and the road south.'

'Germans are attacking from the north. We'll soon be at the rear of the Allied lines,' he said with more confidence than he felt. It would be risky, but the risks far outweighed the danger of staying put.

After they'd helped the nuns and children climb aboard the six-by-six, Ezio shook Vito's hand and wished him luck. 'See you soon,' Vito said. 'We'll be raising a glass of Sangiovese to each other in the red city before you know it.'

* * *

Vito got behind the steering wheel and started the engine. The vehicle juddered into life and soon he was driving the cumbersome beast up a winding, narrow unmetalled road, its massive tyres churning up clods of mud. At least it had stopped raining. But perhaps that was a mixed blessing, for the low-lying clouds of mist had lifted and the lorry full of children and nuns was clearly visible by friend and foe.

The track ahead forked into two. He took the left-hand fork, which led away from Monte Battaglia in the direction of Castel del Rio.

Without warning, a grenade landed on the road and bounced back up again. Vito slammed his foot on the brakes as the bomb exploded, showering the truck with dust and bits of rock. 'Get out,' Vito yelled. 'We need to take cover.'

A couple of dozen enemy soldiers were coming down the road towards them. *Damn.*

Hurriedly, he helped the nuns from the truck, grabbed the little girl, and made for the treeline.

'Follow me,' he shouted.

He stopped dead. A platoon of Blue Devils were approaching from where they'd been waiting to ambush the Germans.

Shots rang out.

Grenades flew in all directions.

Vito, the nuns and children were well and truly caught in the crossfire.

The little girl gave a scream and went limp in his arms.

Oh, dear God, no. A big red gash had appeared on her forehead and she was bleeding profusely.

Vito ran toward the Americans, calling out, 'I'm a partisan. I have an injured child here.'

A loud bang and pain shot through his right buttock. *Merda*, he'd been wounded. Another explosion from behind brought him down. He covered the child with his body while heavy stones fell on top of them. Where was Anna? He struggled to free himself, calling out her name, but his vision had filled with pinpricks of light and all the strength had gone from his limbs.

Is this it? he asked himself calmly. *Am I dying?*

If so, there was nothing he could do about it. He'd made the biggest mistake of his life. His last hope was that he hadn't sacrificed anyone else to his stupidity. The pinpricks of light were soon swallowed up by darkness and he felt himself slipping away.

8

Carrie was sitting on a small patch of dry grass at the base of a grapevine, its fading yellow leaves fluttering in the cool breeze. A brief respite of Indian summer was relieving the cold, rainy Tuscan fall weather, and warm sunshine filtered between the vines. A line of ants crawled diligently towards a fallen grape, oblivious to the human activity around them: the hospital bivouac, the taut ropes stretching from the tents, the shouts of the men.

It was her afternoon off, and Carrie needed to catch up on some mail. She popped a piece of gum into her mouth, picked up her pen, and began to write.

Dear Daddy, Mom and Helen

We've moved location again. Ten days ago, the entire hospital traveled in about eighty trucks loaded with all our equipment along the Arno River to Florence. From there we headed northward through mountain country to the village of Scarperia and set up in a large vineyard here. Like almost all the small Italian towns we've seen, Scarperia is old. The local people told us the town hall had been constructed in the Middle Ages. Its prominent tower, seen against a backdrop of mountains (which the Germans still hold), has a crenelated top, and the courtyard is surrounded by high stone parapets with battlements. I'm looking at the medieval fortress-like building rising above the town, which is on the other side of our bivouac, now as I write. Was it built before the use of gunpowder? Perhaps archers first used those parapets to fire on the enemy? There's so much history here, it's truly awe-inspiring.

When we first got to this site, heavy artillery was installed all around us, and the repeated blasts from 8-inch guns buckled our canvas walls. But the big guns moved away as the front shifted. Everyone hopes the fighting will end by Christmas. We all want to get it over with and come home. Seeing the complete senselessness, devastation and waste of the war in Italy, it's no wonder we can't wait for it to stop. I'm so thankful you're safe and sound in the US of A.

Carrie put down her pen with a sigh. She never conveyed any hint that she was in danger when she wrote to her folks. But, just the other day, Jerry surprised the hospital during a moonlit night by giving the nearby highway a thorough strafing and bombing. The light anti-aircraft guns had been moved forward and the raiding enemy must have realised that this was an occasion that couldn't be missed. The Luftwaffe planes flew quite low, shelling and dropping bombs on the road, onto neighbouring ammo as well as supply dumps and convoys. They continued the attack all night and at four thirty in the morning put a 20-mm shell in the enlisted men's area, mortally wounding Private First-Class Hulon V. Lofton, who died two hours later. After the air raid, the EM shifted their quarters away from the highway to the creek east of the main camp. It started to rain soon after the tents were pitched, making the mud in the area almost a foot deep. Carrie had feared Scarperia would become another Anzio, but thankfully the front soon moved far enough away.

The sound of jive music, coming from the radio in the medics' mess, interrupted her thoughts.

Max sauntered past, crooning, 'Is you is or is you ain't my baby?' She knew he was just singing the words of the song, but she didn't like the way he raked his eyes over her. He was becoming a problem, one she needed to resolve.

She finished her letter home, then picked up another sheet of paper. When she and Bill had gotten engaged, they'd kept it a secret from their families. There'd been no point telling them; they were too far away. So, they'd agreed to present their Rome marriage as a done deal once they'd shipped stateside. She'd been putting off sending a condolence letter to Bill's parents; she couldn't face it. But today, in the beauty of this Tuscan setting, she felt it was time.

She stroked the gold necklace hidden beneath her fatigues, the cameo and diamond ring. Then she picked up her pen again.

Dear Mr and Mrs Ainsworth

I hope you don't mind me writing despite us not knowing each other, but I knew your son Bill well. We met at the General Hospital in Algeria. He worked hard and he was very good at his job. It was an honor to be one of his theater nurses. When we were off duty we grew close. Losing him was like a knife in my heart and I miss him terribly. I'm stationed in Tuscany now, and I can't stop thinking about how much Bill would have enjoyed visiting the sites here. He was so interested in history, art and geography. I guess you don't need me to tell you, but you raised a real fine man. I know your pain and

sorrow must be deep and terrible. Please accept my deepest
condolences.
   Yours sincerely,
   Carrie Adams

She folded the paper and put it in an envelope. The hospital admin would forward her letter to the Ainsworths, of that she had no doubt. She peered at the vine above her, remembered picking the ripe grapes when they'd first arrived. There weren't many left, though, just like the potatoes where the unit's kitchen had been placed, which had provided several good meals until they'd run out.

Last Sunday, ice cream had been served, sourced from Scarperia, from an artisan *gelato* producer, much to the delight of the hospital personnel. Apparently there would be an endless supply. Not too endless, Carrie hoped.

She prayed the 56th would be relocated to Bologna before too long. Problem was, Jerry was putting up harsh resistance on Hitler's Gothic Line. The hospital had been busy with patients coming in from the 88th Infantry Division, casualties from a battle on a mountain known as 'Monte Battaglia'. The torrential rain had hampered the fighting. Attack had followed counter-attack and there were big losses on both sides. She'd heard about the litters carried up to four and a half miles along the steep, treacherous evacuation trail, using stretcher-bearers from among the ground troops forced into service. It was terrible.

The wail of an ambulance siren reverberated and Carrie's heart sank. Yet more wounded. More blood. More gore. When would it ever end?

* * *

Louise arrived in the tent as Carrie was getting ready to go on duty. 'They've just brought in a little girl with an open head injury.'

Carrie gasped. 'Oh, dear Lord, how horrible.'

'Yeah. She has a compound depressed fracture of the skull. Would you believe she was caught in crossfire on the mountain?'

'What was she doing up there?'

'We have no clue. She came in with a bunch of our boys and an Italian civilian.' Louise sat on her cot and pulled off her shoes. 'Theo and the team repaired the kid's fracture. But we'll need to keep her sedated and control her pain while she heals.'

'Is she on a ward?' Carrie couldn't imagine a little girl being cared for with the men. But where else would she be?

'In a curtained-off section,' Louise said. 'I expect you'll be put in charge of her. You speak better Italian than the rest of us.'

It was true. Whenever any civilians admitted to the hospital required nursing, invariably it was Carrie who was called up. How had she managed to pick up the basics of the language so quickly? Probably because she didn't care if she made mistakes with vocabulary or pronunciation; she simply soldiered on till she made herself understood. As for understanding what people said, she got them to repeat themselves again and again until, finally, the light bulb switched on. The fact that Italians conveyed a lot of meaning through hand gestures also helped. She liked chatting with them, it alleviated some of the loneliness of her everyday life.

She left Louise to finish getting ready for a nap and hurried to report for duty. Sure enough, she was assigned to take charge of the ward where the child had been admitted.

The girl was lying on her side, her head swathed in bandages. Carrie read her notes; her temperature, pulse and respiration were due to be recorded, so she checked them. Her vital signs were steady; she wasn't in any immediate danger. *Poor little pumpkin.*

The child's eyelashes fluttered, and she gave a whimper.

'*Non avere paura,*' Carrie whispered. Don't be scared. '*Stai all'ospedale.*' You're in the hospital. '*Prendiamo cura di te.*' We're looking after you.

The little girl blinked her eyes open.

'*Ciao, tesoro.*' Hi, darling. '*Come ti chiami?*' What's your name?

'Mimi.' She attempted a smile.

'*Mi chiamo* Carrie.'

She didn't know if Mimi had heard her, but her breathing stilled and she fell into a deep sleep.

Carrie proceeded with her rounds. On the other side of the long tent, a young man was groaning. She approached his cot and picked up his medical notes. His name was Vito Mancini, and his temperature hadn't been taken recently, so she found a glass thermometer and inserted it into his mouth. Then she touched her hand to his forehead. He was burning up. His groans weren't groans of pain but of delirium.

She removed the thermometer: 104. He had a raging infection. She sent a medic to fetch the physician in charge.

'His temperature's 104,' she said when the doctor arrived.

'Give him a shot of penicillin,' Captain Huxley said. Middle-aged, he was a kind, fatherly figure who'd been with the 56th since the African campaign. 'Monitor him through the night, Lieutenant. Administer aspirin to bring down his fever.' Captain Huxley checked Vito's notes. 'He was suffering from concussion when they found him and he has a flesh wound in his right buttock. Make sure it's properly cleaned up and the dressing is changed.'

'Yes, sir.'

She glanced at Vito, found his face oddly familiar. Where had she seen him before? Then she remembered. Caffè Gilli in Florence. The young man with a face like Michelangelo's statue of David. A face it would be impossible to forget. The partisan. Carrie's chest tightened.

'*Ciao*, Vito,' she said. 'Can you hear me?'

Vito's long, dark eyelashes fluttered. '*Dov'è Anna?*' Where's Anna?

'*Chi è Anna?*' Who's Anna?

But he'd closed his eyes and had slipped into more delirious groans.

She gave him the injection. With the help of a medic, she rolled him over and attended to his wound. Vito's broad shoulders tapered to a trim waist, and his rounded buttocks were muscular with no spare fat. Pus oozed between the sutures, which must have been applied hastily while he was still up on the mountain.

Carrie cleaned the infection site and sprinkled sulfa powder onto it before applying a gauze dressing.

'Keep him lying on his left side, Private,' she said to the medic. 'I'll come back and check on him later.'

She'd turned to go when Vito started calling out, 'Anna,' again. Was she his sweetheart?

And then, he changed his refrain. '*Dov'è la ragazzina?*' Where's the little girl?

'*E' qui*,' Carrie said. She's here. '*Non ti preoccupare.*' Don't worry.

Vito began to thrash around. '*E' colpa mia.*' It's my fault.

Carrie placed her hand on his forehead. 'Try and get some rest, Vito,' she said. She didn't know how to say that in Italian.

'Okay,' he sighed. 'Thank you.'

He spoke English. Maybe he'd be able to tell her more about the little girl. She was about to ask him, but the medication had already kicked in. His eyes had closed and he'd fallen asleep.

She got on with her work, changing linens and helping the patients to wash or giving sponge baths to those who needed them. She left it to the medics to assist them in using the bedpan or urinal.

After supervising the serving of dinner and helping those too sick to feed themselves, she went back to check on Vito and the little girl.

The partisan was still out for the count, but Mimi's eyes were wide open. Such pretty, amber-coloured eyes. A stray ringlet poked from underneath her bandaged forehead. '*Ciao, tesoro.*'

'*Ciao.*' Mimi smiled tentatively.

And Carrie couldn't help smiling with her.

9

Vito was dreaming he was up on a mountain, wandering around in the dark. In the distance a bright light shone and he walked towards it. He blinked his eyes open and sharp pain pierced his head, making him cry out.

'Stay calm,' someone said.

He was tired, so very tired; he just wanted to sleep. He closed his eyes and spiralled back into the darkness.

'Vito, wake up.' His sister Anna's voice came as if from afar. Was he still dreaming?

He shook his head to try to clear it. Dizziness tingled through him. Blinding brightness and the strong smell of disinfectant invaded his senses.

'Vito? Are you with us?' A halo of blonde hair had come into view. An angel? Had he gone to heaven? His confused thoughts fluttered.

'Can you smile for me?' the angel asked.

That he could do.

'Good.'

'How many fingers am I holding up?'

He squinted. 'Two.'

'How about now?'

'Four.'

'Just follow this light with your eyes.'

He found himself doing so, blinking in the intensity.

'Now look straight ahead.'

He stared at the row of cots filled with men.

'Good.'

'What's happened to me?' The words slurred on his tongue.

'You came in three days ago. Concussed and with a severe infection. We had to sedate you as you were extremely agitated,' the woman said. She was a nurse, he realised. Had he met her before? There was something familiar in her face.

'There's a nun here to see you,' she went on. 'Sister Immacolata.'

Anna's religious name. A slow smile spread over his face. He'd been worried about her for some reason. But he couldn't remember why.

Anna came forward and kissed him on the cheek. 'We thought you and the *ragazzina* had been killed. The Americans took us down the mountain, and when we got to the valley we went to the first church we could find. The priest sheltered us, then arranged transport for us to our order's mother house in Florence.'

Vito inhaled a sharp breath. It all came back to him in a rush: his stupid decision to drive Anna, the kids and her fellow nuns along the road below Monte Battaglia. 'Where's the little girl?'

'She's here, Vito. The *americani* are taking good care of her.'

'I never found out her name.'

'She's called Mimi.'

'Her mamma and papà are surely frantic with worry about her.'

'We're trying to find them.' Anna gave a sigh. 'The rest of the children have gone home. Their parents came out of hiding when Florence was liberated. You can imagine how they must have fretted, and how relieved they are to have their children back safe and sound. But Mimi's parents have disappeared off the face of the earth.'

'Poor kid.' He exhaled slowly. 'Have you seen *our* parents?'

'Yes. They wanted to come, but Mamma has a bad cold. They send you their love and want you home as soon as you leave the hospital.'

'How did you discover I was here?'

'Sister Agnese has a cousin in Scarperia who's working for the Americans in the hospital kitchen. She visited him yesterday and he told her about you and Mimi.' Anna's tone had turned joyful. 'God answered my prayers and I came as soon as I could.'

'*Grazie*. What will happen to Mimi?'

'She'll be here for some time yet,' the American nurse chipped in. 'I hope her parents will be found before she's discharged.'

'Me too.' His heart went out to the child. He shifted position, and an ache throbbed in his right buttock. 'When can *I* leave?'

He remembered that he was supposed to join Ezio in Bologna.

'Only after your stitches are out, young man.' The nurse checked his pulse, her fingers cool on his wrist. 'It's just a flesh wound, but it got infected. And you've had concussion so we need to keep you under observation.'

Anna touched his arm. 'I'll go and visit Mimi, now. She must be scared all on her own.'

'She sleeps a lot,' the nurse said. 'But I'm sure she'll be real happy to see you.'

Feeling as helpless as a new-born baby, Vito watched them

until they reached a curtained-off section at the far end of the ward. His head fell back on the pillow and he thought about Mimi, recalling his shock and horror that day in November 1943 when the Nazi-fascists rounded up about three hundred Florentine Jews. They'd herded them onto cattle trucks in the Santa Maria Novella station.

He hoped Mimi's parents hadn't been among them.

* * *

The next day, Vito woke with a clear head. His angel was back on duty and he couldn't take his eyes off her. She was doing her rounds with a young medic, dispensing medicines and changing dressings with a quiet efficiency.

'How are you feeling today?' she asked when she reached his cot.

'A lot better, thanks.'

'My name is Second Lieutenant Adams, US Army Nurse Corps.'

'I'm pleased to meet you, but that's such a mouthful. What's your first name?'

She ignored his question and he gave a wry smile. 'I think we might have met before...'

Her cheeks pinked. 'Caffè Gilli? About a month ago?'

'Ah, yes. Now I remember.'

She stuck a thermometer in his mouth and took his pulse. 'Your vital signs are normal. I'll change your dressing. Roll over for me.'

He did as she requested.

Her warm fingers probed. 'Healing nicely,' she said. 'You can sit up now.'

'How's Mimi?'

'She's making good progress. Maybe you'd like to go see her later?'

'I'd like that.' Guilt panged in his gut. He should never have placed her in danger.

Lieutenant Adams left him to his own devices, and he lay back on his pillows. A group of patients were playing a game of poker nearby, smoking and chewing gum. Should he go and bum a cigarette? He was dying for a smoke. He manoeuvred himself from the cot, but as he stood up, pain shot through his buttock. He inhaled through clenched teeth, shifted his weight to the uninjured side of his body and hobbled towards them.

Later, after a disgusting meal of what was known as Spam – salty canned pork – he managed a wash and a shave. Lights were dimmed and snores soon reverberated around the tent. But Vito wasn't sleepy. All he'd done for the past four days was sleep. So he decided to go and visit Mimi.

He pushed his way through the curtain and did a double-take. Lieutenant Adams was sitting beside Mimi's bed, a book in her hands. She wasn't in uniform; she was wearing an evening dress. God, she was beautiful. 'Sorry to disturb you,' he said, backing away.

'Oh, *ciao*, Vito. Don't go. I came to see Mimi before our weekly dance. I'm reading *The Little Engine That Could* to her but of course she doesn't understand English. Maybe you can translate?'

'I'll try,' he said.

'Which is the theme of the story.' A smile played across her lips.

The tale was charming and he enjoyed translating. A little

blue railroad engine was employed in a station yard, pulling a few cars at a time on and off the switches. One morning it was waiting for the next call when a train full of toys broke down and asked a shiny new engine to take it to the children over the hill. '*I* pull the likes of *you*. Indeed not,' said the shiny new engine built to pull passengers. Then the train asked another engine, and another, only to hear excuses and be refused. In desperation, the train asked the little switch engine to draw it up the slope and down to the other side. 'I think I can,' the little locomotive puffed, and put itself in front of the train full of toys. As it went on, the little engine kept bravely puffing faster and faster, 'I think I can, I think I can, I think I can.' As it neared the top of the hill, it went more slowly. However, it carried on saying, 'I – think – I – can, I – think – I – can.' It reached the top by drawing on bravery and then went on down the slope, congratulating itself by saying, 'I thought I could, I thought I could.'

When Vito and the lieutenant had got to the end of their joint effort, Mimi's eyes had grown heavy. The nurse bent and kissed her on the cheek. 'Good night, honey bunches.'

'*Buonanotte*,' Vito said. He smiled at Lieutenant Adams. 'I enjoyed that story.'

'I found it in our library.'

'You have a library?'

'Yes. Why?'

'Could I borrow a book?'

'Of course.' She glanced at him. 'They're only in English, though.'

'I was enrolled at the Faculty of Letters when the Germans occupied Florence. I was studying English literature.'

'You speak the language well.'

'I'd like to go back and finish my degree when the war is over.'

She inclined her head towards him. 'What was it like having Nazis in Florence?'

'The university term was late starting, but by then I'd joined the Resistance.'

'Someone told me you were a partisan when I first saw you.'

He widened his eyes in surprise. 'Oh? How did they guess?'

'I think those guns you and your friend carried were a sure giveaway.'

He nodded. 'Ah.'

She looked him in the eye. 'What were you doing up on Monte Battaglia?'

He told her the whole sorry saga. 'I made a big mistake. It was my fault Mimi got hurt. I'm only thankful Suora Immacolata, her fellow nuns and the rest of the kids escaped unharmed.'

'I hope the sister will be able to find Mimi's parents.'

'My sister will ask around, I'm sure.'

'She's your actual sister?'

'Yes. She's three years older than me, but still a novice nun. I expect she'll take her final vows in a couple of years.' He kept to himself the terrible story of her losing her fiancé when he was sent to fight on the Eastern Front. It was her tale to tell, not his, but her turning to the religious life had been what had saved her.

'How interesting,' Lieutenant Adams said. 'Maybe I can help? I mean, the Allied military government in Florence could have access to records?'

He was about to express his doubts when a tall blond man came through the gap in the curtain.

'Carrie, I've been looking for you.' The man shot Vito an annoyed look. 'You're missing the start of the dance.'

She visibly stiffened. 'I'm just finishing here, Max,' she said tersely, getting to her feet. She turned to Vito. 'I meant what I said. I'd like to help.'

'*Grazie.*' He thanked her, watched her leave with the blond man.

Was he her sweetheart? Vito couldn't help his chest tightening with disappointment. Don't be ridiculous, he told himself. *She's so far out of your reach it would be like expecting a queen to reciprocate your feelings.*

'I like the nurse.' The little girl had woken.

'Me too. But you should go back to sleep, Mimi. You need to rest.'

'Okay,' she said sweetly. 'Will my *mammina* and *babbo* come and visit me here?'

Her question was so plaintive, he felt for her. 'I hope so.' What else could he say? There was always hope. He'd do everything he could to find them, he resolved.

'*Buonanotte*, Mimi,' he said, wishing her goodnight. 'I'll come and visit you tomorrow.'

Back in his cot, he smoked the cigarette he'd bummed earlier. He couldn't stop himself from thinking about the nurse. *Carrie*, the man had called her. There was a sadness in her beautiful green eyes that tugged at his heart.

Maybe he'd accept her offer to help him search for Mimi's parents...

10

Carrie was on duty in the POW ward. She approached a German officer with a stomach wound, who'd been brought in the day before. He lay there rigid, as if he was about to give a *Sieg Heil* salute. His pale colour, glassy blue eyes, and glistening shaved head had earned him the nickname of China Doll among the nurses. Would he have goose-stepped about the tent if he'd been able to get up from his cot? Carrie wouldn't have been surprised. To her he was the epitome of an evil Nazi, lending credence to all the propaganda she'd heard. She shuddered with disgust. A man like him had launched the bomb that had ended Bill's life.

The German's cold stare fixed on the syringe in her hand. Yet another penicillin injection; he'd gotten one every four hours since he'd arrived. The medics had told her he'd been suspicious of the newly developed antibiotic and had demanded his rights under the Geneva Conventions. He'd only fallen silent when they assured him it was the same treatment given to wounded Americans.

Carrie lifted China Doll's nightshirt and jabbed the needle into the muscle of his thigh. His icy gaze fell on her, probably noting she had lowly yellow bars on her work fatigues rather than silver ones. He bore the shot stoically, of course, his face an impassive mask.

As Captain Huxley arrived to supervise the German's blood transfusion, Carrie caught the Nazi's cold eyes staring at the doctor's insignia, not his face, before they shifted warily to the flask of dark liquid she was hanging on an IV pole.

'From whom was this blood obtained?' China Doll demanded, addressing Captain Huxley in perfect English.

Unperturbed, the physician carried on working, taking his time and ignoring the question. Then he made an off-hand comment, not to China Doll but to the enlisted Wehrmacht soldier in the next bed. 'This was a fine young Jewish man's blood.'

'*Juden blut, juden blut.*' The words chorused through the tent, accompanied by ripples of laughter. The patients, mostly German, were a mixture of adult men and pitifully younger boys, and they knew the Americans took blood from the German POWs in the stockade. Clearly they hadn't shared this fact, or much else, with their superior officer. If the man were a chess player, he'd consider himself a knight while they were mere pawns.

Carrie smirked to herself, enjoying China Doll's horrified expression, then went to carry on with her rounds. She'd heard many stories about the Nazis' cruel and barbaric persecution of the Jews, and it sickened her to the core.

With a bounce in her step, she moved to the next patient.

* * *

Later, she made her way back to her quarters. She'd checked on Mimi earlier in the day so she didn't need to now, and anyway, the little girl would be fast asleep.

It was raining cats and dogs again, had been doing so for days. Carrie undressed and got under her blankets. The wind outside had begun a mad rampage. Her pulse raced. Would it lift the tent off its poles and fling it about her head?

Too agitated to sleep, she picked up John Steinbeck's *The Grapes of Wrath*, switched on her flashlight and turned the first page. The novel had been recommended by Vito, who'd read it after she'd borrowed it from the library for him last week. But she couldn't focus. She listened to the snores of her tentmates, Louise, Betty and Marge. Her heart filled with affection; they were such nice girls and easy to live with. Like in all families they had the occasional quarrel, but they were quickly forgotten. She didn't know what she'd have done without their support these past several months.

Her gaze shifted from the book to her surroundings. The bivouac was a total dive. A pyramid pole held up the canvas in the centre and a laundry line had been strung, on which their 'GI drawers' were doing a dance while the wind howled outside and shook the tent. Carrie sighed. She couldn't remember the last time she'd worn feminine underwear. Local ladies still did their laundry for them, but she and the other nurses insisted on washing the male boxer shorts they'd taken to wearing for the sake of comfort.

They sure were roughing it, but none of them ever complained. Their respect and admiration went to every soldier in uniform, for it was they who were bearing the brunt of the war.

Carrie's chest ached at the thought. The exhausted men came in covered in blood, dirt, mud and grime. When they first opened their eyes and saw her bending over them, they would grin and some of them would even kid her, hurt as they were, saying things like, 'Howdy, babe,' or 'Holy mackerel, an American gal!' or even more indiscreetly, 'How about a kiss?' But she didn't mind. They were someone's brother, someone's father, someone's son. She was rewarded beyond measure when she saw them gradually brought back to life by the hospital personnel.

The GIs stayed with them only a short time, from ten days to possibly two weeks, and she learnt a lot about them, the grit they were made of. The wounded didn't cry. Their buddies came first. She felt humbled by their patience and determination, their courage and fortitude. She was proud to be their nurse. Whenever she longed for home, to soak herself in a hot bath, put on clean clothes over a clean body and crawl in between clean sheets on a soft, springy mattress, she reminded herself why she'd volunteered. She was here because she was needed, so she would endure whatever hardships she had to. Come what may. Even looking after the POW enlisted men. It wasn't their fault they'd been conscripted. They too were someone's brother, father, or son.

Her thoughts turned to the battle up in the mountains. All three corps of the Fifth Army had now reached positions on the northern slopes of the Apennines, an average of ten miles beyond the Gothic Line. Problem was that the fall rains were hampering the advance and making supply lines increasingly difficult to maintain. The troops were weary from continuous and bitter mountain fighting, certain classes of ammunition were running low, and many officers had been killed.

Carrie released a heavy sigh as she remembered how devastated she'd been when she'd learned that the young American captain, who'd commanded the company on Monte Battaglia, had lost his life while shouting words of encouragement to his men. The thousand American troops up there had suffered a hundred casualties a day before being relieved by British Eighth Army forces. The Tommies, as they were called by Jerry, were still up on Battle Mountain, which had earned the moniker of a mini-Monte Cassino.

Carrie flopped back on her pillow as she thought about Vito, the nuns and the children. They'd been lucky not to have been killed. Yet Vito had made a complete recovery since he'd been admitted two weeks ago, and he was due to be discharged tomorrow. Mimi, however, was still on the ward. If only they could find her parents, maybe she'd be able to recover at home. As things were, she required continuous monitoring and it would be many months before she was completely healed. Poor little pumpkin. Her wistful enquiries about the whereabouts of her *mammina* and *babbo* tore at Carrie's heart.

Thankfully, she could carry on nursing her. Just last week, the US 8th EVAC had moved to the vicinity of Pietramala, north of the Futa Pass on the road to Bologna, thus giving the 56th a respite. Mimi's bed wasn't needed by an American soldier, and the colonel in charge of the hospital had given his authorisation for the child to remain with them for the time being. Carrie wrinkled her brow. If the Allies broke through to Bologna, the 56th would move with the front. What would happen to Mimi then? It was vital that her parents were found, and Carrie would do everything she could to help Vito in the task.

She smiled to herself as she thought about him. He was a good soul. She enjoyed their conversations. He said he liked practising speaking English with her and had even taught her more Italian. She felt safe with him – he behaved like a perfect gentleman – and, given that he was five years younger, she could treat him like the younger brother she didn't have. Now that their caseloads had lightened, the hospital personnel were receiving passes to visit places of interest in Allied-occupied Italy. The only place that interested Carrie was Florence, and she'd arranged to meet Vito there after he'd gone home to his family.

Two mornings later, under a pearl-grey sky that was threatening yet more rain, she was standing on the Ponte Vecchio, waiting for Vito. The picturesque old bridge had a dejected air, and the northern end had been reduced to ruins by the mines set off by the Nazis before they'd retreated from the city. How could they have done such a heartless thing? So much artistic heritage wilfully destroyed.

Vito was late, so she went to have a look in the window of one of the tiny jewellery shops that had recently reopened. A tap landed on her shoulder and she spun around.

'*Ciao*, Vito,' she said as she took in his dark blue dress suit, cream shirt and a burgundy-coloured necktie. *Boy, was he handsome.* She'd only ever seen him in his partisan gear or hospital pyjamas. '*Come stai*?' She asked him how he was.

'*Bene.*' He said that he was well. 'It was wonderful to go home to my parents' place after so long. Mamma makes the best *peposo alla fiorentina.*'

'What's that?'

'Beef, slowly cooked over a low flame covered in red wine, garlic and lots and lots of peppercorns.'

'Sounds delicious.'

'It is.' He rubbed his belly. 'Meat was strictly rationed during the German occupation and still is, but my parents managed to save up their coupons for my welcome home dinner. I was truly spoiled. Anna too.'

'How nice.'

So Vito had met up with his sweetheart. They must be close for her to have been invited to a family dinner.

'How's Mimi? I miss her.'

'She's doing great. When I told her I was meeting you, she said to say *ciao*.'

His mouth quirked a smile. 'Say hi to her from me too, please.'

'Were you able to get the last known address of Mimi's parents from your sister?' Carrie got straight to the point.

'Yes.' He pulled a piece of paper from his pocket. 'An apartment in Piazza Santo Spirito in the neighbourhood across the river. Mimi's parents' names are Noemi and Adamo Bettinelli...'

'Lead the way!'

'Yes, ma'am!'

He took her arm and looped it through his.

Carrie's chest fluttered with nerves about their mission. Why had Mimi's folks disappeared?

She walked with Vito through the back streets parallel to the Arno. The riverside road was a mass of rubble, the area of destruction on each side of the Ponte Vecchio. According to Vito, the violence of the explosions was such that it had sucked mortar right out from between the stones of buildings.

They came to what looked to be a temporary bridge built on the ruins of one that had been blown up by the Germans. 'It's known as a Bailey,' Vito explained as they started to walk across the wood and steel structure. 'The British army engineers assembled it in no time at all.'

'I'm so sad for Florence.'

'Me too.' A smile came to his face. 'But I've heard there are already plans to rebuild the original. The Ponte Santa Trinità dates from the sixteenth century.'

They crossed over and Carrie glanced at the enormous piles of debris below. 'I hate this war. I hate everything about it.'

* * *

The street leading to the Bettinellis' last known residence was narrow, the sidewalk practically non-existent, and Vito tucked Carrie into his side as they strode past heavy oak doorways, stores selling a variety of fresh produce, artisan workshops, and ground-floor windows with thick black wrought-iron bars. The buildings were tall, blocking out what little sunlight there was and giving an oppressive feel. But, when they reached the square, Carrie widened her eyes in awe. The rectangular open space was lined with trees, their leaves an array of fall colours, and an octagonal fountain in the centre boasted a marble font from which cascaded a stream of clear water. A church with a plain façade overlooked the far end.

Vito took the address from his pocket again and showed it to an elderly man who was passing by. The man pointed to a row of cream-coloured four-storey buildings with green shuttered windows. Vito thanked him and took Carrie's arm again.

The address was for an apartment on the first floor. Vito pressed the doorbell at the entrance and a lady poked her head out of the window. After listening to Vito's explanation, she came down to open the door for them. She was plump, middle-aged, and introduced herself as Signora Monia Landi. Vito and Carrie gave their names and explained who they were, to which she said, 'Come upstairs, my dears, and tell me how I can help you.'

The woman ushered Carrie and Vito into an elegantly furnished living room with carved wooden sideboards. Beautifully embroidered white linen drapes dressed the windows, and there were beige wool carpets on the pale pink marble-tiled floor.

'Would you like a coffee?' she asked, indicating they should sit on the plush cream sofa opposite the fireplace.

Vito and Carrie thanked her but declined. 'We don't want to disturb you,' Vito said. He then launched into the reason for their visit. When he'd finished explaining, Signora Landi gave a heavy sigh. 'We hid them in our attic,' she said. 'Noemi and Adamo were such a nice young couple, but I think they found it difficult to be cooped up while their friends were working for the Resistance. They left without a word, which was very common when the Nazis were here. Everything was hush-hush. No one trusted anyone else for fear of informers. And no one said anything also because, if the person they told their secrets to was interrogated, they might reveal information under torture.'

'Oh, how horrible,' Carrie said, her heart dropping. 'When did Noemi and Adamo disappear?'

'I can't remember the exact date.' Signora Landi frowned. 'Towards the end of last January, I think.'

'At least they couldn't have been with the group that was sent to a labour camp the previous November.' Vito leaned forward. 'Do you know their political affiliation?'

'They were members of the Action Party, I believe.'

'Thank you for telling us.' He smiled. 'You've been a great help.'

'Are you sure you wouldn't like a coffee?'

'*Grazie*, signora.' Carrie thanked her. 'But I need to head back to the hospital.'

* * *

Half an hour or so later, Carrie was sitting with Vito under the crystal chandeliers in Caffè Gilli, a glass of white wine in hand and a ham panino on the marble-topped table in front of her.

They'd not spoken much on the way there, other than to express their surprise that Mimi's parents had been members of the Resistance like Vito.

'What did the Action Party do during the Nazi occupation?' Carrie asked.

'I'm not sure, to be honest. I was in a small group. We all operated independently of each other. But we all had the same goal, which was to rid Florence of as many Nazis and fascists as we could.'

'How did you do that?' She took a sip of wine.

'My friends and I would go out on our bicycles, one at a time, and shoot them. Then we'd hide until the next opportunity arose to do it again.'

'Sounds really dangerous, Vito.'

He huffed. 'Dangerous maybe, but it was simple and effective.'

'What made you join the Resistance?'

'If I hadn't, I'd have been conscripted into Mussolini's Republican Army, a fate worse than death in my opinion. As a draft dodger, if I'd been caught I'd have been executed. Fighting back was the only option.'

'Goodness gracious,' she said, shocked. There was so much she didn't know about this horrible war.

'There's something I need to tell you, Carrie.' He knocked back a slug of his wine. 'I'm leaving Florence tomorrow to go to Bologna.'

Her heart sank. 'But why?'

'All of us partisans have been ordered to meet up there and fight the Nazi-fascists in preparation for the arrival of the Allies.'

'I was hoping you'd stay and help me find Mimi's parents. She'll need them when the hospital packs up and moves with the front. We won't be able to take her with us.'

'Anna and I have already discussed this with *our* parents. They've offered to take her in temporarily when she's well enough to leave the hospital.'

Carrie wondered which set of parents had offered – his or Anna's. She didn't want to appear nosy so didn't ask. Instead, she said, 'Wow. That's so nice of them.'

He smiled. 'They're nice people.'

'I wish you didn't have to go to Bologna.'

She'd miss him, miss their chats, miss their friendship. She so enjoyed being with him, never thought she would bond with another man since Bill. Vito was taken by Anna. Carrie didn't need to worry that he'd presume something other than friendship with her, which was perfect.

'I'm still a partisan. It's my duty,' he said.

'Maybe I'll see you there when Bologna is liberated?' She couldn't help sounding wistful. God forbid anything might happen to him...

'Maybe.' The corner of his mouth lifted. 'In the meantime, perhaps you'll continue your search for Noemi and Adamo...'

'I wouldn't know where to start.'

'You could try contacting the Action Party, the Partito d'Azione. They're part of the Comitato Nazionale di Liberazione.'

'What's that?'

'The National Liberation Committee. As you know, the Allies have established a military government in Florence, but the Tuscan CNL set up their own administration before the British Eighth Army arrived. It is they who really hold the reins of power. I could ask my father to help you speak to the right people if you like.'

'That would be great. I firmly believe Mimi should be with her parents...'

Vito's face assumed a serious expression. 'I think we should prepare ourselves for the worst. It's highly likely that Mimi is an orphan. I mean, her parents would have come forward by now if they were still alive, wouldn't they?'

Carrie nodded. Vito had put her deepest worry into words. 'I was hoping we'd achieve a happy outcome today, although it was just a slim hope.'

Her voice had caught on a sob, and Vito reached across the table to take her hand. 'What's wrong, Carrie? I sense such sadness in you. It's not just for Mimi, is it?'

His insight took her so much by surprise that she told him. Told him about Anzio. Told him about Bill.

'Don't go and get yourself killed, Vito,' she added. 'I couldn't bear that. You've become a real good friend.'

He got to his feet and helped her up, wrapping his arms around her and holding her while she fought back her tears.

'I'll be careful, Carrie, I promise.'

She remembered begging Bill to promise the same.

'Let's finish our lunch then I'll walk you to the station,' he said. 'You can't miss your ride back to the hospital. And I've got to prepare to leave in the morning.'

She did as he suggested, but the food was no longer appetising to her. 'I'm not hungry,' she said, passing Vito her half-eaten bread roll. 'You eat it.'

He made quick work of the panino and they paid the check. Their ten-minute walk to the station took them past the Santa Maria Novella Basilica.

'Can you leave me here, Vito?' she asked, gazing at the beauty of the marble. 'I'm a little early and I've heard this church is worth a visit.'

She declined his offer to go into the building with her.

'I'd rather we said goodbye outside.'

'*Arrivederci*, Carrie.' He took her hand, lifted it and kissed her wrist. 'Until we meet again.'

'I hope so, Vito. I hope so with all my heart.'

She spun on her heel so he wouldn't notice the tears she could no longer contain, and she went inside the church.

An enormous wooden crucifix hung from the centre of the ceiling above the central nave. With empty air all around it, she was reminded of Christ's actual crucifixion. She picked up a leaflet and read that it had been created by the Florentine painter, Giotto, in 1288–89. She could see his mastery in the shading on the Saviour's body, the waves in his hair, the blood spilling out, the details in the background tapestry. Gory but incredibly beautiful at the same time.

Carrie fell to her knees in the pew beneath and prayed. Oh, how she prayed. She prayed for Bill's soul. She prayed for all the soldiers fighting in this terrible war. She prayed for little Mimi and her vanished parents. She prayed for her family at home in the States. And she prayed for Vito to return safe and sound.

Later, in the Jeep returning her to Scarperia, she sat silent while Captain Huxley, Betty and Marge discussed their tour of the Palazzo Vecchio, from where the Medici family had ruled over the city.

All the way back to hospital, her thoughts chased each other like coyotes chasing rabbits. Why had she been so unhappy when Vito had said he was going to Bologna? Was it because he'd stoked her grief for Bill? Or was it because she'd developed romantic feelings for him? If she had, it was wrong of her. Vito was taken and she loved Bill. She would never betray him with anyone else. Her feelings for Vito were affection for a friend, she told herself. Of course she'd been upset when he'd said he was going off to fight. She simply didn't want him to get killed.

11

Wrapping her coat around herself, Carrie made her way to her bivouac. It was raining again. At least she no longer needed to slosh through the boot-deep muck. The continuous downpours had rendered it necessary for work details to gravel the entire site and install big culverts to handle all the water. Recently, it had also gotten colder and, since GI stoves – portable gas burners – could only be obtained for the wards, the engineers had started building oil heaters for the hospital personnel to keep warm. Potbellied, like old wood stoves, their soot got everywhere, blackening everyone's clothes.

Carrie wiped a particle of the sediment from her eye and pushed her way through the flap of her tent.

She sat on her cot, took off her shoes and rubbed her tired feet. Then she laid herself down for a short rest. She closed her eyes and tried to fall asleep, but thoughts about the progress of the war buzzed through her mind. The Allies were making a last-ditch attempt to reach the Po River before winter. However, the assaulting divisions had sustained a lot of casualties and had only gained a few miles of terrain. Carrie felt so sorry for them.

Cold and drenched by the unending rainfall, infantrymen had needed to walk long distances through seas of sludge. And the many mines, together with the mud, had hampered tank support. Rations and ammunition needed to be carried up steep mountain trails by mule pack, but even mules had been unable to move heavy guns through the massive quantities of mud. The 91st Division had tried oxen, Carrie had heard, but with no greater success. Enemy shelling and mortar fire had been the worst ever encountered during the Italian campaign, and there'd been a big increase in admissions to the hospital.

Carrie couldn't help but worry. US troops were still struggling forward against increasingly strong opposition. With the British Eighth Army immobilised by soft ground and flooded streams on the fringe of the Po plain, the American Fifth Army now faced the best German units in Italy. To make matters even worse, the Field Artillery Battalions had been withdrawn for shipment to France, and ammunition was in such short supply as to require drastic restrictions on its use.

It was all too horrible.

The last straw had come the other day when torrential rains had washed out all the roads and bridges. A patient had said that, in rare intervals of clear weather, the Po Valley was visible in the distance. But Bologna was still nine difficult miles away, crawling with the enemy, and US troops had been ordered to fall back to defensible positions and dig in. For how long was anyone's guess.

Carrie drew her eyebrows together. If Vito had gotten through to Bologna, he'd be fighting the Nazi-fascists in the city in preparation for the arrival of the Allies. What would happen to him now that the front appeared to have stalled? She said a silent prayer.

Dear Lord, please keep him safe.

* * *

Mimi was sitting up in bed when Carrie arrived to check on her before going to the usual weekly dance. She perched beside her on the cot and smiled. 'Hi, honey bunch. How are you feeling?'

'I'm okay,' Mimi replied in English. Carrie had started teaching her the language recently and she was doing great.

'Would you like me to read you a story?'

'*The Little Engine*?'

Carrie giggled. 'Of course.'

She'd read it so many times that Mimi remembered what came next and repeated the words with her. It was a great way for her to learn English.

When they'd gotten to the end of the tale, both saying together, 'I – thought – I could,' Carrie put the book down.

She waited for the inevitable question, which came immediately.

'Will my *mammina* and *babbo* come visit soon?' The small voice was so wistful Carrie's throat tightened.

'I don't know, pumpkin, but I'm going to Florence tomorrow and will try and find them.' She'd been invited to have lunch with Vito's parents and his sister, and prayed there would be some news about the Bettinellis. Vito wouldn't be there, of course. He was still in Bologna.

Carrie took Mimi's hand. 'I promise I'll do everything I can.'

A hollow promise, but there was always hope.

'They could be at our house,' Mimi said in Italian. 'You should go there.'

Carrie's ears pricked up. 'Can you remember the address?'

'Of course. Mammina and Babbo made sure I knew it by heart in case I ever got lost.' She went on to recite a street name and number which meant nothing to Carrie, so she got Mimi to repeat it slowly while she wrote it on one of the pieces of paper the child used for sketching.

'You're so smart, Mimi.' Carrie couldn't help praising the girl. Neither she nor Vito and his sister had thought to ask about the address. Carrie, for one, had never guessed that she'd know it.

Carrie caught Mimi eyeing the pencil she'd used. Mimi was a fine artist for someone of her age, and the activity kept her from getting bored.

'Would you like to draw me a picture, darlin'?'

Mimi nodded solemnly.

Carrie plumped up Mimi's pillows, then watched her sketch. 'I'll get you some coloured pencils when I'm in town, if you like.'

'*Grazie*.' Mimi's smile touched Carrie to the core.

'You're so welcome.'

'You look very pretty.' Mimi was staring at her blue evening dress.

'We have dances every Friday night, honey. Maybe you can come to one when you're feeling better?'

'I don't know how to dance.'

'Then I'll teach you.'

Mimi smiled again and handed Carrie the picture she'd just drawn. 'It's you.'

'Wow. I love it.' Mimi had captured the lines of her outfit perfectly. 'You're incredibly talented.' Carrie brushed a kiss to her soft, rounded cheek. 'I should go or someone will come looking for me.'

That someone being Max.

'*Ciao, tesoro. A domani*.' Bye, darling, see you tomorrow.

'*A domani*, Carrie,' Mimi said.

* * *

'*Piacere di conoscerla,*' Carrie said, shaking Vito's dad's hand. It's a pleasure to meet you.

She stood at the entrance to a three-storey stone palazzo, which overlooked the Medici Chapels at the back of the San Lorenzo Basilica. Sister Immacolata, dressed as always in her nun's habit, had walked Carrie there from where she'd gotten a ride to the railway station.

Vito's sister kissed her father then said to Carrie, 'Our apartment is at the top, but the many stairs are worth it. The panorama is fantastic.'

Signora Mancini was waiting for them on the landing. 'Welcome,' she said, and her smile was so like Vito's that Carrie's chest fluttered.

Both his parents were in their late fifties, he'd told her. His dad would soon retire from his legal practice and was looking forward to drawing his pension in peace.

Carrie beamed a smile at them. 'Thank you for inviting me.'

'You are most welcome.' Signor Mancini turned to Vito's sister. 'Anna, show Carrie the view before I take her coat.'

Carrie gasped. 'I thought your name was Immacolata, not Anna...'

The nun laughed. 'Suora Immacolata is my religious name.'

Carrie's heart gladdened, which was wrong of her, she knew. But she couldn't help smiling at the news that a girl called Anna wasn't Vito's sweetheart, but his sister.

Anna led her across the living room towards floor-to-ceiling windows, which she opened with a sharp exhale of breath.

'Oh, my...' Carrie stepped onto a wide terrace and gazed at the panorama of Florence's hundreds of terracotta-tiled rooftops, the domed red cupula of the cathedral, its pearly bell tower, and the fortified turrets of the Palazzo Vecchio. 'So beautiful.'

Signor Mancini approached. 'Come inside, my dears. It's cold out here and lunch is ready.'

He took Carrie's coat and she followed him through to the dining room, which also boasted stunning vistas of the city. Vito had told Carrie a while back that his father was a lawyer and that his mother devoted herself to charity work. The apartment's luxurious art nouveau furnishings and prestigious location reflected the family's apparent wealth, but Signora Mancini did her own cooking and cleaning, having given up employing a cook and a maid at the start of the war.

Vito's mom had made *crespelle alla fiorentina* – crepes stuffed with ricotta cheese – for their first course.

'This is delicious,' Carrie complimented her. The thin layers melted on her tongue they were so light.

Signor Mancini poured red wine into their crystal glasses. 'Vito should be here,' he said. 'We didn't want him to go to Bologna.'

Carrie echoed his sentiment but kept it to herself. 'He's very brave,' she said instead.

Signor Mancini huffed and wiped his moustache with a linen napkin. 'Brave and sometimes foolhardy. I worry about his safety. So many of his fellow *gappisti* urban guerrillas have been killed by the *tedeschi* – Germans. Vito was lucky to have got away with his life. And the risk he took with Anna, her fellow nuns and the children.'

'I'm keeping him in my prayers,' Carrie said. Fear for him sent a shiver through her. 'I hope the Allies break through to Bologna soon and then he'll be able to come home.'

'Our Lord Jesus will look after him.' Anna got up and began to clear the dishes. 'In the meantime, we can focus on finding out what has happened to Mimi's parents. Papà has a contact in the

Action Party. He can tell you what he has discovered while I go and help Mamma in the kitchen.'

As Signor Mancini spoke, Carrie concentrated hard on what he was saying. Her Italian had come a long way since she'd arrived in Tuscany, but she still needed him to repeat himself several times. Finally, following his hand gestures, and listening to his repetitions, she understood that no one with the names of Noemi and Adamo Bettinelli had been *Partito d'Azione* partisans.

'But that doesn't mean to say that they weren't,' he added. 'They would have had aliases like all the others. If we could discover what they called themselves, we'd stand a better chance of discovering what happened to them.'

A sinking feeling came over Carrie. 'It would be like looking for a needle in a haystack.'

'Shame you don't have any photographs of them.'

Carrie thought for a moment. 'Mimi gave me their address.'

She pulled the piece of paper from her dress uniform pocket and showed it to Vito's dad.

He took it and read out loud, 'Via Benedetto Varchi, 22.' His face turned pale. 'The first of the *ville tristi*.'

'*Ville tristi*?'

'There's no other way to put this.' He took a deep breath before speaking again. '*Ville tristi* were locations where the *fascisti* tortured people for information. In Florence they were led by a despicable man called Mario Carità. He started his heinous activities in Benedetto Varchi street, then moved on to bigger places as his band of evil-doers grew too big to be accommodated there.'

'But why were they in the Bettinellis' house?'

'They'd have sequestered it because it belonged to Jews.'

'Oh, dear Lord, how awful.' Carrie shuddered.

* * *

When lunch was over – a main course of tasty roasted guinea fowl and chestnuts, followed by a succulent fresh fruit salad of grapes, apples, pears and pomegranate – and after Carrie had helped with the dishes, Anna offered to accompany her to Via Benedetto Varchi.

'We can ask about Noemi and Adamo there,' she said. 'Someone might remember them.'

'Why don't I go with you,' Signor Mancini suggested. 'I need to get out for a walk and it has stopped raining for once.'

'I'll put my feet up and catch up on some reading while you're gone,' Signora Mancini said. She smiled at Carrie. 'Thank you for taking such good care of Vito and Mimi. I hope to see you again soon.'

'I hope so too. And *grazie* for the delicious meal. I really enjoyed it.'

To be honest, she hadn't eaten much after learning about the *villa triste* and hoped she hadn't caused any offence.

Carrie stayed silent during the brisk twenty-minute walk across the centre of Florence, listening to Anna and her dad discuss the practicalities of Mimi moving in after she was discharged from the hospital, as a temporary measure. It was clear that they already believed her to be an orphan, and Carrie had started to believe so too. But she owed it to the little girl to find out the truth, terrible though it might be. How Carrie's heart broke for her.

The house, when they got to it, was set back from the road in a small garden overgrown with weeds and surrounded by a wrought-iron fence. Built of brown stone with the usual terra-cotta-tiled roof, the dwelling was accessed by a short flight of steps that led to a loggia behind which was a boarded-up front door. The ground-floor windows had been boarded up as well, and the second-floor window shutters were all closed.

'It looks deserted.' She sighed.

'I'll try the entrance bell, just in case,' Anna said.

They waited and waited, but no one came.

'I guess I should make tracks to the station.' Carrie's arms drooped by her sides. 'My ride back to the hospital is due to leave soon.'

'We'll go with you.' Anna touched her hand to Carrie's. 'But before we leave, let's just try next door.'

Without waiting for a response, Anna stepped away to press the doorbell of a big villa overlooking the Bettinellis'. A mature woman in a maid's uniform came down the front path.

'How can I help you?'

Anna and her father explained, and the maid shook her head. 'The fascists took away all the valuables in the house and burnt the rest.'

'Do you know anyone in the neighbourhood who might have been friends with the Bettinellis?'

'Why?' she asked, a stern expression on her face.

'We need to find them. Their daughter is in the American hospital.'

The maid's demeanour softened. 'Poor little thing. I remember she was such a sweet child. I'll ask around for you. Adamo Bettinelli was a brilliant engineer and well liked. And his wife, Noemi, a gifted artist.'

Signor Mancini thanked the maid and handed his business card to her. He turned to Carrie. 'We've done all we can for now. Anna and I will keep our ears open, no need to be anxious.'

'*Grazie*.' Carrie forced a smile. 'We just have to pray someone comes forward.'

'Indeed. Anna and I will walk you back to the station now. Otherwise you might get lost.'

Again, they set off at a quick pace. Carrie eyed every store they passed until, at last, they came to a stationer's.

'I promised Mimi I'd get her some coloured pencils,' she said.

Inside the shop, she bought the biggest box on offer. 'I'll take that too.' She pointed to a cute cloth doll in a pink dress. She wasn't sure if Mimi liked dolls, but the toy's happy expression – rosy red cupid lips and twinkling blue eyes stitched onto its chubby face – would surely sugar the bitter pill of disappointment that Carrie hadn't managed to find her parents.

At the Piazza Santa Maria Novella, she thanked Anna and her father.

'We'll telephone the hospital and leave a message if there's any news,' they promised before waving her off.

The Jeep was parked where it had dropped her off at midday and Carrie climbed aboard. She was the only passenger and glad she didn't need to make polite conversation. Soon they'd left the city behind and were motoring up into the hills towards the mountains above Florence. The road they were on would lead to Bologna eventually via the Futa Pass, but the final stretch was still in enemy hands. Vito had planned to cycle along the route as far as he could go before sneaking behind German lines. Had he made it through safely? If only she had news of him. She thought about the *ville tristi*, and a dark cloak of fear for Vito fell over her shoulders. Anna was his sister, not his sweetheart. Apparently, he wasn't taken. But she felt concerned for him as a friend. And that meant she had every right to worry about him, didn't she?

12

Vito sat on a rickety chair in the crumbling destroyed fortress-like ruins of the old hospital building, which overlooked the steep banks of the Reno Canal in Bologna. He and Ezio were in the white-tiled lobby, smoking Nazionale cigarettes. Surrounded by about one hundred and fifty men – *gappisti* urban guerrillas and Bianconini's *partigiani* from the mountains – Vito contemplated the stock of submachine guns and hand grenades they'd requisitioned from an attack on a train. He was in the only part of the Ospedale Maggiore left intact after the Americans had bombed it over a year ago, supposedly by accident, when they'd targeted the nearby railway.

'I'm bored,' he said, tapping ash from his smoke. 'I wish the *inglesi* and *americani* would damn well hurry up.'

For days now, he and the others had spent their time playing the waiting game. They slept on mouldy old beds in the derelict hospital wards and local people brought them food. They'd been reduced to drinking the water collected in barrels, as the faucets had run dry. Vito gritted his teeth. Rumour had it that the Allies had been delayed by the recent bad weather. The endless rain had turned the ground between their front lines and Bologna into a quagmire. Roads and bridges had been bombed to bits. It was a complete disaster.

But that afternoon, the commander of the National Liberation Committee, a wiry man with a hook nose, had arrived with a proclamation. Vito and his comrades had formed a circle around him while he declared, 'The Allies have announced a new offensive and soon we will go into action to liberate the city from within.' He went on to congratulate the *partigiani* on the efficiency of their organisation and on their high morale. 'The Germans are in retreat along their entire front and the time for insurrection is fast approaching.'

He added that it was difficult to establish exactly when that would be. Everything depended on the movement of the US Fifth and British Eighth armies.

Vito hoped the tide had turned and they would get here soon. His thoughts turned to Carrie; she was never far from his mind. When he'd met her in Florence last month, she'd looked so beautiful in her dress uniform, her little officer's cap perched on her pretty blonde curls. Her concern for Mimi had touched him deeply and he'd wanted to kiss her so badly that he'd had to use all his willpower not to gather her into his arms. He'd fallen for her hook, line and sinker. But he'd told himself she was so beyond his reach, a goddess to a lowly mortal, that to think for one minute that she would ever reciprocate his feelings would be absurd. Besides, she was in mourning for her fiancé. How could he compete with a dead man? From what she'd said, Bill had been everything that he, himself, was not. Mature. Eminently qualified in his profession. Competent. Carrie obviously still loved him and it would take a long time before she would love anyone else.

'The battle is at hand,' Ezio said, interrupting Vito's thoughts.

'There's a band of partisans in the old municipal slaughterhouse near Porta Lame who'll join us, I've heard.'

Porta Lame was one of the nine remaining gates to the five-hundred-year-old battlements that once encircled Bologna and were demolished in the early part of the century. Given their strategic position nearby, both Vito's group and the one in the abattoir would be used as backup to the Allies when they entered the city.

'I hope you're right,' Vito said. 'I can't wait for it to be over and done with.'

'Let's try and get some sleep.' Ezio stubbed out his cigarette. 'Tomorrow is another day.'

Fully clothed, Vito stretched out on his cot. His stomach rolled as he remembered the battle to liberate Florence last August. The Allies had taken their time to arrive then, as well. Hopefully, history wasn't repeating itself. In the euphoria of believing liberation was imminent, the Florentine partisans had relaxed their vigilance, and as a result, one of them had been captured and tortured by Mario Carità and his band in the Villa Triste. The *partigiano* went on to reveal vital information about his comrades which led to many arrests, horrific acts of torture, indiscriminate brutality and deaths by firing squad.

The fascists then departed, leaving Firenze to about one thousand German troops, commanded by a Colonel Fuchs, who'd been given the task of acting as a rear guard for the retreating Wehrmacht. The only good thing that came out of this was that Florence, like Rome, was to be considered an 'open city', which meant it shouldn't be bombed because of its artistic heritage.

Partisan groups who'd been fighting in the mountains and countryside, who'd been armed by the Allies via air drops, had entered Florence to fight alongside Vito, Ezio and the few who were left of the *gappisti*. But the Germans, who everyone referred to with the pejorative name *crucchi*, ordered the evacuation of citizens living on both sides of the Arno after cutting off electricity and water supplies. About one hundred and fifty thousand civilians including the sick, the elderly and the very young had to leave their homes forthwith. Taken by surprise, Vito and his comrades helped them load their belongings onto hand carts which they trundled to empty barracks, school buildings, and even the magnificent Pitti Palace. He couldn't help marvelling at the solidarity shown by the humblest people during that trying time. Problem was that the order to evacuate had split the partisans into two groups, one third on the left-hand side of the Arno and two thirds on the right. And, what was worse, despite their guarantees not to bomb Florence, the bastard Nazis had mined the bridges.

As soon as he'd found out what the Nazis had done, Vito rushed to the Ponte della Carraia with a company of fellow partisans to try to stop its destruction. But there was nothing they could do – *crucchi* soldiers were defending the bridge with machine guns and lookouts – and not long afterwards massive explosions rocked the city. Only the Ponte Vecchio had been left standing; however, it was impossible to cross over as the approaches on each side had also been bombed. When the Allies arrived, they found Florence split into two. Vito and his group were stuck on the left-hand bank of the Arno. There, they were allowed to keep their arms to help the British, New Zealanders and South Africans round up enemy snipers and those Wehrmacht troops who'd been cut off.

Vito had been beside himself with worry for Mamma and Papà, who were on the other side of the river in the part of the city still under German occupation. He and Ezio had snuck across, clambering over the rubble in the middle of the night. At their parents', they found there was no food, no water, no electricity. In the August heat, rotting rubbish had accumulated in the roads and the stinking corpses of the dead had been left unburied. Wehrmacht soldiers patrolled the empty streets, firing into any open windows.

The only thing that kept Vito going was the hope that the nightmare was coming to an end. And come to an end it did. Finally, the Liberation Committee gave the order for an uprising. After the tolling of La Campana del Popolo – the people's bell – in Palazzo Vecchio, every church bell in Florence began to sound and all the partisans in the city went on the attack. Bitter fighting ensued and, when the Allies made it across the Arno, they learned that Florence had liberated itself.

Vito and Ezio stayed with their families. In early September, shortly after meeting Carrie for the first time in Caffè Gilli, they set off for the mountains. He thought about her now with such longing. Would he ever see her again?

Ezio's snores rumbled in his ears. His friend had been with him through thick and thin, like he'd been with Ezio. The upcoming battle would put them both to the test, but Vito was confident they'd win through. Morale was high and they were defending their country. One day, Italy would be free. A better future beckoned. He rolled over on the cot and let sleep claim him.

* * *

Vito woke to Ezio nudging him. 'One of our scouts has just spotted a big group of militia going from house to house,' he muttered. 'Uniformed officers of the Feldendarmerie and the fascist Police Assault Department appear to be in charge.'

Vito leapt up and ran to the window that overlooked the open space between the old hospital and the abattoir.

Oh, shit... Shots were coming from the upper windows of the building opposite. The partisans inside seemed to be using pistols. What hope did they have?

'Do we go to their assistance?' he asked Bianconini, who'd come to stand next to him.

'I think they've got it under control.'

And it was true. The *gappisti* in the former slaughterhouse had started lobbing grenades and it looked as if they were inflicting many casualties. Black-shirted fascists and Wehrmacht soldiers were falling left, right and centre. The Nazi-fascists made several attempts to occupy the structure, with assaults as furious as they were fruitless, but the partisans were winning the day. They kept on firing and the enemy returned fire without seeming to get anywhere.

Vito grabbed hold of Ezio's arm and nodded down towards the street. An armoured car had rolled into the area in front of the *ospedale*. Black cross with a white background on its sides, the vehicle trained the barrel of its long-range 88-mm cannon on the abattoir.

Boom-boom-boom. Shells arched through the air and exploded against the exterior wall, sending bits of brick flying. Vito winced. It looked as if the roof had caved in. Smouldering rubble, stone and tiles had been scattered everywhere. Black smoke billowed, stinging his eyes.

One of the German crew opened the car's hatch at that point, and rather complacently stuck his head out to peer around. He was joined by another fellow and they both lit cigarettes.

'We must counter-attack, *partigiani*.' The order came from Bianconini. 'Our comrades in the abattoir will be able to escape if we do so. Speed is of the essence. That vehicle is a cumbersome beast, the crew aren't expecting us and they won't see us very easily with all this smoke.'

Adrenaline pumped through Vito's veins and perspiration prickled his brow. He grabbed a grenade and slung his Sten over his shoulder.

Stealthily, he made his way outside with Ezio. They crept up to the armoured car.

'Give me a leg up,' Vito whispered. 'I'll take those men down.'

Vito clambered onto the plating at the side of the vehicle. Then he gripped the thin cord of the grenade with his teeth and threw it into the open flap.

A barrage of noise erupted: the explosion of the grenade, the screams of the men in the car, the *whack-whack-whack* of the partisans' submachine guns as they converged on the vehicle.

Crucchi began running towards them from where they'd been attacking the slaughterhouse. But they were outnumbered, getting mowed down by Vito and the others as they approached. It was over almost as soon as it had started.

'Come with me,' Bianconini said to Vito and Ezio after giving orders to the rest of the men to deal with the dead and wounded.

They went into the bombed-out building and picked their way through the rubble, but all they found were four bodies.

'There were about seventy *gappisti* in here.' Bianconini smiled. 'They've succeeded in getting away.'

* * *

By the time Vito and Ezio managed to wheel their bicycles past the German position just south of the town of Pianoro, it was snowing. It was the dead of night, and dressed in the stolen black uniforms of fascist militia, they had succeeded in escaping the enemy's notice.

Vito's stomach clenched with disappointment as he thought about how, a couple of days ago, he and his comrades had listened open-mouthed to a broadcasted message on the Allied radio station *Italia Combatte*. A proclamation on behalf of General Harold Alexander, Supreme Commander of the Allied Forces in Italy, had come over the airwaves addressed to the Italian Resistance.

'The summer campaign, which began on 11 May and has been conducted without interruption, is over. The winter campaign will now begin. This means ceasing large-scale operations and preparing yourselves for a new phase of struggle to face a new enemy, the winter itself.'

'It only mentions large-scale operations,' Bianconini had muttered in the Garibaldi partisans' hideout. But then the wiry, hook-nosed man from the National Liberation Committee came to inform them that they should all return to their families until the spring.

'If you stay here, you'll risk being rounded up by the Nazi-fascists. They're paying informers to reveal information on where you're all quartered.'

There was nothing to be done but follow his advice. Morale had plummeted after the radio broadcast. Everyone felt dejected and hopelessness had taken hold. The realisation that victory had been snatched from their grasp, when they'd all believed it was just around the corner, had been too much to bear.

Vito shivered in the cold light of the November dawn. Up on the road to the Futa Pass, the snow had turned to sleet and the narrow road ahead became slippery as he and Ezio mounted their bicycles and pedalled on. The going was tough and the hairpin bends were all uphill. At places, it was incredibly steep and Vito's calves ached.

At last, they reached the top of the pass. Tiredness washed over him and nausea swelled his gullet.

'I'm going to puke,' he said as he dismounted from his bike. At the side of the road, he vomited up the meagre meal he'd eaten before leaving Bologna. 'I feel like crap.'

Ezio glanced at him. 'You don't look that great.'

Vito groaned. 'It's at least another four to five hours' cycling until we get to Florence.'

'Hmmm.' Ezio tapped his stubbled chin. 'Maybe we should rest.'

'It's okay. I'll carry on.' Icy sweat beaded Vito's forehead, but his body felt as if it had caught fire. 'The way is downhill from here.'

A kilometre or so from Firenzuola, though, they came to a roadblock manned by Americans. Groaning inwardly, Vito brought his bike to a halt. He and Ezio were dressed as fascist militiamen. *Damn!*

'Halt!' A US sergeant stepped forward and raised his weapon.

Vito put his hands up. 'We're friends.'

'Identify yourselves!'

He and Ezio gave their names and explained that they were partisans.

'You shouldn't be armed,' the sergeant said, his eyes on the Stens slung around their necks.

'We came from Bologna,' Vito said.

'You got through German lines?' The sergeant sounded incredulous.

'Probably by fluke, but here we are.'

The sergeant barked an order to his men and they relieved Vito and Ezio of their guns.

'Where are you headed?'

'Florence.'

Vito's legs suddenly lost all their strength and he crumpled to the ground.

Ezio crouched next to him then gave a visible start. 'The whites of your eyes have gone yellow.'

The sergeant came and looked down at Vito. 'You've got jaundice. We'll take you to the hospital.'

Vito retched and threw up again.

13

Carrie was watching Mimi play with the doll she'd bought her in Florence, which she'd named Stella and seemed to really love. Carrie tied a bow in Mimi's dark brown ringlets, thankful she hadn't suffered any side effects from the fracture in her skull. Mimi's bandage had been taken off and the stitches in the upper part of her forehead had been removed. Her physical scar – a vivid red – would heal eventually and be covered by her hair once it had grown back. Carrie only hoped any psychological ones would do the same.

Too many days had gone by since Mimi had asked about her parents, and Carrie feared the silence suggested she was hiding her feelings. Not knowing what had happened to Adamo and Noemi made it difficult for Carrie to help Mimi. Yesterday, Anna had visited, bringing clothes and colouring books for the child, but Anna still had no news. 'We seem to have dug a hole in water,' she'd said in Italian, which Carrie guessed meant they'd failed to get the answer they were looking for.

'Can we make Stella a new outfit?' Mimi's voice broke into Carrie's thoughts.

'That's a great idea, honey.' Carrie chewed at her lip. 'We'll need some fabric.'

'What kind of fabric?'

'I think I have just the thing,' Carrie said. 'I'll be straight back.'

Carrie rushed to her bivouac. She only had a couple of evening dresses, but what the heck. She would do anything for Mimi, even cutting up one of her gowns. She hadn't worn the green silk dress since Bill's tragic death; it reminded her too much of when they used to dance together in Algeria. She lifted the gown from where she'd folded it neatly in her footlocker, then rummaged for a pair of scissors, needles and thread.

The sound of footfalls alerted her to Betty's arrival. 'What'ya doin', hon?'

Carrie explained and Betty shook her head. 'Try not to get too attached to the little girl, darlin'. It'll be a big wrench when we move with the front.'

'I know.' Carrie heaved a sigh. 'But I can't help it. The poor baby, she really needs a friend. And I love the little pumpkin. She's such a great kid.'

'You just take care, sweetie.' Betty sat on her cot and pulled off her boots. 'Doesn't look as if we'll be pushing off anytime soon. But we'll do so eventually, and we won't be able to take her with us.'

'Yeah, I know, but for however long I'm here, I wanna take care of her.'

Hospital work had been light recently. The troops were now engaged in patrolling activities and reinforcing defence posi-tions. German artillery fire was no longer as intense, so there were fewer casualties. The armies seemed to have settled down into static warfare; only reconnaissance activity went ahead with patrols on both sides probing enemy lines. Carrie wished she had news of Vito. Anna said she thought he was still in Bologna but couldn't be sure. Apparently, the partisans had been told to stand down until the spring. Possibly, he would come home to Florence to sit it out. How Carrie hoped that would be so. She'd ask him to help step up the search for Mimi's parents.

'I'd better get back to her,' Carrie said. 'Have a nice nap...'

'I will.' Betty yawned.

Outside, enlisted men were hard at work winterising the tents by adding wooden side walls, floors and doors. Carrie couldn't wait for them to get to hers; the weather had gotten so cold that not even the stove could keep them warm.

Mimi glanced up when she approached her bed, and Carrie was rewarded with a wide smile.

'Stella will like her new dress,' Mimi said when she saw the green silk in Carrie's hands.

'I do believe you're right.'

Carrie cut out a chunk of the cloth and laid the doll on top of it. She vaguely remembered how to make clothes for toys from when she used to sew them for her own dolls when she was little. It wouldn't be too different than making clothes for herself. She'd made the dress she was cutting up while she was in college.

She picked up a pen and made a small mark on the material next to Stella's shoulders. Then she cut holes big enough for the doll's arms before sliding her into them. After wrapping the fabric around Stella, she cut a further section to make a belt. All that remained to be done was sew the edges so the silk wouldn't fray. She handed Mimi the larger piece and taught her how to do a blanket stitch. 'You're doing great, pumpkin,' she said.

'*Mi piace farlo.*' I like doing it.

'*Sei bravissima.*' You're very good.

'*Grazie.*'

Mimi's manners were impeccable, Carrie thought as she finished stitching the belt.

They dressed the doll together, then Carrie suggested going for a short walk. It was important for Mimi to do a little exercise every day, to regain her muscle strength. Carrie wrapped her up warmly in the clothes Anna had brought and then, with Stella tucked into Mimi's coat, they made their way down the ward. It was half-empty due to the fall in casualties. Louise, Theo and some of the others had gone on a return trip to Rome to take in the sights they'd missed seeing back in June. Shame Max hadn't gone with them. He was still hanging around like a bad smell, as welcome as a skunk at a lawn party.

That evening, Carrie was having dinner in the officers' mess. She took a forkful of spaghetti with meatballs and chewed thoughtfully. Mimi had been so cute on their walk; she'd chatted non-stop to everyone they met, introducing Stella and, not caring at all if they didn't speak Italian, she'd used her ever-increasing knowledge of English whenever she could. Carrie hoped she hadn't made her overtired. When she had taken her back to the ward, Mimi ate her lunch then went straight to sleep, Stella cuddled in the crook of her arm.

Carrie groaned inwardly as Max came up to her table, tray in hand. He pulled out the chair next to hers and sat himself down.

'You remember that Italian partisan we treated last month?'

'Yeah,' she said indifferently. What did Max know about her friendship with Vito?

'Well, he's back.'

'What?' Her heart pounded painfully. 'Has he been injured?'

Maybe he stepped on a German box mine while making his

way back to Florence. So many of their recent admissions had been because of anti-personnel explosives.

'Nope. He's in with jaundice.'

'Oh, no!' *Poor Vito.* 'How come he's been admitted to this hospital?'

'He got sick on his way down from the Futa Pass by one of our roadblocks. So they brought him here. He's on the hepatitis ward.'

It was a common illness among the troops. Little was known about the disease, but the general consensus was that it was caused by the lack of sanitation in the field. The only treatment was bedrest and plenty of food. Vito was in the right place.

'I'll go and see him,' she said.

'Why?' Max shot her a look that spoke words. Jealousy mixed with feigned surprise.

'I'm friends with his sister.'

'The nun?'

Max seemed to know a lot about Vito. Carrie narrowed her eyes. 'What's it to you?'

'Nothing.' He shrugged, took a sip of water. 'Hey, it's Thanksgiving tomorrow. I'm looking forward to a real feast.'

'Yeah. Me too.' She got to her feet and gave him a wave. 'I'll see you later, Max.'

Without waiting for a reply, she hurried out into the cold night air and made her way to Vito. She found him immediately. He was fast asleep, so she pulled up a chair next to his cot and waited for a medic to come and check on him. She didn't need to wait long.

After his temperature had been taken, Vito stared at her with jaundiced eyes. 'My angel,' he said.

Was he hallucinating?

'*Ciao, come stai?*' Hi, how are you?

He winced. 'My head aches.'

'You need to rest, Vito. I'll come back and see you tomorrow.'

'Yes, ma'am.' He chuckled then groaned.

She wanted to press a kiss to his cheek, but she didn't.

'I'll phone your sister so she can get a message to your parents.'

'*Grazie.*' He closed his eyes and his breathing deepened.

She placed her hand on his. Poor Vito, but at least he was in one piece. Thank heaven for small mercies.

After speaking with the physician in charge of the hepatitis ward, Carrie headed for the hospital admin tent and put through a call to the convent in Borgo Pinti, Florence – she didn't have Vito's parents' number.

Anna expressed a mixture of relief that Vito had made it out of Bologna followed by concern about his illness. 'I pray it isn't too serious.'

'They expect him to be over the worst in about two to three weeks.' Carrie sighed. 'I'll find out when you can come visit.'

'*Grazie.* I'll tell Mamma and Papà.'

Next day, Carrie went to see Vito as promised, after she'd finished her rounds.

'How's your head?' she asked as she pulled up a chair.

'A lot better.' He gave her a wan smile. 'But I still feel nauseated.'

'Just give it time.' She paused to gather her thoughts. 'So, you decided to come back from Bologna...' She was stating the obvious but was unaccountably lost for words.

'We fought the Nazi-fascists at the city gates and won a big battle. It was supposed to clear the way for the Allies.' He gave a frown. 'Let's not talk about it, Carrie. It's too upsetting. On a different note, did you manage find out about Mimi's parents?'

She told him about her lunch at his parents' and their walk to see the child's former home. 'It was a *villa triste*, would you believe?'

'That bastard Carità. I want to get my hands on him and give him as good as he gave.'

'He sounds like a horrible man.'

'Unfortunately, he ran away from Florence, like a coward, before we could make him pay for his crimes.' Vito growled softly. 'When the front finally moves, my friend Ezio and I have resolved to find him.'

Fear for Vito pounded in her chest.

'Can't someone else do that?'

'There are reasons why it has to be us. I'll explain later. Now is not the time or the place.'

'Okay.' What else could she say?

Vito's eyes had closed. He'd fallen asleep.

Once more, she wanted to brush a kiss to his cheek, but that would have been entirely inappropriate. With a sigh, she got to her feet and made her way out of the ward. He didn't want to talk about the Allies reaching Bologna.

Whyever not?

* * *

A week later, Carrie was sitting on her cot, writing a letter to her family.

Dear Daddy, Mom, and Helen

   I hope you are well and had a good Thanksgiving. I'm glad to write that here we celebrated in real American fashion, with turkey and all the trimmings served as it should be. It's hard to believe it was my second Thanksgiving overseas and that it's well over a year since I last saw you. I miss you so much and can't wait for this war to be over so I can come home.

The weather is cold now and we have been 'winterized'. They put wooden sides on all the tents, which has helped a lot.

I've just finished cleaning my clothes – they get so dirty from the soot. Our stoves burn crude oil, and even the tents are soot-blackened.

You asked me what gifts I would like for Christmas. We have an adorable five-year-old girl called Mimi in the hospital with us. She was injured when she was caught in crossfire during one of the battles. Praise the Lord she's making a full recovery. We can only get second-hand clothes for her as she appears to be an orphan, so I was wondering if you could send an overcoat and maybe a couple of sweaters? She's the average size for a child of her age with dark brown hair. I'll leave it to you to choose something suitable. Thank you so much!

All my love
Carrie x

She put her pen down and sealed the letter in an envelope before writing her parents' address on it. Then she swung her legs off the cot and reached for her coat. She would go see Vito to say goodbye. Tomorrow, his dad was coming to collect him. There was no point in him staying in the hospital when his folks could take care of him. It had been different when he'd been wounded. Now, eight days after being admitted, all he needed do was to rest and eat well. Already he was less jaundiced and it would just be a question of time before he got completely better.

When she made her way to Vito's cot, she saw that most of the patients in the hepatitis ward were asleep, but he was sitting up reading *Stamboul Train*, by Graham Greene.

He smiled as she approached. '*Ciao*, Carrie.'

'Hi. Is that a good book?'

'It's very entertaining. First time I've read this author.'

She perched on the edge of his mattress. 'I've been meaning to ask you. What got you so interested in English?'

'Ah. Well, pre-war Florence was full of what they called Anglo-Florentines.'

'Anglo-Florentines? Who were they?'

'Expats who'd made it their home. When I was growing up, I used to hear them speaking English in the cafés and squares.'

'How amazing. Did they all live in the town?'

'The wealthier of them lived on the hills at Fiesole and Settignano. Unmarried less wealthy ladies rented apartments in the city centre and, to earn extra money, they would give English lessons.'

'Did you meet any of them?'

'My parents sent me and Anna to a Miss Roberts. Anna didn't enjoy the classes and soon gave up. But I loved them and decided I would be an English professor once day.'

'So that's why your partisan friend called you *Professore*.' Carrie took his hand, decided to broach the topic festering between them. 'I'm sorry things didn't work out as planned in Bologna...'

'It was a huge disappointment that the Allies stalled their advance.' Vito's voice was tinged with anger. 'They threw the partisans to the lions, you know. I doubt they have any idea how hard we've been fighting to liberate our country. Not only from the Nazis, but also the fascists.'

'You realise that since the start of this Gothic Line offensive in

September, the Fifth Army has lost over twelve thousand men?' The words trembled on her tongue. 'That's equivalent to more than an entire division. And we don't just have a front in Italy. There's another campaign going on in France.'

'The partisans' harassment of the Germans has prevented them from sending more of their troops to France, I believe. I still think we've been treated extremely badly.'

Carrie shook her head. 'My fiancé gave his life, but I don't point the finger of blame at the Italians. I could do. I mean, didn't your king abandon his army to their fate? If he'd been a better king he'd have made sure they got the right orders to fight along-side the Allies before he fled from Rome. Instead, they ran away from their barracks.'

'Most of them have been sent to labour camps in Germany, Carrie. The rest have joined the Resistance. But I agree with you about the king. No one wants a monarchy any more. Italy will be a democratic republic when all this is over.'

'It's all too horrible,' she said, the tears starting to fall. 'So many lives ruined because of Hitler and Mussolini.'

Vito drew her into his arms, then wiped the tears from her cheeks with his thumb. 'You are right, *tesoro*. War is a terrible thing.'

It felt good to be held, to feel strong arms cradle her, to have someone show that they cared. She was surprised by how much she'd missed it. 'I'm glad you got out of Bologna safely.'

He lifted her chin and met her gaze. 'You are?'

'Of course.'

Before she could say another word, he was kissing her.

He eased her into the kiss, soft but firmly, without hesitation. He pressed his mouth down, waiting for her to open for him. And God help her, she did. She threaded her fingers into his hair, and he held her in place, his hand around the nape of her neck.

He kissed her so thoroughly she lost her breath.

She pulled back with a horrified gasp.

'What's wrong?'

'We can't do this.'

'I thought you wanted to.'

'That's not the point. One, I'm still mourning Bill. Two, I'm not the kind of girl to play fast and loose. This must never happen again. We can only be friends.'

He held her wrist and brought it to his lips. '*Mi dispiace tanto.*' I'm so sorry.

A tingle went through her, but she pushed her free hand into his chest. 'Goodnight, Vito. I'll bring Mimi to Florence to see you and your parents before Christmas.'

'*Va bene. A presto,*' he said. Okay. See you soon.

It was only as she was leaving the ward that it occurred to her that she'd kissed a man with hepatitis. How totally irresponsible. She'd let her profession down; she'd let Bill down; and she'd let herself down.

Bill would be disgusted with her, and it would serve her right if she came down with jaundice as well.

14

Idiota! Standing in front of the basin in the corner of his bedroom, razor in hand, Vito reproached himself for the umpteenth time. He should never have kissed Carrie.

She was coming to lunch today, bringing Mimi to meet his parents and familiarise herself with the apartment. The dear little girl would start to live with them after Christmas, which was only a week away. Vito frowned. How would Carrie react when she saw him again? He'd been such a fool with her. For a few seconds, when he'd kissed her, she'd reciprocated with an intensity as passionate as his own. But her fleeting response must have been purely physical.

When she'd pushed him away so abruptly, he'd wanted the ground to swallow him up. *Idiota!* How could he have misread her so badly?

Vito's tired eyes stared back at him in the mirror as he scraped the stubble from his chin. At least the whites were no longer yellow. The Mancinis' family doctor had said that his liver had cleared the bilirubin from his blood in record time and that, luckily, his bout of hepatitis had been short-lived. Nevertheless,

Vito was under strict orders to refrain from drinking alcohol, to eat as much protein as he could lay his hands on, and to intersperse periods of rest with light exercise.

He dried his face and glanced at his wristwatch. Papà had gone to pick up Carrie and Mimi from the station in his Lancia automobile – it would have been too far for Mimi to walk in her condition. Vito's chest tightened with anticipation. *Anticipation mixed with trepidation.* He'd been such a fool.

The sound of voices came from the hallway. He pushed open the door of his room and went into the corridor.

Before he could say anything, Mimi ran towards him, calling out his name.

He caught her and swung her up to kiss her on both cheeks. '*Ciao*, Mimi.'

'*Ciao*, Vito.' She extracted a ragdoll from where she'd tucked it into her coat. 'This is Stella.'

'*Ciao*, Stella. I'm very pleased to meet you.'

Mimi put her ear to the doll's mouth, and then proclaimed, 'She says she's very pleased to meet you too.'

Vito put Mimi down and Mamma stepped forward to take her coat. She received an introduction to Stella as well.

'Come and see the apartment, Mimi,' Mamma said.

'I'll go with you,' Papà chipped in.

Vito caught Carrie gazing at him. She glanced away and, as he took her coat, she didn't say a word.

'Please come through.' Vito ushered her into the sitting room where she sat next to him on the sofa.

She shot him another glance, and then finally spoke. 'You're looking so much better, Vito.'

'I'm fine. No more headaches or nausea.'

'Good.' She twisted her hands in her lap. 'Any news about Mimi's parents?'

He shook his head. 'Sorry.'

They lapsed into an awkward silence, which was only broken when Mimi skipped into the room and sat between them.

'I'm thirsty,' she said.

'Would you like a glass of water?' Vito asked.

'*Si, grazie.*'

'How about you, Carrie?'

'Thank you. I'd love one too.' A soft smile feathered her lips, a smile that made his heart beat like a drum. *Idiota!*

Papà had followed Mimi into the room and went to fetch the water, which he brought to them before going to help Mamma in the kitchen. 'I'll call you when lunch is ready,' he said.

'So, Mimi.' Vito chucked her under the chin. 'What have you been doing since I last saw you?'

'Carrie took me to the Friday night dance and I learnt to do the Texas two-step.'

He was speechless. Literally.

'If you can put on some music, we'll show you.' Carrie laughed. 'Anything you'd dance a foxtrot to would work great.'

Vito went to the gramophone in the corner of the room and flicked through a stack of records until he came across an old Beniamino Gigli record, 'La Paloma'.

Giggling, Mimi asked Carrie to dance. They extended their arms and took each other's hands before dancing the quick-quick-slow-slow steps. After they'd shown Vito Mimi's new dancing skills, Mimi eyed her doll, which was still perched on the sofa.

'I want to dance with Stella. You dance with Carrie, Vito.'

Her tone left no room for argument, and Vito found himself with Carrie in his arms.

'You're a good dancer,' she said.

He held her gently, not too close.

Idiota.

'It's good to see Mimi having fun.'

'She loves that doll.'

The record came to an end and Papà arrived to tell them to go through to the dining room.

'Oh, good,' Mimi said. 'Stella and I are so hungry.'

* * *

Later, after Mamma had outdone herself by serving homemade *ribollita* vegetable soup, followed by roast pork and then fruit salad with whipped cream, Mimi said she wanted to take a nap.

'Would you like to go to Anna's old room, *tesoro*?' Mamma smiled at her.

'If Anna doesn't mind.'

'She doesn't live here any more and I'm sure she'd be pleased for you to lie down on her bed.'

'Can Stella come too?'

'Of course.'

Mimi rocked the doll in her arms.

'Come, little one. You're tired,' Mamma said. 'I'll take you for that rest.'

Trustingly, Mimi placed her hand in Mamma's and Vito's heart melted.

'I'll go and make us all a coffee,' he said. 'We managed to get the real thing on the black market.'

'Let me help with the dishes.' Carrie got to her feet and followed him into the kitchen, leaving Papà to go into the living room for his habitual post-prandial forty winks.

Vito spooned ground coffee into a Bialetti coffee pot, then set it on the stove. He grabbed a dishtowel. 'You wash, Carrie, and I'll dry.'

'Yes, sir!' She giggled.

'Remember my partisan friend? The guy I was with in Caffè Gilli the first time we met? Well, his name is Ezio and his sweetheart is called Stella,' he said. 'Like Mimi's doll.'

'I guess it's quite a common name in Florence.'

He stared down at his hands, released a heavy sigh. 'Ezio's Stella was one of our bravest lady partisans.' He wiped at a plate. 'Last February, she and Ezio even went to carry out an action in the Paskowski Bar in Piazza Vittorio Emanuele, the place frequented by Nazi officers and senior Italian fascist militiamen.'

Carrie glanced at him. 'What kind of action?'

'They intended to plant a small bomb. They were supposed to attach the device to the underside of a table.'

'Did something go wrong?'

Vito's eyes filled with sadness.

He dried the dish and put it on a shelf. 'They lit the fuse but the explosive fell to the floor. Stella managed to snuff it out quickly and put it back in her bag.'

'Oh, my God! Did anyone notice?'

'Unfortunately, yes. A customer saw smoke coming from the fuse and he shouted the alarm.'

Carrie gave a gasp. 'Oh, no!'

'Ezio snatched up Stella's handbag and they both ran for their lives. But Stella couldn't run as fast as him. She was caught and taken to Carità and his band of torturers in the Villa Triste. They'd moved to Via Bolognese by then, and she was brutalised. Later, we learnt that she'd refused to divulge any information, denied all knowledge of the device, and said she'd gone to the Paskowski to meet her sweetheart.

'Ezio was distraught. They'd planned to get married when the war ends, they're so in love. He and I went to the Verdiana women's prison, where she was incarcerated, a former cloister near the Santa Croce Basilica. We'd met up with a Wehrmacht defector, who'd joined up with the *gappisti*. We told the governor of the jail that we'd come to take Stella to our barracks to face a firing squad. The German captain was dressed in his old uniform. Ezio and I disguised ourselves as Republican Guard militiamen. You can imagine our relief when the prison governor believed us and handed Stella over.'

'Thanks be to God.' Carrie heaved a sigh of relief.

'We took her to a safe house where she stayed until Florence was liberated. She's at home with her family now, recuperating. She's severely disfigured – she had so many cigarettes stubbed out on her face, poor girl, and she walks with a limp from the beatings. Carità and his henchmen were trying to get her to reveal Ezio's whereabouts, but she remained silent throughout the entire horrifying process.'

'That's so awful. She must be incredibly courageous.'

'She is. Like Ezio. They're my best friends.'

'I'd love to meet them.'

'As they would you, I'm sure.'

With a hiss, the coffeemaker bubbled up aromatic steam and they both gave a start. Vito took four little cups from the cupboard and filled them to the brim.

'Could I have a dash of milk in mine, please?' Carrie asked. 'I'm not a big fan of espresso coffee. It's so strong it could practically walk by itself into my cup, I reckon.'

He laughed. 'Of course.' You can have anything you desire. *Idiota!*

* * *

The next day, Vito was on his way to meet Ezio at the Caffè Gilli in Piazza Vittorio Emanuele. Would the square keep the name of the discredited king after the war ended? Probably not. It would be changed as soon as the entire country was liberated and a referendum could be called for a vote on abolishing the monarchy.

While strolling the short distance from home, he thought about Carrie and Mimi's visit. Despite still feeling like the biggest idiot on the planet, he'd been relieved when he and Carrie had relaxed into their erstwhile close friendship. The awkwardness seemed to have vanished, as he'd told her about Stella, and the horrors of the German occupation.

He walked past the brass doors of the octagonal marble clad St John's Baptistry, then headed down a side street. Caffè Gilli was on the corner of Piazza Vittorio Emanuele, next to the Paskowski where Ezio and Stella's mission had gone so horribly wrong.

He found Ezio sitting at a small marble-topped table opposite the big solid oak bar counter. Vito ordered himself an espresso and went to join him.

'You're looking well,' Ezio said. 'Have you fully recovered?'

'I still get a little bit tired, but I'm over the worst. I'll need to be 100 per cent by the time the Allies get off their backsides and make a move on Bologna.'

'Not gonna happen for a while yet, *Professore*. But I can't wait to go after that bastard Carità.'

'Last I heard, he was in Ferrara.' Vito gritted his teeth.

'We'll go after him soon enough. What have you been up to since I saw you last week?'

Vito told him about Carrie bringing Mimi to the apartment.

'I remember Mimi from San Ruffillo. And that American nurse too,' Ezio said when Vito had finished recounting his tale. 'Quite a beauty, as I recall.'

'Hey, you're engaged, don't forget!' Vito smiled, picturing the 'beauty' in his arms as they danced. 'But, seriously, she's been extremely kind to Mimi and is truly concerned about her welfare.'

Ezio shot him a look. 'Is there something you're not telling me?'

'What do you mean?' Vito knocked back his coffee.

'You've fallen for her, haven't you? I can see it in your eyes.'

How well Ezio knew him.

'I don't stand a chance,' he said in a mournful tone. 'We can only just be friends.'

Idiota, he said to himself again after he'd taken his leave of Ezio. He'd truly burned his bridges as far as Carrie was concerned. But he did not have time to dwell on that. His thoughts turned to Mimi. Her dear little face. That horrific scar on her forehead. He would focus on trying to find out what had happened to Noemi and Adamo. It would take his mind off longing for Carrie.

15

Carrie sat at the makeshift desk in the corner of the bivouac – a couple of crates one on top of the other – and picked up her pen.

Dear Mom, Daddy, and Helen

Thank you so much for the gifts you sent for Mimi. The wool coat is gorgeous, and I'm sure she'll love the adorable red skirt and sweater. So Christmassy! I've saved my present to open tomorrow, and I can't wait to see what you got me. I hope you like the leather belts and bags I mailed you. They were handmade in Florence.

The scene is very festive here. The hills behind Scarperia are blanketed with snow, and the hospital is all decked out for the holidays. We nurses spent a lot of time decorating the wards with holly, pinecones, wreaths, and candy canes. Now Jack Frost has arrived to complete the picture and sprinkle his magic over the tents. Thankfully, we're warm and cozy inside.

Today, we held a party for the enlisted men, which included a banquet, a huge tree, decorated by us, and a stage show – yours truly dressed up as Santa's elf and performed

'Jingle Bells' with her tentmates – and there were presents for all. Christmas trees and mistletoe adorn each ward and mess. Earlier this evening, there was a service in the chapel. When we sang 'Hark the Herald Angel' and got to the words, 'Peace on Earth', there wasn't a dry eye in the house. The lyrics made me think how far we are from achieving that, and also about the bereaved families, the devastation of homes, the unhappiness and separation. I just pray it will all be over soon.

Tomorrow, we're giving all the patients a stocking each. We stitched them ourselves from whatever fabric we could find. We also made one for every enlisted man in the detachment and in them, among other things, we've placed a 12-ounce bottle of grappa – Italian eau de vie – bought by our physicians and surgeons.

Well, I'd better get some sleep now. I'll be up early to hand Mimi her gifts. I'll finish this letter in a day or two and let you know how it all went.

Carrie put her pen down. Her eyes prickled with tears as she remembered last Christmas in Naples. Midnight Mass with Bill in Bagnoli then lunch with him on Christmas Day followed by his proposal of marriage. She trailed her fingers to the ring and cameo pendant on her necklace. How she wished she had a photo of him; it was becoming more and more difficult to visualise his handsome face.

Carrie's chest lightened at the thought of watching Mimi open her gifts in the morning. Vito had sent a message that he and his family would also visit in the afternoon. Seeing him at his folks' last week, when he'd behaved like the perfect gentleman he was, had calmed her nerves after she'd let him kiss her. She moved her fingers from the necklace to her lips, recalling his kiss with unexpected yearning. Then she gave herself a little shake and came back down to earth again. There could never be a romance between the two of them. She was grieving for Bill and, when the war was over, she'd be returning to the States. She liked Vito, though, and his friendship meant the world to her. She must keep a level head or risk hurting him, and she couldn't bear to do that.

* * *

Next morning, it was still dark when Carrie woke. She switched on her flashlight and checked the time. Seven a.m. It wouldn't get light until at least eight. Her tentmates had placed a stocking at the foot of her cot, but they were still asleep so she'd open it later. She'd done the same for them. Her gifts from her parents were another matter, however, and with eager fingers she unwrapped a gorgeous green cashmere sweater and a pair of warm grey woollen slacks. She'd showered last night, so she quickly dressed in her new clothes – she was off duty today – and headed out.

After using the latrines, she made her way to Mimi's curtained-off section of the general medical ward.

'Merry Christmas, pumpkin,' she said, giving her the stocking and packages she'd hidden underneath the cot last night. 'And Happy Hanukkah,' she added.

Yesterday morning, when Anna had visited, she'd said that the nuns had celebrated the Jewish festival with the children on Christmas Day last year – even though it finished the week beforehand – so Carrie had decided to do the same.

Excitedly, Mimi tore open the paper Carrie had used to wrap the red sweater and skirt.

'They're *bellissimi*,' she said, smiling from ear to ear. 'Please say thank you to your mammina and babbo from me.' She breathed a sigh but didn't mention her own parents.

How Carrie's heart pained for her.

She handed her the stocking she'd made from felt material, which she'd filled with candy, nuts, pencils, watercolour paints, a small jigsaw puzzle, marzipan animals and chocolate. Mimi's eyes glowed as she extracted the gifts.

'Are all these from you, Carrie?'

'They're from Santa. Remember I told you about him?'

'Yes.' Mimi picked up a piece of paper from her bedside table. 'I did this for you.'

'Oh, wow.' Mimi had drawn a picture of a doll that could only be Stella and had coloured it in beautifully. 'It's perfect. Thanks, honey.'

Carrie kissed her, then reached for the last gift she'd stashed under Mimi's cot. She handed it over and Mimi ripped off the paper to reveal a new edition of *The Little Engine That Could*. Carrie's parents had gotten it for her a month ago.

'It's yours to keep,' she said.

'*Grazie*, Carrie.' Mimi threw her arms around her. 'I love it.'

The sound of a cart being wheeled down the ward alerted Carrie to the arrival of Mimi's breakfast. She went to fetch the bread, strawberry jam and milk the child had every morning, then watched her eat her fill. Afterwards, she gave her a sponge bath and dressed her in her new clothes.

'Come with me to my bivouac, sweetie,' she said. 'My friends will be waking up now and we can see what Santa has brought them.'

* * *

When Vito and his parents arrived in the afternoon, a group of medics were touring the wards, singing Christmas carols. They joined in with 'O Come, All Ye Faithful', intoning the words in Latin. Mimi clapped her hands in evident delight.

Carrie pulled up chairs for everyone, and they sat around Mimi's cot, exchanging gifts.

Mimi opened hers first. A gorgeous pink dress for Stella, knitted by Signora Mancini.

The little girl hugged her, then put her ear to the doll's mouth. 'Stella says *grazie*. She loves it and so do I.'

Vito – looking incredibly attractive in his dark blue dress pants, open-neck white shirt and burgundy sweater – gave Carrie a small parcel wrapped in red tissue with a green bow.

'It's from us all,' he said.

She unwrapped the gift, a beautiful handmade ladies' leather wallet. 'It's lovely, thank you.'

She kissed Vito and his parents on both cheeks.

'I got this for everyone.' She handed a big box of assorted American candies to Vito's mom. 'I hope y'all like it.'

'*Grazie*, Carrie.' Signora Mancini smiled warmly. 'We'll enjoy these so much.'

'How about we take Mimi for a short walk around the camp?' Carrie suggested. 'She needs to get a little exercise every day and, for once, the weather's dry.'

'*Buon'idea*,' Vito said.

They put on their coats and went outside. Mimi skipped ahead, in between Vito's mom and dad, her hands in theirs.

Vito fell into step beside Carrie.

She tripped on a tent peg and reached for Vito. He held her close. 'Sorry,' she said.

'No need to apologise...'

She pressed her cheek to his chest and inhaled his wonderful, clean scent. She couldn't help herself. Stepping out of his hold, she brushed a kiss to his cheek.

Movement in the periphery of her vision startled her. Max was striding down the row of tents to the left. Had he seen her in Vito's arms? 'We've fallen behind your parents and Mimi,' she said to Vito quickly. 'Let's go catch up.'

* * *

After dinner in the officers' mess – roast turkey and ham, pumpkin pie, chestnuts, mashed potatoes and locally grown broccoli, served with endless flasks of Tuscan Chianti, followed by a traditional Italian Christmas sweet bread called *panettone* and glasses of grappa – Carrie, her fellow nurses, and their higher-ranking officers moved the tables to make room for dancing.

Sadness prickled Carrie's eyes as she helped her friends. Bad news had arrived shortly before they'd sat down to eat. American troops in France were being slaughtered by the German 6th Panzer Army, which included the elite of the Waffen-SS, in the densely forested Ardennes region between Belgium and Luxembourg. Known as 'the Battle of the Bulge', Hitler had launched a 'Blitzkrieg' surprise attack on the weakly defended US forces: a mixture of raw recruits sent for training and war weary soldiers who were resting. Apparently, the Allied High Command had mistakenly believed it to be a quiet sector and that the Germans would be focusing on defence rather than going on the offensive.

Carrie's shoulders drooped. General Clark's prediction that the year 1944 would see the end of the war in the European Theatre had not come true like many had expected. The optimism of last summer had changed to a grim realisation that Germany was by no means defeated. It would be some time before Carrie would be shipping back to the States. The thought filled her with sorrow but made her feel guilty at the same time.

She was dreading having to say goodbye to Mimi and Vito. They'd become extremely important to her.

More important than going home to her folks? A guilty lump formed at the back of her throat. She swallowed it down and went to help Louise position chairs around the edge of the tent.

'Hey, cheer up, Tex.' Kenny gave her a nudge.

'You're very perceptive.'

'Tell me about it later, okay?'

'Sure.' She forced a smile.

They sat next to each other and it wasn't long before they were whisked off to dance to lively music provided by the combo the unit had hired from Florence.

Captain Huxley danced a fast jive with Carrie before Theo cut in and invited her to jitterbug. She sat the next dance out, then the band launched into the slower tempo of a foxtrot. Before Carrie realised what was happening, she found herself being pulled to her feet by Max and led onto the floor.

Stay calm, she told herself. Someone will cut in, and if they don't it will soon be over.

She caught the whiff of alcohol on Max's breath; he was as drunk as a skunk. Clearly, he'd had more than one glass of grappa. She was about to squirm from his hold when he brought them to a halt beneath the mistletoe that had been tied by the nurses to the side of the mess.

Carrie stiffened. 'Let me go, Max.'

'Aw, babe. It's Christmas and we're under the mistletoe. Know what that means?' His words slurred and he inclined his head.

She made to turn away, but it was too late. His wet lips met hers and he shoved his tongue into her mouth. 'Stop!' She pushed her hands against his stomach and took a step back.

'I want you to be my girl, Carrie.' He sounded like a spoiled child who'd been denied his favourite candy.

'I'm still in love with Bill and I'll never stop loving him,' she said firmly.

'Ha. I saw you with that wop this afternoon. You're a two-faced bitch.'

'How dare you!'

Her slap came from nowhere, landing on the side of Max's face.

He smirked and rubbed at his reddened cheek. 'You'd better watch out, Lieutenant. You've assaulted a superior officer. I'll be keeping my eye on you.'

'Just keep your distance, Captain.' Carrie huffed and spun on her heel, his sneering laughter echoing in her ears.

16

Carrie was packing a small suitcase, her stomach fluttering with anticipation. She'd applied for three days' leave at a hotel in Florence, where the Army had rented a set of rooms designated for the Nurse Corps. Tomorrow, Vito and his dad would come to pick her and Mimi up.

Poor little pumpkin. Finding Florence bereft of her parents will be so hard for her.

Carrie folded her pyjamas and placed them in the case. She was alone in the bivouac as her tentmates had all gone to the Isle of Capri for R&R. They'd wanted her to go with them, but it was somewhere she and Bill had planned to vacation; she couldn't face going without him.

She gave a sigh. Thank God Max had steered clear of her since Christmas. She prayed he was sorry for his behaviour, although he hadn't made any attempt to apologise. His warning that he'd be keeping an eye on her was just sour grapes, she hoped. When she'd told Louise about it, Kenny had pulled an angry face and said if he tried it again, Carrie should kick him where it would count.

At the New Year's Eve party last week, she'd been relieved when he hadn't invited her to dance. Hopefully, he'd leave her in peace from now on.

She finished her packing and headed to the mess for dinner. The tent was practically empty on account of the number of hospital personnel having reduced to half its usual strength. Only around four hundred of their seven hundred and fifty beds were occupied, which meant that staff had been given time off. Large-scale military operations had been officially postponed until spring, Carrie had been told. By then, reinforcements would be available, adequate supply levels would have been attained, and the weather would be more favourable for rapid exploitation by armour and motorised infantry. Most of the hospital admissions nowadays were cases of trench foot, hepatitis and the occasional land mine injury. Carrie was grateful she was no longer run off her feet.

She ate her C-rations quickly and went to visit Mimi, who she found sitting on a chair next to her cot, drawing.

'*Ciao*, sweetie.' She kissed her on both cheeks. 'Would you like to show me your picture?'

Mimi held out a sketch of what was clearly the Bettinellis' house.

'That's beautiful. You're very talented.' The little girl's smile almost broke Carrie's heart. She took a deep breath. 'I need to talk to you about something sad,' she said, lowering herself onto the seat beside Mimi's and taking her hand.

'Is it about Mammina and Babbo?' Mimi's voice trembled.

Carrie squeezed her fingers. 'We don't know what's happened to them, but we're trying to find out.'

A tear trickled down Mimi's cheek. 'Why haven't they come to look for me?'

'Something must have stopped them from doing that, I think.'

Carrie smoothed the tear from Mimi's face. 'You're gonna have to be brave, honey.'

'Brave like Mammina and Babbo? They're brave.'

'They are, I'm sure.' Carrie held out her arms and Mimi climbed into them. 'Vito and his parents are fixin' to take real good care of you. There ain't no need for you to worry about that. You've seen how nice they are.'

Mimi squirmed from Carrie's hold. 'I like them. A lot.' She reached for her doll. 'And so does Stella.'

'I like them a lot too.' Carrie took Mimi's hand again. 'You know I'll be staying in Florence for a few days while you settle in. Maybe we can go to the Boboli Gardens together?'

A shadow passed over Mimi's face. 'I used to have picnics there with Mammina and Babbo.'

Carrie gave an inward groan. It would be hard to avoid raking up the past with the little girl. How sad she felt for her.

'What's your favourite place, darlin'?' she asked.

'Piazza Santa Croce. I like to ride my bike in the big square.'

'We'll do that together.'

Mimi's eyes lit up. 'Will Vito come with us?'

'Of course.'

Mimi nodded. 'Good.' She played with her doll's hair, then yawned. 'I think I'm ready to go to bed now.'

Carrie went to fetch a bowl of water to give Mimi a sponge bath, but when she returned the child was already tucked up under her blankets, fast asleep.

* * *

Two mornings later in Florence, Carrie stepped onto her private terrace to gaze at the view of the terracotta-tiled rooftops and church spires. The hotel where the Army rented rooms for its nurses, in a quiet street five minutes' walk from the railway station, was beautifully clean and spacious. She'd luxuriated in a wonderful warm bath last night before going to bed and sleeping on a comfy, springy mattress under crisp linen sheets. She was still in her pyjamas and shivered as a cold wind blew the hair back from her face. The mountains forming a backdrop to the scenic panorama were white with snow. She went back inside and put on her dress uniform – a requirement of all military personnel on leave – before heading down to the dining room for breakfast.

She found an empty table and ordered a cappuccino and bread rolls from the waiter. While she ate, she thought about the day before. When Vito and his dad had come to pick her and Mimi up, she'd spotted Max hovering by the hospital entrance.

He'd stared at her, making her flesh crawl. Why was he so obsessed? Maybe he was the kind of guy who only wanted girls he couldn't have. She curled her lip in disgust.

But the day had been all about Mimi. She'd been so cute when she'd said goodbye to the hospital staff, giving them hugs and pictures she'd drawn and coloured in for them. She'd been excited about returning to the city but hadn't mentioned her parents once. Carrie was only glad she appeared to have settled in with the Mancinis.

Carrie sighed. How she wished she could take her back to the States. But that would be impossible, and there was no point longing for something she could never have. Besides, Mimi needed stability in her life and uprooting her would be heartless on Carrie's part.

After breakfast, she decided to explore the city a little. She wouldn't be meeting Vito until lunchtime when they'd grab a bite to eat together. The Santa Maria Novella Basilica called for a second visit. After admiring Giotto's wooden crucifix again,

Carrie sat in silent contemplation of the solemnity of her surroundings – a tad gloomy, to be honest – and her mind drifted back to Mimi. Vito's mom had made Anna's old bedroom nice and cosy for her. A new multi-coloured quilt covered the bed, fresh white embroidered linen drapes hung from the window, and a sunny pale-yellow rug held place of honour on the parquet floor. Signora Mancini said she regretted having donated Anna's old stuffed toy animals and childhood clothes to charity, but promised she would get Mimi new ones little by little whenever she could.

A warm feeling of gratitude washed over Carrie. Thank God Mimi had been taken in by the Mancinis. Vito had let slip that his mom had always wanted more children, but they'd never come along. It was one of the reasons why she'd devoted herself to helping others, he'd said. Now Mimi would receive Signora Mancini's full attention, and Carrie knew she would be loved. Mimi would feel safe and cared for.

But for how long?

With an exhale of breath, Carrie rose to her feet and exited the church. She was meeting Vito at the entrance to the Ponte Vecchio at midday, so there would be time to take in the sights en route. All around her there were signs of reconstruction work. Jerry sure had inflicted cruel and callous harm to the city last August, when the force of the explosions blowing up the bridges had damaged buildings in other parts of town. She passed the scaffolded cube-shaped Orsanmichele Church, whose roof and upper windows were being repaired. She'd heard that tiles were scarce and glass scarcer still, so waxed paper was being used as a temporary substitute.

Soon, she'd arrived at her destination: the Ponte Vecchio. She leaned over a parapet at the centre of the structure and gazed at the eastern section of the Arno. The remnants of the nearest destroyed bridge sat in the water like the rubble of a broken sluice. With a frown, she crossed to the opposite parapet. Downstream, beyond the Bailey bridge she'd traversed with Vito last October, four piers encased in brick stood ready for rebuilding work. The signs of energetic preparedness for reconstruction gave her a feeling of hope.

* * *

They went to the Gilli for a quick panino lunch, during which Vito told Carrie that Mimi was settling in well and looking forward to seeing the friends she'd made while staying with the nuns at the San Ruffillo Convent.

'Mamma is going to have them all over for a party on Mimi's birthday,' he said.

'Will she invite me too?' Carrie looked him in the eye.

'Of course. It's on 23 March.'

'I know.' She smiled. 'Mimi told me already.'

He offered her a cigarette, which she accepted. She leaned in for a light, took a puff, and coughed.

'I don't smoke much,' she said by way of explanation. 'Just when I'm nervous.'

'Why are you nervous, Carrie?'

'I'm worried what will happen to Mimi when the war ends. If we don't find her parents, she'll have to go to an orphanage...'

'Let's cross that bridge when we come to it. A lot of water will pass before that happens. I mean, the future is uncertain for all of us. It's better to live in the present.'

Carrie nodded. 'You're right, I suppose.'

'One thing I can't help looking forward to, though, is returning to my studies at the university. I'll do that as soon as we rid Italy of the Nazis.'

His youthful optimism reminded her of how much younger he was than her. That, and the fact that he had yet to finish college. 'Just don't go and get yourself killed first,' she said, tickles of worry prickling her chest.

'I won't.' His certainty tempted fate, in her opinion. But she kept her superstitious thoughts to herself.

They finished their cigarettes, then paid the check.

Outside it was cold and damp. Carrie was tall, but Vito was taller and she had to lengthen her steps to keep up with him.

'I'd better go back to my hotel,' she said.

'You're not spending the rest of the day on your own. You can spend it with Mimi,' he suggested. 'I'm sure you've been missing her and it will take your mind off things.'

'You're so perceptive, Vito,' she said, linking her arm with his while they made their way across the square.

* * *

Mimi ran towards them as they stepped into the Mancinis' apartment.

'*Ciao*, Carrie.'

'Ciao, pumpkin.'

'Nonna took me shopping,' Mimi said.

It had been agreed that she'd call Vito's mom 'Nonna', *Grandma*. 'Signora Mancini' had been considered too formal, and her first name, Rita, too informal. Vito's dad would be 'Nonno', *Grandpa*, for the same reasons. Mimi had said her own grandparents had passed away, and she was happy to have new ones.

'We got some new shoes. Look!' Her voice bubbled with excitement, and she pointed to her new black leather pumps.

'They're gorgeous, honey.' Carrie kissed her.

'Only a few shops have stock, but I know just the place.' Rita smiled, walking in behind the boisterous child, and Carrie felt a rush of affection towards her.

'Thanks, Rita,' Carrie said, glad she'd been encouraged to call Vito's mom by her first name.

Vito took Carrie's coat and ushered her through to the living room, where Signor Mancini was on the phone. He hung up his call and got to his feet.

'*Buongiorno*, Signor Mancini.'

'Please, call me Jacopo.'

'Thanks, Jacopo.' Again, Carrie felt a rush of affection. Vito's parents sure were nice folks.

Mimi took her through to her bedroom, and Carrie spent the rest of the afternoon giving her an English lesson by inventing scenarios with her doll and drawing pictures. At around seven they went to help Rita with supper. Carrie was given the task of stirring a risotto, while Mimi was sent to fetch Vito from his room, where he was catching up on reading the assigned texts for his university course.

They ate at the wooden kitchen table, Mimi chatting non-stop about the shopping trip. Carrie held her breath, worried she'd bring up her missing parents, but she didn't. It was as if she, too, were waiting for news.

* * *

Later, Carrie was once again linking arms with Vito as he walked her back to her hotel.

'I'm feeling so sad that we haven't found Mimi's parents yet,' she said.

'I'm feeling sad too.' He squeezed her arm. 'How are we ever going to tell her the truth if we can't find them?'

'We'll figure it out,' Carrie said, feigning confidence.

He walked her to the entrance of the building, but when it came to saying goodbye, she just couldn't do it.

'Please, stay with me a while, Vito. I don't want to be alone...'

'Neither do I.'

They went up to her room, but as soon as they stepped through the door and had taken off their coats, she began to shake. Ripples of sadness washed over her. She hugged herself but couldn't stop trembling.

'Hold me, Vito, please.'

He took her in his arms and held her tight. 'Is that better?'

'No.' Her teeth chattered. She was shivering violently now and feeling dizzy. 'I need to lie down.'

He walked her backwards until they reached the bed, where he laid her down gently and stretched out beside her, warming her with his body.

'Breathe in slowly through your nose, Carrie. Then exhale slow, deep and gently through your mouth. Try to relax.'

She closed her eyes and focused on her breathing and, before too long, the shakes eased. She gazed at him and he gazed back at her.

'I feel a little silly now,' she said.

'You're not silly at all.' He stroked a finger down her cheek. 'Didn't you go through hell in Anzio? And the way you nurse the sick, the injured and the dying. I'm full of admiration for you.'

'You are?' Her heartbeat quickened.

'Yes.'

Without thinking, she wrapped her arms around him and kissed him on the lips.

Don't think, Carrie. Just kiss him.

He jerked his head back in evident surprise, his eyes questioning. He'd never looked more handsome, his hair tousled, his Michelangelo's *David* profile so beautiful.

She pressed her hand to his chest, felt the beating of his heart. *Thud-thud, thud-thud.*

He took a breath and covered her hand with his.

She didn't make a sound as his lips brushed her forehead. Then, with a deep sigh, she melted into his embrace.

Their eyes locked.

He kissed her again.

His kiss was intoxicating and she wanted more. She wanted *him*. Was it so wrong? Everything that had happened thus far had brought her to this moment. The past didn't matter. Neither did the future, for there might not even be one. What mattered was now. Here. With Vito. She needed him. 'Make love to me, please,' she said.

Carrie rolled over in bed the next morning and burrowed into the spot on the bed where Vito had made love to her. Her necklace with Bill's ring and the cameo pendant on the nightstand caught her eye. Vito had removed it carefully last night and, at that moment, had asked her if she was sure she wanted to keep going.

Her only concern had been that perhaps she shouldn't sleep with him while he was still recovering from hepatitis, and she'd said so. He'd assured her he felt fine, that following his doctor's advice had cured him, but that he'd leave it up to her.

A warm feeling spread through her at the memory; he was so different to Bill, but he was also a good man. She wouldn't have agreed if he'd been pushy. Except now, in the cold light of day, she wondered if she'd done the right thing. She'd needed Vito so much, his concern for her, the warmth of his godlike body. Kissing him had been like cutting loose the ties that bound her to earth and she'd floated in a cloud of such desire that she'd allowed herself to be carried away. When she'd parted her thighs for him, she'd lost all sense of time, of space, of reality. Afterwards, he'd held her close and a great wave of affection had washed over her. Affection, not love.

She mustn't fall in love with Vito.

They'd fallen asleep in each other's arms, only waking when Vito had kissed her goodbye, passionate kisses that had begged for more. Carrie had been concerned they'd made love without using a rubber. It was her 'safe period', but even so, it wasn't infallible. She wouldn't let herself take any further risks, so she'd seen him to the door.

The chiming bells of Santa Maria Novella echoed through the windowpane. It was the Feast of the Epiphany, 6 January, and Carrie had been invited to spend the day with the Mancinis. Vito's sister would be joining them for lunch, a family celebration. The holiday was an important one in Italy, almost as important as Christmas, Vito had explained.

* * *

At around midday, Carrie left the hotel and made her way towards San Lorenzo. People were thronging the streets, all gussied up in their finest clothes. *How hard they'd fought for their freedom.*

An unexpected chill prickled her spine. Vito had said that he and Ezio planned to go after Mario Carità once the Allied front moved again. But that evil man was a sadistic monster; he wouldn't let himself be captured without a fight. She hoped Vito wouldn't be reckless, like when he'd been caught in the crossfire up on Monte Battaglia.

She pressed the doorbell at the palazzo housing the Mancinis' apartment and Vito came downstairs to let her in. On the top floor, Mimi opened the door with a big smile. 'Look what the Befana has brought me!' She showed Carrie a handmade stocking overflowing with dried fruits, candies and an assortment of cookies.

'Who's the Befana?' Carrie asked Vito as he took her coat.

'According to tradition, she was a witchy old woman who hosted the Magi when they were travelling to Bethlehem. They invited her to accompany them, but she was too busy cleaning her house. When she had second thoughts, she filled a basket with gifts for the baby Jesus and set off alone. But she was unable to find the stable with the manger and so, ever since, she has travelled the world on Epiphany Eve, searching every house for the Christ child, leaving candies and chocolates for the good children and lumps of coal for those who've been bad.' Vito laughed. 'Of course, Mimi didn't get any coal.'

They stepped into the living room. Anna was there already and she kissed Carrie's cheeks. They sat together on the sofa, with Mimi between them. She looked adorable in her festive red skirt and sweater.

Vito brought Carrie and Anna each a flute of sparkling white wine; he was still avoiding alcohol because of his hepatitis. He raised a glass of mineral water. '*Salute!*' Good health.

Mimi clinked her beaker of orange juice with them. Then she pretended to give her doll a sip and they all smiled.

'Does your mamma need any help?' Carrie asked Vito.

He shook his head. 'We have strict orders to stay out of the kitchen. We can do the washing up afterwards.'

Carrie's eyes met his and her insides melted. Stop it, she told herself. You must *not* fall in love with him. Focus on Mimi instead.

* * *

Lunch was delicious. Chicken liver pâté on toasted bread, followed by *tagliata* – grilled beef, thinly sliced from a massive T-bone steak, *bistecca alla fiorentina*, which Vito said he and his parents had saved their meat rations to purchase – accompanied by roast potatoes and cannellini beans. For dessert, Rita served *cavallucci senesi*, traditional spiced biscuits made with honey, aniseed, walnuts and candied fruit, which everyone except Vito and Mimi dipped into *vin santo* sweet wine.

While Carrie helped Vito and Anna in the kitchen, Rita took Mimi for her nap and Jacopo also went for a rest.

Dealing with the dishes, they chatted about how best to approach telling Mimi that they might never find her parents.

'We need to use words that are clear and direct,' Anna said as she scrubbed a plate in the sink. 'Mimi hasn't seen them for well over a year. It's a long time in the life of a child of her age.'

'I think she needs to be reassured that we'll look after her.' Vito took the plate from Anna and dried it.

'She should be encouraged to talk about her parents and remember them,' Carrie said, taking another plate from Anna. 'She's been bottling up her feelings.'

They carried on discussing Mimi until the washing up was finished, then went into the living room to wait for her.

She didn't take long to appear; her afternoon naps seemed to be getting shorter. '*Ciao*,' she said, skipping across the parquet floor.

'Sit here, sweetie.' Carrie patted the space between her and Vito. 'I'm afraid we have something very sad that we need to share with you.'

'Yes, *tesoro*,' Vito added, putting his arm around the child as she snuggled into his side. 'We are so sorry to have to tell you this, but your mammina and babbo... they're missing.'

Mimi nodded, tears streaming down her face. 'Is that why they never came to find me?'

Carrie and Vito both put their arms around her.

'You don't need to worry,' Anna said. 'We'll take good care of you. This will be your home for now.'

'I like it here.' Mimi sighed. 'And so does Stella.' She cradled her doll. 'But I love the garden in my old house.'

'Tell us about it, darlin'.' Carrie smoothed the hair back from Mimi's tear-stained face.

'I like to ride my bicycle up and down the path.' Mimi took a shuddering breath. 'And Babbo has a shed where he's always making things. And Mammina grows tomatoes and lettuce and green beans.'

Vito hugged her to him. 'Would you like a bicycle for your birthday?'

'Oh, yes, please.' A tentative smile brushed Mimi's lips. 'We could go for bike rides together in Piazza Santa Croce like I used to with Mammina and Babbo.'

'Sounds like a fantastic idea.' Anna chucked Mimi under the chin. 'But I'm not sure how I'd cope on a bicycle in my nun's habit.'

Carrie caught Vito's eye and they both smiled.

'I'd like to draw you a picture of my garden,' Mimi said, from where she still sat in between them.

'And we'd love you to do that, wouldn't we, Anna and Vito?' Carrie said.

* * *

Carrie and the entire Mancini family spent the rest of the afternoon focusing on Mimi, encouraging her to talk about her parents, giving her hugs and watching her make art. In the early evening, with Mimi holding their hands, Carrie and Vito walked Anna back to her convent in the Borgo Pinti district.

After eating such a big lunch, they only had a light dinner of fruit and cheese.

Rita took Mimi to get ready for bed, then Vito and Carrie went to tuck her in.

'Do you think Mammina and Babbo will be gone forever?' Mimi asked in a wistful tone. 'I really want to see them again.'

Carrie's heart filled with pain for the little girl. She couldn't answer the question, so she kissed her gently on the forehead instead.

Mimi sighed. 'I wish you weren't returning to the hospital tomorrow. I'll miss you, Carrie.'

'I'll miss you too, sweetie.' And she would. The ward would be so empty without her.

'When will you be back?' Mimi looked her in the eye.

'On my next day off. I promise.'

'*Va bene.*' Okay.

Vito brushed a kiss to Mimi's cheek. 'I'll be here for you, *tesoro*. And Carrie will visit as soon as she can.'

'*Grazie.*' Mimi's eyelashes fluttered and she gave a sleepy yawn. '*Buonanotte*, Carrie. *Buonanotte*, Vito.'

Her heart aching, Carrie placed her hand in Vito's. Thank God he was there. 'I'd better make tracks for my hotel now,' she said. 'I have to be up early for my ride to Scarperia.'

Vito suggested they go for a drink in the hotel bar as he walked Carrie in the direction of Santa Maria Novella.

'We need to talk,' he added.

They found a quiet corner where they sat next to each other

on a two-person seat. His firm thigh pressed against hers, making her ache for his touch.

'It's boiling in here,' Vito said.

'Yes, it is,' Carrie agreed, though she felt he'd said it on purpose. The heat between them was hot enough to fry an egg. She caught his gaze, the smouldering look in his eyes, and she couldn't help but lean into him.

Vito ordered them both herbal tea. Their drinks arrived and he took her hand.

'I hope you don't think I was taking advantage of you last night,' he said.

A flush flamed across her face, warming her even further. 'It was more like me taking advantage of you, Vito. I'm sorry.'

'Why are you sorry?' He frowned.

'I... I...' She struggled to find the right words. 'This... thing between us. You know it can never be permanent.'

'Why not?' He raised a brow.

'Because... because I'm going back to the States and your life is in Italy.'

'I could move to America to be with you.'

She shook her head. 'You need to finish your college degree. And Mimi needs you to be here.'

How Carrie wished it could be her to be with the child.

'She could come with me. We could adopt her, the two of us.'

Vito's words fanned a flame of longing in Carrie. A family of three. Her, Vito and Mimi. It was a fantasy, though. The world was in turmoil. And what she felt for Vito wasn't love, was it?

'Mimi needs stability,' she said firmly. 'It would be selfish to uproot her.'

He huffed. 'You don't love me. I get it.'

He'd sounded so young that guilt burned through her. 'That's not what I'm saying. It's not about us. It's about Mimi.'

His beautiful brown eyes glowed. 'Then you do love me?'

'We can't fall in love with each other. It would be crazy.' She sipped her tea, trying to be sensible as she considered what to say next. 'I care about you. Very much. But we mustn't make plans for the future.'

She was utterly torn, confused and miserable.

'I can't stop myself from loving you. You're the most wonderful woman.' His voice came out choked.

'Please don't try to persuade me. It would only cause sadness. For both of us.'

'If that's really what you want.'

'It is.' She sighed, her heart breaking. 'It's probably a good thing I'm going back to the hospital in the morning. By the time we see each other again, you'll have realised that I'm right.'

'My feelings for you will never change, *amore*.'

He'd called her *love*. The word made her stupid chest flutter. 'I'm tired. Let's just say goodnight.'

'When will I see you again?' He helped her to her feet.

'I'll phone when I find out about my next day off.'

He walked her to the elevator. Then he cupped her face with his hands and kissed her. She melted into his embrace – she couldn't help herself – and his kiss captured her breath, her heart and her soul. It took every ounce of her will to whisper, 'Goodnight,' and then step into the elevator alone.

18

Carrie was sitting on a tuft of dry grass under a grapevine in Scarperia, chewing on a piece of gum, lost in thought. Birdsong and warm sunshine lent a feeling of spring to the air. It hadn't rained for two weeks and the snow on the hills surrounding the camp had melted. Time seemed to have flown since Christmas, and now it was the middle of March. Over the winter, the Allies had contented themselves with resting, receiving reinforcements, and stockpiling munitions like artillery shells as well as other supplies. During the months of January and February, a rotation of replacement Army units had given all the GIs a brief rest from frontline duty at the spa town of Montecatini, near Florence. But the war front would be moving before too long. Recently, a battalion of the US 10th Mountain Division had mounted a one-shot action, successfully climbing the cliff face of the Riva Ridge, surprising enemy forces there and forcing them to retreat. And now, after continuing their attacks to the north-east, the Americans had captured Monte Belvedere overlooking Pianoro on the Futa Pass.

Carrie breathed a sigh. She should be feeling happy about

prospects of the war finally coming to an end, but the thought of saying goodbye to Mimi, Vito and the Mancinis gave her a feeling of loss. How would she cope when the time came to leave them forever? Vito's family had become almost as important to her as her own folks. She'd been going to Florence every ten days or so to visit with them, and their kindness touched her to the core. Vito had been the epitome of thoughtfulness; he'd respected her request not to try to persuade her to change her mind about their relationship. If only things could have been different, if only the oceans soon to separate them both physically and metaphorically weren't so wide.

She was grateful Mimi had settled in well and was adapting to her new life. It was clear that she felt loved and protected. Whenever she asked about her parents, answers were given in terms she could understand. Carrie was confident Mimi would eventually cope if her parents were never found. As for herself, she knew she'd have to be strong when the time came to say goodbye to the child. If she broke down, Mimi would be upset.

The sound of the radio blaring from the enlisted men's quarters interrupted Carrie's thoughts. She was expected on the ward soon, so she'd better get on with the task at hand. Balancing a sheet of crisp cream-coloured paper on her knees, Carrie began to write a letter home.

Dear Daddy, Mom, and Helen

Thank you for your last letter and for sending more clothes for Mimi. She truly loves the green velvet dress you got for her. The cute little white cardigan also goes with it perfectly. She asked me to send you her thanks.

It's a beautiful day here; the sun is shining, and we don't have the fire on in our tent in the daytime anymore. Rumors are flying about an imminent push off. We've gotten kind of used to life here in Tuscany. Our unit has been in its present location for almost six months now, which is a record in comparison with the frequent moves made last spring and summer. Because of the inactivity on the frontline, we only have a moderate patient load. The majority are medical cases, of which hepatitis has been the biggest problem. The men get extra meat rations to help them recover.

My big news is that I'm now a First Lieutenant! They changed the regulations so that after eighteen months' service we'd be eligible for promotion. I had to buy some silver bars for my uniform.

Next week, I have another couple of days' leave at the hotel in Florence where I stayed in January. It will be nice to have a break from my daily routine and to spend time with Mimi and the Mancini family. They're hosting a party for her birthday, which I'm looking forward to attending. I'll write you all about it.

All my love
Carrie x

She rested her pen on the grass and folded the letter into its envelope. Footfalls sounded as Louise approached. 'Hi, Tex. Ain't it a beautiful day?'

'Howdy.' Carrie shaded her eyes. 'I'm hoping it will be good weather when I'm in Florence.'

Louise sat next to her, took out her corncob pipe, stuffed it with tobacco and lit it. 'Are you visiting Mimi again?'

Carrie nodded. 'Sure am. It'll be her sixth birthday.'

'Poor kid. I can't imagine having my parents go missing at her age.'

Carrie had told Louise the whole tragic story. 'Mimi is very resilient. She's coping really well.'

'She has you. And Vito.' Louise shot Carrie a glance. 'I'm glad you met him but please take care. Max was asking Theo about him, insinuating that you're fraternising with what he called "a wop".'

'That's a horrible, bigoted word. Vito is my friend. And it ain't any of Max's business what I do during my time off.'

'He's your superior officer and has the authority to stop you from seeing Vito if he thinks it would adversely affect the unit. Just be careful, honey. If you give him any excuse, Max will take it.'

Carrie groaned. 'What is it with him? He acts like the sun comes up simply to hear him crow.'

'He's an egotistical womaniser. I heard he had his way with several nurses in the 95th EVAC at Anzio. He can't take it that you haven't swooned for him like they did, I reckon.'

'He's slicker than a boiled onion, and he gives me the creeps.' A sour taste tanged in Carrie's mouth. She changed the subject. 'How are things with you and Theo?' Louise had told her that he'd proposed when they were on leave in Capri but they'd yet to set a date.

Kenny's face assumed a dreamy expression as she exhaled a puff of smoke. 'He wants to start a family as soon as we're married.'

'How do you feel about that?'

'I can't wait. I don't wanna be a nurse once we're shipped home. I've seen too much death.' She glanced at Carrie. 'How about you?'

'I think I might go back to school and study to be a paediatrician.' The idea had recently occurred to her, but this was the first time she'd told anyone about it. 'I've so enjoyed looking after Mimi.'

Louise smiled. 'You'd be really good at it.'

'Thanks.' Carrie smiled back at her friend.

* * *

The next week, in Florence, Carrie woke to the chiming bells of Santa Maria Novella. She'd slept deeply, tired from the exertions of the day before. Mimi's birthday party, attended by five of her friends from when she'd been living at the convent, had been exhausting. Carrie remembered the games Mom and Dad had organised at her own parties, so she'd gotten the kids playing hide-and-seek, musical chairs and pin the tail on the donkey (drawn by Mimi on a massive sheet of paper beforehand). Rita – with Anna's help – had outdone herself on the food side of things; there'd been cake, cookies galore, homemade candies and ice cream. Jacopo had been in charge of the gramophone record player. And Vito had behaved like a big kid himself, joining in the fun with them all. Afterwards, he'd walked Carrie back to the hotel, saying a chaste goodnight to her at the front door.

This morning, she and Vito were taking Mimi for a bike ride around Piazza Santa Croce. True to his word, Vito had managed to get Mimi a bicycle for her birthday. It was second-hand, but it had a fresh coat of paint and training wheels. Mimi had said her old bike had actually been a tricycle, but she was adamant she wanted a two-wheeler.

After a continental breakfast of cappuccino and sweet bread rolls, Carrie made her way to the Mancinis' apartment, where upstairs, Mimi and Vito were waiting for her. The three of them immediately went down to the basement, where Vito had parked Mimi's bike next to his own. Only Mimi would be riding, though. Carrie and Vito had already agreed that they would walk on either side of her while she walked her bicycle along the side-walks to the square.

They set off and, about ten minutes later, they'd arrived at Santa Croce. The Basilica overlooked the rectangular-shaped piazza and contained the tombs of several illustrious Italians – including Michelangelo Buonarroti, Niccolò Machiavelli, and Galileo Galilei – and it was famous for its sixteen chapels, many of them decorated by the fourteenth-century Florentine artist, Giotto. But the façade of the church had been walled up to protect it from war damage and had yet to be completely uncovered. Warm sunshine bathed an assortment of magnificent ochre, cream and pale pink palazzi of varying sizes lining the big, open flag-stoned space in front.

'Can I get on my bike now?' Mimi asked.

'Of course, honey bunches.' Carrie smiled.

Mimi pedalled as fast as her legs would go, and soon she was criss-crossing the square with ease. It was quiet at this time of the day – mid-morning – just a small group of boys kicking a football and an elderly couple walking arm in arm.

'Would you like a coffee, Carrie?' Vito indicated towards the umbrella-shaded round metal tables on the terrace of a *caffè* opposite. 'We can keep an eye on Mimi while we chat.'

'*Grazie.*'

They told Mimi where she could find them, then pulled out chairs. A waiter came to take their orders, and they talked about the fun of the birthday party while they waited.

Their coffees arrived, and they stirred sugar into their cups.

Vito reached for Carrie's hand. 'I'm leaving next week, *tesoro.*'

Carrie's breath hitched. 'Do you have to go?'

'The call has gone out for us partisans to fight with the Allies as soon as they move the front.' He squeezed her fingers. 'Ezio and I will join our comrades up in the mountains. We'll help the Americans as we know the terrain. Then we'll march on Bologna.'

'Why do you have to go there?'

'You know why, Carrie.' His eyes blazed with the fire of revenge.

'Surely someone else can go after Mario Carità? The authorities will deal with him, won't they?'

'He'll be long gone by the time they get round to it. Justice must come from the people he hurt most.'

'Oh, Vito. I wish you'd reconsider. How will Mimi and your family cope if you get killed?'

Vito huffed. 'I'll make sure that doesn't happen.'

Carrie sighed. 'Please don't take any risks.'

'I won't.'

He seemed about to add to his statement, but Mimi came cycling up to their table.

'I can go really fast now. Did you see?' she said, her little face so bright and happy.

Carrie forced a smile through her worries. 'Yes, darlin', you're the bee's knees.'

* * *

Carrie found herself going through the motions for the rest of the day. Her heart was as heavy as lead. Whenever she thought about saying goodbye to Vito, nausea gripped her stomach. Their paths were about to separate and she doubted she'd see him again, even if he did survive. She feared he wouldn't make it, though; she was scared his luck had run out and that he would be killed. This wasn't her first rodeo; she'd gone through it all before with Bill. But she couldn't show her fear to Mimi and Vito's family, so she pretended tiredness when they asked her if anything was wrong. Thankfully, Mimi could talk the ears off a mule and she filled Carrie's silences with chat about her party, her friends and her presents.

Feeling so low she couldn't jump off a dime if she tried, Carrie made her excuses after dinner and said she wanted to head back to her hotel.

'You'll visit soon, I hope?' Rita said.

'Of course.' Carrie kissed her and Jacopo.

Mimi threw her arms around her. 'Thank you again for the nice clothes from your family and for the books.'

Carrie had given her *The Story of Babar the Elephant* and *Little House in the Big Woods*.

'You're so welcome, Mimi. I'm looking forward to reading them to you.'

Vito looked Carrie in the eye. 'I'll walk you back to the hotel.'

Not a question, but a statement.

'*Grazie*,' she said.

Outside, she gave a shiver.

'It's turned as cold as hell with the furnace out.'

'Is that another of your Texan expressions?' He quirked a brow.

She laughed despite her sadness. 'The days are so warm now, it's kind of a shock when it turns chilly at night.'

He put his arm around her and tucked her into his side. It felt so right. How could this be the last time she saw him?

Her breathing slowed.

She couldn't let that happen.

Something shifted within her. Something monumental.

Not planning a future with Vito would be the biggest mistake of her life. Life was too short to say no to happiness. And life was far, far too short to say no to love.

At the hotel entrance they came to a halt and faced each other. Her skin tingled as his eyes questioned. She nodded.

His head bowed, his mouth found hers. Then he kissed her. Oh, God, how he kissed her. His body pressed to hers and heat sparked between them. She wanted him desperately.

'Come up to my room, Vito.'

'Are you sure?'

'Absolutely.'

In the elevator, he kissed the corner of her lips, her cheeks, her eyelids.

At the door to her room, he took the key from her, unlocked it and lifted her in his arms.

Inside, he carried her to the bed.

She loved him. *She was in love with him.* The words danced in her heart, desperate to be said. He was her alpha and her omega. How did this happen?

She tried to speak, but he wouldn't let her; he pressed a finger to her mouth.

'Don't you want to hear what I have to say?' she whispered as his fingers trailed down her body.

'Tell me after.'

He undressed her and then undressed himself. She smiled as he put on a rubber, wanting to tease him for coming prepared, but at the same time not wanting to spoil the moment. She'd joke with him about it later. She kissed his jaw, his cheeks, his lips.

'You're so beautiful, Carrie. *Ti amo.*' I love you.

She straddled him and eased herself onto him, gasping with pleasure as she took him deep. Their eyes locked and he rolled her over, covering her with his gorgeous body while they moved together, their passion building until they both cried out their release.

They kept their arms around each other, waiting for their gasping breaths to still.

She caressed his shoulders. 'Will you let me tell you now?'

'Tell me what?' His eyes met hers and they seemed anxious.

'That I love you.'

He gave a gasp of evident surprise. 'You're not just saying that?'

'No, Vito. I'm not just saying that.'

'You love me?'

'I love you. *Ti amo.* I'm in love with you. I've been in denial of my feelings for weeks. It was the realisation that we might never see each other again that made me face the truth.'

A big smile spread across his handsome face. Then he stole her lips, kissing her with both roughness and gentleness.

'You've made me so happy. I thought you wanted to tell me it was over between us, that this would be our last time. Do you think we're crazy? I mean, crazy to be falling in love with no idea of what the future holds?'

'I used to think it would be crazy.' She stroked his chest. 'But now I think it's the only thing that will keep me sane.'

19

The track rose sharply ahead of Vito as he climbed into the steep hills above Florence, under cover of darkness. He and Ezio had managed to arm themselves with Sten guns from a secret stash and now, under cover of darkness, they needed to hike during the night. Although there wouldn't be any Nazis on this side of the frontline, there'd still be fascist sympathisers who might wish them harm. Vito wasn't afraid, however. He didn't feel the need to overcome fear with courage: for him fear simply didn't exist. Even danger had no meaning for him after all he'd gone through the past couple of years; danger had become so much a part of his existence that he welcomed it like an old friend.

The temperature had dropped and he hunched into his coat, remembering how Carrie had reacted to the cold night air last week. God, how he loved her. He'd been walking on clouds with a silly grin on his face ever since she'd told him she loved him back. When they'd made love a second time, and she'd teased him about having rubbers on him, he'd said he didn't normally carry *preservativi* in his pocket but had been concerned he might have got her pregnant back in January. There was nothing he wanted more than to father a child with her, except now was not the moment.

When she'd said that she, too, would love to have his children one day, joy had flooded through him. A little girl like Mimi would be perfect. But they hadn't made any plans for the future before saying goodbye; they'd decided to put plans on hold.

'Bill and I made plans and look what happened to them,' Carrie had said with a sigh.

Vito had wrapped his arms around her soothingly. She'd made him promise to be careful while they were apart and he said he'd send a message to her in Bologna to arrange somewhere to meet up. Until the hospital packed up and followed the front, she'd carry on visiting Mimi whenever she could.

Dear little Mimi. She'd burst into tears when he'd told her he was leaving. Guilt had cracked in his voice as he'd explained that he needed to help his comrades fight the Germans. 'I hope they don't shoot you,' she'd said, sobbing.

'I won't let them.' He'd ruffled her curls. 'Try not to worry, *tesoro*. The war will be over soon and I'll come back to Florence. We can go for bike rides together then as I'm sure you won't be needing your training wheels anymore.'

'Will Carrie come with us?' Mimi's tears had dried. 'She'll need her own *bicicletta*, though.'

'We'll get her one.' He'd hugged Mimi tight.

The next day, Anna, Mimi and his parents had waved him off. Mamma and Papà had tried to persuade him not to go – to no avail – and Anna had said she would pray for him. He gritted his teeth. Carrie's happiness was paramount, and so was Mimi's and his family's. He would change his modus operandi and try not to take any risks.

The night wore on, the only sound the tramping of his and

Ezio's feet on the stony path. Towards dawn, they came upon a village nestling in a bowl-like valley between the hills. In the soft, pink light of early morning, a stream came tumbling down to a mill. The steep sides of the 'bowl' were thick with chestnut trees budding into leaf and, in the village, people were stirring, mules were being saddled, and a peasant was heading for the fields with his hoe. It was time to take cover until nightfall.

'This place is safe,' Ezio said, on reaching a long, rambling farmhouse. 'It was recommended to me.'

Vito didn't ask where the recommendation had come from. He was tired and hungry. All he could think about was food and rest.

An elderly man with grey sideburns and a fringe of moustache on his lip opened the door. He listened to Vito and Ezio's explanation, then took them across the flag-stoned kitchen to a solid oak table. A big woman, whom he introduced as his wife, offered to heat up some milk, which they accepted with thanks. They dunked bread into it and ate hungrily while the man, who told them his name was Carlo, talked of his enemies: the state and its inspectors, the Duce and Hitler. Like many of his fellow-farmers, fascism to him meant authority. Fascism took his wheat for the communal grain pool, his copper pots for the driving bands of shells, his sons for the war. It gave him nothing in return. The enemies of fascism, to his way of thinking, were his friends. He clapped Vito and Ezio on the shoulder and said they were welcome to stay as long as they liked.

After they'd eaten, he showed them upstairs. They slept for the rest of the day on a couple of mattresses on the wooden floor. There was nothing else in the room except bags of seed, onions, shallots, gaudy heads of maize, and apples and pears wizening in a corner. They woke at dusk and Carlo's wife, Maria, offered them a plate of rabbit stew. They ate enthusiastically, savouring the taste of the meat, which had been braised in onions, toma-toes, garlic, fennel, rosemary, and white wine. Smacking their lips, they thanked them both, and gave them some lire to pay for their kindness.

Another long, tiring walk took them close to the Futa Pass. They camped in a derelict house and decided to hike during daylight henceforth, given that they would be following moun-tain tracks to avoid the main road. Their mission was unofficial; they needed to fly under the radar – not only of the Germans but also of the Americans – until they'd rendezvoused with Bian-conini and his second-in-command.

The rough terrain taxed Vito's energy levels: the mule paths they were following rose almost vertically in places and his muscles complained with every step. To distract himself from his tiredness, he filled his mind with thoughts of Carrie. He'd known the moment they'd first met that there was something special about her. It was the way she'd looked at him, as if she was seeing into his soul. When his body had slipped into hers, and her breath had entered his lungs, and her kisses had captured his lips, he'd felt their connection grow even stronger. There had to be a future for them, for he would never be able to live without her. He'd go to America if she wanted him to, he'd give up every-thing to be with her.

No ifs, ands or buts.

* * *

The sharp Apennine ridges towered above them. The paths doubled to and fro, sometimes falling to torrents – yellowy-white with snow-water – before climbing again to traverse the opposite wall of the ravines. At the tops, there were plateaux, high among the chestnuts, and often single stone huts. Vito and Ezio hiked towards the loneliest of them, where they came across a man, who told them he worked as a charcoal burner. He was a widower with two children who went by the name of Alfredo. The adolescent girl, Stefania, kept house. The young son, Giorgio, laboured with his father, leading their mule up the rain-channelled paths, through the bedraggled woods, to clearings where wood smouldered beneath a cone of divots to be turned into charcoal.

The little family exuded warmth and comradeship, making Vito and Ezio feel at home. Stefania smiled proudly while her father recounted that, when he was young, he'd travelled north through France to the Clydeside in Scotland, where he'd peddled plaster Madonna statuettes to devout Irish Catholics in the industrial slums. Having sold his wares, Alfredo had gone into the pits to work. But the great economic depression of the early thirties had driven him back to Italy. Alfredo didn't say what had happened to his wife, and neither Vito nor Ezio asked. A harsh life had taken its toll, no doubt.

Stefania began to mix a paste of a coarse pinkish flour, and Vito dipped his finger in the bowl and licked it: it was sweet with a bitter edge. Chestnut flour. She lifted a big pair of tongs from the chimney-side and warmed them in the fire. Each arm ended in a circular plate: a diminutive gridle, on which she dropped a little olive oil. The oil hissed and smoked on the hot metal. She added a blob of the paste, closed the tongs firmly and thrust them back into the flames.

Carrie would have been fascinated by the process.

'Hold out your hands,' Stefania commanded, lifting the tongs from the fire.

Hot, thin pancakes landed on Vito and then Ezio's palms. The nutty aroma made Vito's mouth water. They ate them, topped with creamy cheese, before retiring to the hayloft above the mule which, for the entire night, clattered in its stall.

The next day was Sunday, the day of rest. And so Vito and Ezio rested, but only until late afternoon. They needed to head for their rendezvous with Bianconini near the village of Brento. Last October, despite numerous losses suffered as a result of the German counterattack, the Allies had conquered the nearby area. The enemy defence, positioned on Monte Adone above Brento, had resisted to the point of exhaustion, turning the zone into a scene of heinous battles where, unfortunately, many US soldiers had died. The Germans were still there: it was their last bastion on the Gothic Line. And they'd become a real thorn in the side of the Americans.

When he was in high school, Vito used to enjoy climbing Monte Adone with the mountaineering club on the weekends. Adone – Adonis in English – a mythological name for a natural fortress 665 metres high, the mountain boasted rock towers made of sandstone, cut by caves and canyons. Its ravines were well known to both Vito and Ezio, and for this reason Bianconini had chosen them to work as scouts for the Americans as they began their final assault.

The day lengthened, and soon it was dusk. Vito and Ezio bade farewell to Alfredo and his children after a meal of roasted chestnuts and wild boar stew. The charcoal burner refused their money, but they'd left a wad of lire behind in the hayloft to compensate.

They followed a zigzagging track and, before too long, Monte Adone rose like a jagged whaleback against the darkening skyline. Soon, the village of Brento, cut high into the mountain's side like a scar and under German occupation, came into sight. It would be foolhardy to go anywhere near it yet. But there was no need to do that. Bianconini and his second-in-command were waiting for Vito and Ezio in an abandoned farmhouse up ahead.

'You got here just in time,' their commander muttered. 'We need to go down to the cellar. The *'mericani* are due to flatten Brento with everything they've got.'

20

Carrie was getting ready for bed when Louise ran into the tent, a dazed look on her face. 'President Roosevelt has died,' she said.

'Oh, my God,' Carrie gasped. 'That happened suddenly.'

She wrapped her arms around Louise, and they both wept.

'He was such a big personality,' Carrie said.

'Yeah. I liked him a lot.'

'So, what happens now?' Carrie said as she dried her tears with the back of her hands.

'We'll have thirty days of mourning. No more dances. But we'll still get days off, of course.'

'I'm due to go to Florence tomorrow. Gotta say goodbye to Mimi.' Carrie drew her brows together. 'Not lookin' forward to that.'

'She'll be okay with Vito's folks, though, won't she?' Louise sat on her cot and took off her shoes.

Carrie sighed. The front would move soon. 'I'm gonna miss her so much.'

'I bet.' Louise put on her pyjamas. 'I'm bushed, Tex. Let's talk about it in the morning, eh?'

Carrie brushed her teeth and crawled under the blankets. The nights were still cold and her feet felt like blocks of ice. While she waited to warm up and for sleep to claim her, thoughts of Vito filled her mind. Her love for him was an all-consuming emotion, and she clung to it like a lifeline. He was strong, and brave, and kind and gentle. His only apparent fault appeared to be his reckless assumption that he was invincible. Touching her fingers to her mouth, she recalled the feel of his lips on hers: tender at first, then deliberate and relentless until she'd moaned for the wanting of him. He'd given her so much pleasure that every cell in her body quivered now with remembered delight. She'd cried like a baby when they'd said goodbye.

'Promise me you'll be careful,' she'd begged.

He'd brushed off her fear. 'Nothing bad will happen to me, Carrie. I once had my fortune told by a gypsy and she predicted a long life.'

She wasn't sure if he'd made that up on the spot, and the statement had done little to calm her worries. They hadn't spoken about the future; she'd forbidden it. Her future with Bill had been taken from them, so it was better that she and Vito lived in the moment. Yet she couldn't stop herself from dwelling on the obstacles they'd need to overcome. Apart from the war, there were so many practical, tangible barriers in their way. Live in the moment, she kept reminding herself. *But it was so difficult with him not being there.*

* * *

'I can ride my bike without the training wheels,' Mimi announced when Anna let Carrie into the apartment the next day. 'Let me show you!'

'We'll go to Piazza Santa Croce after lunch, my dearest,' Anna said. 'I'm sure Carrie is hungry.'

Rita had prepared her signature *peposo*, and Carrie's taste buds couldn't help but respond. The apartment felt strange without Vito. His vibrant presence had been the linchpin that held everyone together. The entire family seemed lost without him.

After helping Carrie and Anna with the dishes, Mimi declared she was too old to take a nap. 'I'm six now and my head is better.' She pointed to the bangs which had grown to cover the scar on her forehead. '*Andiamo!*' Let's go!

Carrie laughed. When she was with Mimi, her troubles seemed far away. How she loved the little girl. She would miss her horribly.

She said as much to Anna while they were sitting at the same *caffè* where she'd sat with Vito last month, watching Mimi pedal across the square, scattering pigeons in her wake.

The spring sunshine warmed them, but Carrie still felt the coldness of missing Vito chilling her bones.

'You'll be back in Florence before too long, I hope,' Anna said as their waiter brought their coffees.

Carrie stirred sugar into her cappuccino. 'I don't know. The uncertainty is killing me. Who knows where the front will move after Bologna?'

Anna reached across the table and squeezed her hand. 'The Lord will lead you where you are needed.'

'I want to believe that His will is for me to return.'

'I pray that will be so.' Anna's smile warmed her eyes. 'Vito loves you and I think you love him too. Am I right?'

'Oh, yes.' Carrie gazed into the distance. 'I thought it would be crazy to fall for him, but now I can't imagine not doing so... if you know what I mean.'

'We don't choose love. It chooses us.'

'And you, Anna? Have you ever been in love?' Carrie risked the question. She knew Vito's sister well enough by now, and her Italian had improved so much she no longer tripped over the words.

'My sweetheart, Giordano, was conscripted into the army and sent to Russia to fight in Hitler's Operation Barbarossa.' Anna's voice trembled. 'He died near Stalingrad in December 1942.'

'I'm so sorry.' It was Carrie's turn to squeeze Anna's hand. 'Is that when you decided to become a nun?'

'Yes. I was always attracted to the religious life.' She stared down at her lap. 'So, when Giordano was killed, I found my solace in the convent.'

'Did Vito tell you about Bill?'

'No.' Anna tilted her head to the side in question.

Grateful for Vito's discretion, Carrie told his sister the whole tragic story. 'I truly believed I would never love anyone else after I lost him. Now I'm terrified Vito will suffer the same fate.'

Anna took Carrie's hands in hers. Then she prayed, and Carrie prayed with her for God's protection of the man they both loved.

'What are you doing?' Mimi asked as she cycled up.

'We're praying, sweetie.' Carrie gave her a wan smile. 'But we saw how well you did on your bike. We're so proud of you.'

'*Grazie.*' Mimi grinned from ear to ear.

'And now there's something I need to tell you.'

'What?' Mimi propped her bike against the table and sat on a chair.

'I'm going away for a while, darlin'.'

'Why?' the little girl asked with a frown.

'Because the hospital will be moving to Bologna.'

Mimi's face fell. 'When will you come back?'

'I don't know, pumpkin. Soon, I hope. In the meantime, Nonno, Nonna, and Anna will take real good care of you. You don't need to worry.'

Mimi threw her arms around her. 'Please don't go!'

'I have to obey orders, darlin'. I'm in the Army, remember? But I'll miss you such a lot.'

'I'll miss you too,' Mimi sobbed. 'Come back soon!'

'I'll try.' Carrie's voice rasped with unshed tears. She pulled Mimi onto her lap and cuddled her, kissing her wet cheeks and smoothing her hair. 'How about I get us all an ice cream? It will cheer us up.'

'*Grazie.*' The corners of Mimi's downturned mouth lifted as she turned to look at Carrie. 'Can I have a chocolate one?'

'Of course you can, honey.' Carrie signalled to the waiter. 'How about you, Anna. What flavour would you like?'

'*Fragola, per favore,*' she responded, asking for strawberry flavour.

Carrie ordered the *gelati*, including a vanilla cone for herself. There was nothing like Italian ice cream. Nothing like the people she'd met in Italy, to be honest. How would she ever bear it when she had to leave?

* * *

The ride back to Scarperia took slightly over an hour. Carrie climbed down from the Jeep, thanked the driver, then made her way along the narrow path between the tents.

Her skin prickled as she perceived a man was coming towards her.

Max. She thought about turning around and heading down a different route but decided against it. She'd face up to him, show she wasn't concerned.

He halted in front of her and raked his eyes over her body. 'Salute your superior officer, Lieutenant,' he barked.

She did as he'd requested, not saying a word.

'Have you been visiting with that "wop"?' he sneered.

She shook her head. 'I went to see Mimi.'

'She's a kike, I believe?'

'And *you* are a bigot...'

'Watch yourself, Lieutenant.'

He brushed past, his body pushing against hers, his foul-smelling breath sliding over her face and making her cringe.

She rushed to her tent and collapsed onto her cot. *The nerve of the man!* If he ever tried anything like that again, she'd follow Louise's advice and kick him where it counted, damn the consequences.

Voices came from outside, and before too long, Betty and Marge were bustling into the tent, chatting excitedly.

'What's up?' Carrie asked.

'The stingy ammunition allocations of last year have now loosened up like a drunk's tongue.' Marge sat on her cot. 'And our artillerymen up in the mountains are pumping out shells like there's no tomorrow.'

'Yeah,' Betty chipped in. 'Apparently we're softening up the enemy's defences.'

'I don't get what that means,' Carrie said.

Betty smiled indulgently. 'Information gathered throughout the winter has been consolidated and every possible target is being fired upon. Jerry can't afford to take any chances, so he's probably having to alert all his forces to brace themselves, thinking this might be the preparation behind which US troops plan to jump off.'

'Of course, there's no follow-up happening at present. Jerry is simply being fooled,' Marge clarified. 'He'll be experiencing a let-down and losing a lot of sleep. After many such false starts, it's hoped he'll become unnerved or else become somewhat calloused and drop his guard when the real attack comes along.'

'I see,' Carrie said. 'Kinda like a re-enactment of the story about the boy who called "Wolf!"'

'Absolutely.' Betty nodded.

With a flurry of footfalls, the tent flap opened and Louise erupted into the bivouac.

'Orders have arrived.' She took a deep breath. 'Tomorrow we start packing up the hospital.'

Carrie's heart skittered. Where was Vito in all this commotion? She prayed with every ounce of her being that he was safe.

21

Vito was cleaning his Sten in the kitchen of the abandoned farmhouse outside Brento, reflecting on how, that first night, Bianconini and Merlo, his second-in-command, had told them about what had been happening in Bologna the past several months. Taking refuge in the cellar, they'd spoken of reprisals against the partisans, perpetrated by the fascists. They'd described the stool pigeons, marching through the city centre, accompanied by *fascisti* in civilian clothing. They'd recounted how collaborators were going into bars and meeting places and pointing out members of the *resistanza* with a simple nod. In the meantime, the *gappisti*, anonymous in their secret bases, had been hunting down the fascist spies.

'It's been a difficult winter filled with evil and hatred,' Bianconini had said. 'But the light is at the end of the tunnel. Those *bastardi* will get their payback, mark my words.'

Vito wished time would speed up; they'd been waiting for days for the action to start, subsisting on a diet of foraged dandelion leaves, nettles and wild fennel. It had been impossible to hunt for game; firing their weapons would have attracted undue attention.

A stream trickled nearby, providing them with fresh water, but there was no coffee to be had, and he found himself longing to get back to civilisation almost as much as he was longing to see Carrie. He missed her with an ache that throbbed through his soul.

A cuckoo called from the woods beyond, the familiar sound reminding him of the clock he used to hear in his grandparents' apartment before they passed away. The daylight hours here were filled with birdsong, mingling with the babbling of the brook rippling down through the field outside. Vito got to his feet and went to the open window. It had rained last night, and the sun was a huge orb of melted butter, shining out of a cloudless sky. Everything was dripping wet, every blade of grass and every leaf seemed to sparkle with drops of moisture. He inhaled the sweet smell of damp vegetation and gazed up towards Brento. A low mist hung over the village, rising like steam from a giant bath. Monte Adone towered atop, similar to a whale erupting from the sea, its head an enormous, vertical cliff.

Without warning, the birds fell silent. Vito's skin prickled. The drone of aeroplane engines resounded, followed by the hissing noise of bombs dropping.

'Air raid,' he yelled to the others, who were sitting at the table behind him.

'The curtain is going up at last,' Ezio said as they hurried down to the basement.

'At last,' Vito said, a huge grin on his face.

* * *

They spent most of the following two days sheltering from the aerial bombardments. Vito couldn't help ducking his head with each explosion. The entire cellar vibrated and the ground beneath his feet shook as if they were experiencing an earthquake. Acrid smoke seeped through the ventilation shafts along with the echoing whistles and thuds of the bombs.

On the third day, the bombardments ceased. 'The American troops should be arriving now,' Bianconini said. 'I'll go up top and have a look around.'

But, before he could climb the staircase to the ground floor, more explosions rent the air.

'Those aren't coming from planes,' Vito said. 'The Germans must be shelling the GIs from their positions in Brento.'

'Doubt there's anything left of the village.' Ezio took a deep draw from his cigarette.

'I'll be back as soon as possible,' Bianconini said, making his way out of the basement.

Vito listened to the blasts while they waited. There were at least a thousand explosions, he estimated. He hoped Bianconini was all right.

About sixty minutes or so later, the feisty commander returned.

'There's a company of US infantry pinned down by arching machine gun fire and mortars. I talked with the captain and offered to help,' he said. 'The Germans have plenty of fight left in them, it seems. We'll do a reconnoitre first thing tomorrow and find which Brento building is their base. Meanwhile, the American sappers are clearing mines from the approach road.'

* * *

After a meagre breakfast of foraged food, Vito and his friends crept up the stairs and out of the farmhouse. They kept to the treeline, following a mule path which led to Brento. Their breath steamed in the chill of early morning and mud clung to their boots.

'*Gesu Maria*,' Vito exclaimed as the village came into sight.

The American bombs had reduced Brento to rubble. The stench of death and decay made him retch. Piles of debris blocked the road. Blackened corpses lay draped over mutilated machinery. Dead animals were already attracting flies. Only one structure had been left standing: a three-storey edifice which looked to be the town hall. Sure enough, big guns had been mounted on its roof. Vito and his comrades returned to their hideout immediately, and Bianconini went to inform the Americans.

The US troops wasted no time in launching their assault. Vito, Ezio, Bianconini and Merlo stood with them as they walloped the edifice with 'time on target' artillery. Vito had never seen anything like it: a massive coordination of fire so that all the munitions were aimed to arrive at exactly the same time. The Americans pumped in ten direct hits and Vito's ears rang with the resulting explosions.

'Hooah!' the Americans shouted their battle cry.

'*Partigiani all'assalto!*' Bianconini ordered Vito and the others to attack.

Adrenaline pumping through him, Vito raced forward.

Everyone began yelling as they turned on the heat with their Tommy guns. *Thwack-thwack-thwack-thwack-thwack.*

Vito's breaths came in short, sharp bursts.

There was no return fire.

Without any warning, around fifty Germans exited the building with their hands raised, leaving their dead and wounded in the blazing ruins.

An American colonel, hollow-eyed with tiredness, then appeared. He held out the scarlet and gold colours of the 916th

Field Artillery Battalion, to whom the company belonged, and handed them to Bianconini.

'You know the terrain. I want you and your men to fly this flag from the top of Mount Adone,' he said.

* * *

After the Americans had set off for their camp on the other side of the mountain, Vito took a moment to glug down water from his canteen. He smoked a quick cigarette, then, with Ezio, Bianconini, and Merlo by his side, he shouldered his Sten and told the group to follow him.

'I know the safest route to the summit.'

The rain-channelled path above the village was steep and stony, like the dry bed of a stream. As he led his comrades through woodland, Vito felt he could relax, but when they came to open terraces, criss-crossed with enemy trenches, from where they could easily be seen, he chose the more obscure, almost vertical goat tracks through the scrub.

After about an hour, two clay-coloured stone towers – as tall as skyscrapers – emerged from the base of a jagged wall of rock and vegetation. Vito decided he would plant the flag on top of the tallest crag, which was etched against the infinite sky. The Americans would be able to see it clearly from their bivouac below.

So far, they hadn't come across any Germans, thank God. Had they already beaten a retreat?

No such luck.

Guttural Teutonic voices echoed from a foxhole up ahead.

Sweat beaded Vito's brow.

He indicated with his hands that his comrades should flatten themselves.

Stealthily, he inched his way forward, crawling with his stomach pressed to the ground.

Don't take any risks, Vito reminded himself.

Only one solution presented itself. They had to overcome the enemy by surprise.

Kill or be killed.

His finger squeezed the trigger of his weapon. At the edge of the dugout, he unleashed a hail of bullets, firing at the two men inside until they tumbled backwards in a pool of blood and sinew.

Bianconini came from behind and jumped down into the trench to kick the enemy bodies and make sure they were lifeless. Then he took their submachine guns and placed them in his backpack.

'Onwards!' he said.

Vito stared at the vertical cliff above. Last time he'd scaled it, he'd had rope and a harness. But he couldn't back out now. He took the flag from Bianconini and tucked it into his lanyard.

'Best I do this alone,' he said.

He climbed at a snail's pace, feeling for footholds in the crevices, grasping at intermittent protruding rocks.

At one point, with a scatter of stones, he slipped and fell about a metre to land on a narrow ledge, his heart almost thudding out of his chest.

He gritted his teeth and set off again, his muscles straining, his arms aching as he heaved himself ever upwards.

Finally, he reached the summit. He planted the colours into the soft ground. They hung limply as there was no breeze. It didn't matter, though. The flag was a symbol of victory. One small step in many to come.

He gazed at the 360-degree view beneath him: the hills and valleys of his beloved Tuscany on one side, the geometric fields of the Emilia-Romagna region on the other. From up here, it was hard to believe there was a war on, that below humans were hell-bent on destruction. Surely it would be ending soon.

Vito exhaled slowly. His next stop would be Bologna, where he'd meet up with Carrie, he hoped. Then, there'd be Mario Carità to be dealt with.

But, *prima cosa* – first things first – he told himself, he had to get down from this goddammed mountain. With a wry grin, he began the treacherous descent.

22

The grapevines amid the hospital tents had budded into leaf, their branches outstretched as if they were holding hands. Sunshine dappled the newly unfurled leaves while Carrie made her way between the plants on her way to the medical ward. Her chest fluttered with conflicting emotions. Just four days ago, the Supreme Commander of the Allied Forces had broadcast the message that the moment had come to take to the field for the final fray, which would end the war in Europe. And now, from all accounts, after 'softening up' the enemy with aerial bombardments, American soldiers were fighting bitter battles up in the mountains. Vito had said that was where he was heading. Had he heeded her plea to be careful?

She breathed in the delicate lilac-like scent of the bluish-purple wisteria blossom, which was cascading from a support outside the ward tent. Springtime in Tuscany sure was beautiful.

She went to check on the few patients yet to be evacuated, but Captain Huxley came and stood in front of her. 'Bologna has fallen to the Allies,' he said without preamble. 'We're shipping out tomorrow.'

'So soon?'

Although she knew the push had been imminent – in fact, she'd been helping with the packing of medical supplies for days – the order still set her pulse racing.

'I hope this is our last tactical move, Carrie. I, for one, will be glad to go home.'

'Yeah, me too.' It was true. She longed to see Mom, Daddy and Helen, of course she did. But the thought of leaving Vito, Mimi and the Mancinis turned her stomach to lead.

'I'll take over here,' Captain Huxley said. 'Transport will be arriving imminently to carry our remaining patients to Florence. Go and help dismantle the hospital, Lieutenant.' He smiled. 'We need to be ready by sundown.'

The next day, Carrie and her tentmates rose at 5 a.m. They ate a quick breakfast, then helped load all the equipment onto trucks.

Was the war finally coming to an end? How long they would stay in Bologna was anyone's guess. Would Vito be there? How she prayed that would be so. She knew little about the city. Just that a sandwich meat at home had been named after it and had given rise to the word 'baloney'. She'd asked Captain Huxley why Jerry had fought so fiercely to prevent the Allies from taking Bologna, and he'd told her it was strategically important as an industrial and railway hub, a vital centre from where they transported goods and material north to the Reich.

After lunch, she sat next to Louise, both women on their footlockers and surrounded by their kitbags while they waited to climb on board a six-by-six. A cool breeze ruffled her hair as she gazed at her surroundings for the last time. Seven months of Tuscan living were coming to an end and her chest squeezed with sadness. The pretty town of Scarperia would forever be imprinted in her memories, though it was Florence that held her heart.

'What are you thinking?' Louise asked, turning to face her.

'How much I'll miss this place.' A sob quivered in Carrie's throat.

Kenny reached across the space between them and gave her a hug. 'Focus on the fact we're going home soon, Tex. Remember how we used to talk about missing our folks?'

'Seems another lifetime.'

Louise gave her an understanding smile. 'I know...'

A couple of hours later, Carrie found herself sitting on a bench in the back of a five-tonne truck, bumping over the shell-pitted road taking the convoy towards the Futa Pass. At first, she marvelled at the beauty of the scenery: the hills rolling below as far as her eye could see. But then a small village came into view and she gasped. It had been completely flattened. Nothing but rubble. Her heart went out to the poor people who'd once called it their home.

As the hospital transport made its laborious way up into the high reaches of the Apennines, they passed yet more devastation: houses and hamlets shelled to bits. In places, the hillsides were so densely pockmarked with craters that it seemed impossible to find a single square foot of soil that hadn't been hit by shellfire.

Carrie grabbed hold of Louise and they hugged each other with sorrow, expressing their shock at what the soldiers they'd cared for had gone through, while they'd so gallantly attempted to break through to Bologna. The war for those men had been hell on earth, and now, for the first time, she really understood why.

The 56th motor convoy was part of countless others snaking along the winding road to the Po Valley. They crawled at the pace of a tortoise, dust furling around them. A few miles south of the city, devastation from intense bombing and shelling became apparent. Not an inch of the outskirts remained unaffected. Every building had been reduced to debris or left open to the elements. Carrie was reminded of the ride to Rome last year: the sight of all the mutilated vehicles, trash, and the stink of unburied corpses. She wrapped her arms around herself to stop her shoulders from quaking. Where was Vito? Had he made it through all this death and destruction?

At around sundown, the convoy arrived at a big arena to the south of the city, encircled by walls that made Carrie think of the Roman Colosseum. After the trucks had parked up outside, her eyes were drawn to a long line of colonnaded red porticoes that led up a nearby hill to where a golden-yellow church, layered like a wedding cake, perched on the summit. She wondered if it would be okay to visit one day. Maybe with Vito.

Inside the stadium, an enormous statue of a horse on a plinth overlooked the bleachers.

'There used to be a sculpture of Mussolini sitting on its saddle, but the Bolognese tore it down in July 1943, after he'd been deposed,' Captain Huxley said as they unloaded the hospital equipment.

'Gee whiz. That man sure has a lot to answer for.'

'Him and Hitler,' Captain Huxley agreed.

Max came up and Carrie glanced away in disgust. He positioned himself far too close for her liking, between her and Captain Huxley. He handed her a bag of supplies. 'Go put those over there, Lieutenant.' He indicated towards the far side of the stadium, where other bags had been piled.

'Yes, sir!'

She saluted, did as he'd ordered, then went to join the chow line for her C-rations. *Good damn riddance!*

* * *

By darkness, Carrie and the others had eaten dinner, finished unloading the trucks, piled the equipment, pitched their tents, unrolled their blankets, washed their faces, and flopped into bed.

This time, she and Louise were sharing a bivouac for two, their cots next to each other on the grass of the soccer field.

'It feels strange to be here,' Carrie whispered.

'What do ya mean, Tex?'

'I dunno. Like I'm in the middle of a dream, or something...'

The drone of plane engines interrupted her. Probably their own guys heading to bomb German lines.

Then came the dreaded loud whistle of bombs falling. Carrie sat bolt upright, her veins turned to ice.

'Jesus!' she exclaimed.

Massive explosions rocked the tent.

'Oh, my God, Tex.' Louise's voice went up by nearly an octave. 'We haven't had time to place any Red Cross markers.'

'We didn't think they'd be needed. Jerry is supposed to be in retreat.' The words trembled on Carrie's lips.

Boom!

The noise was so deafening, a bomb must have come down on one of the huge troop and vehicle concentrations in the vicinity.

Ack-ack-ack!

'They're strafing us!' Carrie rolled from her cot and slid under it, fear beading her forehead in cold sweat.

'This is Anzio all over again,' Louise muttered.

And it was. The German planes came back again and again, strafing and bombing and wreaking havoc. They hadn't dug any foxholes; there was nowhere to hide. If a bomb fell on their tent, their number would be up.

Carrie put her hands over her ears and squeezed her eyes shut. She thought about Vito, Mimi and everyone she loved. *Would she ever see them again?*

23

EARLIER THAT DAY

Not long after sunrise, Vito sat smoking with Ezio and around twenty of Bianconini's men on the steps of the town hall in the ruins of the main square of Bazzano. They'd taken control of the small town two days ago, and now were about to march on to Bologna, twenty kilometres away. Vito raised his gaze to the medieval red-brick castle on the crag above; its high clock tower adjacent to the palatial building had been severely damaged by aerial bombing. Big chunks blasted out of the structure bore witness to the fact that *tedeschi* troops had camped in the town prior to starting their retreat.

A pigeon strutted across the piazza, pecking at the gravel between the piles of ruined cobblestones, which were all that remained of the surface of the square. But the cheerful sound of children playing, their sing-song voices echoing through the rubble, lifted Vito's spirits. He thought about Mimi, missing her with an intense longing. She was such a sweet child and he loved her as if she were his own. How long would it be before he saw her and Carrie again?

He took a deep draw of his cigarette. By all accounts, the

goddamned Germans had abandoned Bologna yesterday, leaving it open for the Allied forces and partisans. 'The Nazis are like cowardly rats abandoning a sinking ship,' Ezio had said when he and Vito had heard the news.

'Is Bologna a sinking ship?' Vito replied.

Ezio shook his head. 'I trust not.'

With a wry smile, Vito exhaled a puff of smoke. At least he'd be able to fulfil his promise to Carrie that he'd be careful. There wouldn't be any liberation battle like there'd been in Florence last August. In fact, the only risks he'd taken since saying goodbye to her had been in Brento, when he'd climbed Monte Adone. His descent after planting the American colours had been without incident, thankfully. Then he'd gone with Ezio, Bianconini and Merlo to the US bivouac on the other side of the mountain, where they'd been given a good feed and had enjoyed a shower and a shave before spending the night in a tent.

The following morning, the Americans had left for Bologna and Vito and his comrades had met up with Bianconini's men here. Fresh from acting as scouts for the Allies, helping to liberate the nearby Caprara, Sole, and Abelle highlands ahead of chasing the enemy across the River Po, they were buzzing with the success of their mission and raring to take the subsequent step.

'Time to go,' Bianconini announced. 'Bologna is waiting for us.'

Vito gave a whoop. Bologna first. Mario Carità next. Then home to Florence and future plans with Carrie.

He hoped.

* * *

It was mid-afternoon by the time they'd made their way through the battle-scarred countryside and the rubble-strewn outskirts to arrive at the San Vitale gate to the city. There, they met up with partisans from the surrounding area, who were keen to take part in the victory parade and rid the city of any remaining fascists. Cartridge belts slung around their necks and pistols in their waistbands, Vito and his friends clambered aboard trucks which would take them to the historic centre. Sappers with minesweepers checked the road in front while they waited. Finally, with a rumble of their engines, the vehicles lurched forwards.

Crowds of people lined the streets, waving white handkerchiefs and clapping. Tears of emotion filled Vito's eyes as he listened to the tintinnabulation of the city's bells. He couldn't help thinking about Carrie and wishing she was here with him to witness the joy of this celebration.

Their route took them past the 'two towers', the taller Asinelli and the shorter, leaning Garisenda, both of which dated from the thirteenth century, a time when Bologna had resembled a medieval Manhattan. It occurred to Vito that he might invite Carrie to climb to the top of Asinelli and show her the view. Surely her hospital wouldn't be far behind the American troops who'd arrived that morning...

Soon the truck on which he and his comrades were riding was surrounded by hordes of Bolognese, passing them bottles of wine, and singing patriotic songs. They were joined by the *gappisti* – the city's urban freedom fighters – who were marching with banners displaying the names of their formations. Vito was startled as a man on the pavement raised his hand to give the Roman salute to Bianconini's Italian green, white and red flag. Someone nudged the man, and he quickly closed his fist. It was ironic that the Nazis had assumed the rigid extended hand saluting gesture, which had originated with the Caesars and had been adopted by the Italian fascists well before the Germans had appropriated it for their 'Heil Hitler' salutes. Vito fervently hoped never to see the greeting used again.

The crowds blocked the road now, slowing down their progress. Up ahead were Allied tanks and Jeeps and eventually they all ground to a halt in Neptune's Square.

Vito's gaze widened. Groups of women were laying flowers and posting photographs on the external wall of a building that looked to be the town hall.

He grabbed hold of Ezio's arm and pointed. 'Let's go see what that's all about.'

They jumped off the lorry and approached a middle-aged woman dressed in black, who told them that the pictures were of loved ones who'd been killed by the Nazi-fascists.

'They called this place "the rest stop for the partisans",' she said.

'Why, signora?' Ezio asked.

'They were being sarcastic and cruel. This is where many *gappisti* were executed,' the woman said, tears in her eyes. 'One of them was my son, Paolo.'

Vito's throat tightened with sympathy. 'I'm so sorry for your loss, signora.'

She touched her hand to his. 'We can only pray for the future of our country, and for peace to come soon.'

'I second that,' Ezio said.

The woman gave them a melancholy smile. 'You're from Florence, are you not? I can tell from your accents.' Their pronunciation of the letter 'c' like an 'h' was a dead giveaway. 'Why are you here?' She looked them both in the eye.

They explained that they too were *partigiani* like her son and that they'd been fighting with the Allies.

'They took their time breaking through to Bologna,' she huffed.

Vito decided not to elaborate, out of respect for Carrie and the American soldiers he'd fought with. He bowed his head to the woman, wished her well and took his leave.

The mass of people carried him and Ezio past the fountain, in the centre of which stood the majestic figure of Neptune, a trident in his right hand. They arrived at Piazza Vittorio Emanuele II, the principal square, which was overflowing with the citizens of Bologna as well as partisans, Allied soldiers and armoured vehicles on which young people – mostly girls with flowers in their hair and waving Italian tricolour flags – had climbed. Vito glanced around, trying to spot any American nurses, but there were only British Eighth Army and American Fifth Army soldiers to be seen.

Disappointed, his gaze fell on Bianconini. Their commander had joined a group of men dressed in smart suits.

Vito bumped shoulders with Ezio. 'Let's go find out what the boss is up to,' he said.

* * *

An hour or so later, at about 9.30 p.m., Vito and Ezio were sitting with Bianconini at a table in the Bologna headquarters of the Liberation Committee in Piazza Aldrovandi, having given a report to Signor Sarti, the wiry man with a hook nose who'd visited them in the ruins of the Ospedale Maggiore last November.

'The situation in Bologna is about to become apocalyptic,' Sarti informed them when they'd finished telling of their activities with the Americans. 'Because of the sudden departure of the Germans, the city is still full of fascists. Given their brutal treatment of our freedom fighters during the occupation, the people will set up courts to try them and execute them for their crimes.'

'By "people", do you mean "partisans"?' Bianconini asked.

Sarti nodded.

Vito leant forward. 'Do you have any information on the whereabouts of Mario Carità?'

Sarti steepled his fingers. 'He was in Padova, last I heard, collaborating with the SS. Between them, they captured almost all the members of the Veneto Liberation Committee, torturing them dreadfully.'

'Padova will still be in German hands,' Ezio said. 'But now the Allies are on the move, it probably won't be for long. Carità needs to be stopped from escaping like he did from Florence. The people should deal with him...'

'By "people" we mean "us",' Vito chipped in. 'Florentines.'

'It will be difficult to travel to Padova.' Bianconini raised a brow.

'How difficult?' Ezio asked.

'Impossible, I would say.' Sarti shook his head.

'Where's there's a will there's a way.' Vito smiled. 'We can follow the front, keep a low profile, and when the Eighth Army arrives in the city, we'll join the local partisans in rounding up fascists.'

'Following the front won't be easy,' Bianconini said in warning. 'In fact, it'll be highly dangerous. You could be mistaken for spies.'

Carrie's plea for Vito to be careful echoed in his head, but he put it to one side.

'We can borrow bicycles. Disguise ourselves as peasants.'

Bianconini sighed. 'Foolhardy. But I can't stop you...'

With a crash, the door to the meeting room burst open and a young man rushed in.

'The Luftwaffe are bombing the Americans near the Littoriale Stadium,' he said. 'They've set up a hospital inside the grounds and it looks as if it might have been hit.'

Vito leapt to his feet. *Carrie. Oh, my God, Carrie.*

* * *

Vito and Ezio borrowed bikes from Sarti's men and cycled as if all the demons of hell were chasing them. It was slow going; the roads were generally blocked by rubble and those that weren't were overflowing with people celebrating the liberation of Bologna.

But the closer they got to the stadium, the quieter the streets became and no wonder: they were being dive-bombed by German Stuka planes.

Vito squinted in the gloom. A military roadblock made up of barricades and Jeeps barred their path.

He and Ezio dismounted from their bikes and approached.

A young soldier raised his rifle. 'This is a restricted area,' he said with an American accent. 'Turn back or I'll shoot.'

'Yes, sir.' Vito saluted. What else could he do? Aeroplane engines droned overhead, and his heart thudded with fear for Carrie.

A couple of Luftwaffe planes swooped down. *Boom!* From what he could see, they were attacking the area behind the stadium, but not the stadium itself.

'Come on,' he whispered to Ezio. 'Let's find a different way round.'

Under cover of darkness, it was relatively easy to avoid being seen. They wheeled their bikes around the perimeter of the colosseum-like arena, but there was only one entrance, and that was heavily guarded.

When the German planes came back again, bombing the vicinity once more, Vito flinched. All it would take was one stray bomb and the hospital would go up in flames.

'Let's wait it out,' he suggested.

'We can rest over there.' Ezio indicated towards the ruins of an apartment block.

Vito agreed and they hunkered down for the night in what remained of a ground-floor room, making their beds on old armchairs, catching short periods of sleep in between the German air raids. As time wore on, they became more sporadic, thank God, and by dawn they'd stopped altogether.

The next morning, as sunshine filtered through the shattered glass in the side window of their quarters, Ezio turned to him, rubbing the sleep from his eyes. 'What shall we do now?'

'I've been thinking,' Vito said, 'and I remember Carrie once told me that local women did the nurses' washing. Maybe the hospital has arranged the same set-up here and I could give a washerwoman some lire to deliver a message...'

'Ha.' Ezio snorted. 'That's a slim hope. I mean, we could be waiting for ages.' He looked Vito in the eye. 'Have you got paper and a pen?'

'I'll see if I can find something over there.' He indicated the splintered remains of a desk in the corner of the room. 'You don't need to wait with me, Ezio,' he added. 'I'll meet you back at the Committee headquarters.'

'Hey. We're in this together, *amico mio*.' Ezio's dark brown eyes glowed with a smile. 'Where you go, I'll follow, and where I go, you will follow too, I hope.'

'Absolutely.' Vito clapped him on the shoulder. 'Friends till the end of our days.'

'Long might they be,' Ezio said.

His words sent a chill through Vito. He shrugged it off. Of

course there was danger ahead, but life and danger went together. No one knew what was around the corner. The only thing to do was believe that all would be well in the end.

Holding on to that thought, he made his way across the room, and began to rifle through the contents of what was left of the desk.

He'd attempt to see her, remind her how much he loved her, and then continue his journey with Ezio. They'd deal with Carità and then head back to Florence. There, he'd wait to be reunited with Carrie and also carry on searching for answers to the question of the disappearance of Mimi's parents.

24

Carrie woke with a thumping headache. 'What an awful night,' she said as she rolled off her cot. She'd only crept back onto it in the early hours when the Luftwaffe had finally stopped its action.

Louise sat up with a groan. 'It'll be tough having to set up the hospital after so little sleep.'

Carrie wriggled out of her pyjamas. 'Someone said there're showers in the soccer teams' changing rooms.' She pulled on her fatigues. 'Hope there's hot water. I'd love to wash my hair.'

'And make yourself pretty for Vito?' Louise winked. 'I recall you said you hoped he'd be in Bologna.'

'I wish there was some way I could find out.' Carrie picked up a towel. 'He promised he'd get in touch with me. But how?'

'He'll find a way. Remember you told me how capable he is?'

A warm feeling tingled through Carrie. 'I keep reminding myself he's only twenty. It's easy to forget...'

'Age really doesn't matter.' Louise placed a hand over her heart. 'What matters is how you feel.'

'Yeah.' Carrie slipped on her shoes. 'I'll be twenty-six in August, though. There's a big gap between us.' She sighed. 'Bill was seven years older than me. I can't believe it's over a year now since he was killed. Sometimes I feel guilty I've fallen in love with Vito...'

'Bill would want you to be happy, Tex. I'm certain he'd tell you in person if he could.'

Carried nodded. 'I know.' She gave another sigh. 'The ring and the cameo he gave me are my only reminders of him, and I'll keep them with me forever.'

'It's so sad.' Louise pulled off her pyjamas and slipped into her fatigues. 'Why don't we go take that shower then grab some chow?'

Outside, Carrie's eyes stung. She still missed Bill a lot. But she no longer cried for him. It was the lingering acrid smoke from the bombing making her weep.

* * *

Later, in the chow line, everyone was talking about the air raid last night and how someone should have informed the Luftwaffe the Wehrmacht was in retreat. Thankfully, no one had been killed in the bombardment, although munitions and fuel dumps had gone up in flames.

'Won't make much difference,' Betty said. 'Supplies aren't a problem for us any more.'

Captain Huxley approached, spreading his arms out wide. 'Sorry, everyone, but Bologna has been declared off-limits to Allied military personnel. There'll be no sightseeing in the city while we are here.'

'Why?' Carrie's question reeked of disappointment.

'Too dangerous. The city has descended into anarchy. The partisans have started rounding up the fascists, trying them in secret courts and executing them.'

'But can't the Allies prevent them from doing that? Nothing like that happened in Florence...'

'There's nothing we can do. We'll be pulling out soon. In any case, Florence was different. The fascists had all fled by the time the city was liberated.'

Mario Carità had been one of them, Carrie recalled with a shudder. *Vito's nemesis.* Was Vito in Bologna now? And, if so, would he be one of those partisans seeking revenge? How she wished she had news of him...

Her thoughts were interrupted by the PA system calling all personnel to work. Carrie found herself allocated to unpacking medical supplies with Louise, which they took to the big ward tent once it had been erected by the enlisted men.

A heap of grimy sheets had travelled with them from Scarperia.

'There wasn't time for them to be laundered before we left,' Marge explained. 'But a couple of washerwomen are due to come and collect them this afternoon. If you've got anything which needs washing, just add it to the pile.'

'Thanks,' Carrie said. 'I'll do that.'

She spent the rest of the morning working, and while she worked she thought about Vito. Was he thinking about her as much as she was thinking about him? She longed to be in his arms, longed for his kisses, longed for him to make love to her. All she could do was wait, hope and pray.

The box of bandages she'd been unpacking was now empty, the rolls of packaged sterile gauze neatly stacked in the supply tent. She decided to go and collect her dirty ward dress.

Back on the ward, she discovered she was too late. Marge was supervising the medics making up the beds. She told Carrie that the washerwomen had already collected the soiled sheets and had left fifteen minutes ago. Carrie huffed out a breath. *Dang!*

Marge smiled broadly. 'One of the women left this for you.' She handed Carrie a folded piece of what looked to be wallpaper.

Carrie unfolded it. Words had been scrawled with what must have been a charred stick, from what she could make out. She read the signature and gasped.

Dearest Carrie
I am outside the stadium, but the entrance is guarded so I can't come in.
Please try and meet me. I will be here until sundown.
Ti amo, I love you, and can't wait to see you again.
Yours forever
Vito

Carrie's pulse raced. Leaving the stadium for a short time wasn't the same as going into the city, surely. She could barely contain her excitement.

'Are you okay?' Marge gave her a searching look.

'I'm feeling a little shaky. Think I'll go for a rest.'

'Sure.' Marge nodded. 'You're due a break.'

Carrie hurried to her tent, where she brushed her hair and put on fresh lipstick. And then, her heart in her mouth, she sauntered nonchalantly towards the stadium exit.

She stopped.

Max was standing at the gate, chatting to one of the guards.

Drat!

She squared her shoulders and marched up to them.

'I'd like to take a look at our surroundings,' she said.

'Sorry, Lieutenant,' the sentry said, saluting. 'It's an off-limits zone.'

'I won't go far.' She gave him her best smile.

He turned to Max. 'Would that be okay, Captain?'

Max looked Carrie up and down. 'Are you planning on meeting your wop out there?'

'What's it to you if I am?' she retorted, her blood boiling.

'You're ordered to stand down, Lieutenant,' Max shot right back at her. 'For your own safety.' He narrowed his eyes. 'Or else.'

She knew full well what he meant. She wouldn't bring shame on herself and her family by disobeying an order. She saluted Max and gritted out, 'Yes, sir.'

* * *

Carrie tried several times to sneak out and meet Vito, but each time she found it impossible. Max was always lurking in the vicinity of the heavily guarded gate. Her only hope would be to convince new sentries when they changed duty, except by the time that happened, night would have fallen and she knew Vito would no longer be there.

She returned to her bivouac and collapsed on her cot in floods of tears.

Louise came and sat next to her. 'What's wrong, honey?'

Between sobs, Carrie explained. 'It's not fair,' she wept. 'Max is such a bastard.'

Louise put her arm around her and rubbed her back. 'He sure has an axe to grind where you're concerned. I'm really sorry you missed seeing Vito.'

'I wanted to talk to him, to try and convince him not to get caught up in revenge against the fascists.' Carrie dried her eyes with the handkerchief Louise handed her and wiped her nose. 'I'm so scared he'll get himself killed.'

Then she told Louise about Mario Carità and his involvement in the deaths of so many Florentines.

'He also tortured Vito's friend Ezio's girlfriend, Stella,' she added.

'What a monster!'

'It's why they're going after him. Problem is, the man is evil and wouldn't think twice about killing them first...'

'I get that. But you worryin' yourself sick ain't gonna help him, darlin'. The war in Europe will end real soon and then you and he can be together.'

'If he survives.' Carrie sighed.

'All we can do is pray he will.'

'I do that all the time.'

'Good.' Louise got to her feet. 'Time to get some sleep, Tex. I'm all tuckered out and you must be too.'

'I am. Thanks for comforting me.'

'Any time.'

Carrie washed her face and changed into her pyjamas. She climbed into her cot, closed her eyes, but sleep eluded her. All she could think about was how Vito must have waited for hours for her to appear. How disappointed he'd have been. How he might even be doubting her love for him.

No, that wouldn't have happened. He knew she loved him. He'd have realised something must have prevented her from showing up.

She tossed and turned for ages, playing the events of the day over and over in her mind. If only Max hadn't been around when she'd tried to exit the stadium. The sentry would have let her go out for a few minutes, she was sure of it.

Her thoughts went to Mimi. She missed her almost as much as she missed Vito. Wouldn't it be wonderful if she could get some leave and go to Florence sometime soon? All would depend on how the war progressed. Was Jerry really on the run? Maybe he'd decided to give up on Italy and was heading back to

Germany where he belonged? As for Mario Carità, Vito and Ezio wouldn't be the only partisans out to get him. How she hoped the grim task would fall to others, and that Vito would come back to her safe and sound.

* * *

On 25 April, Carrie learnt that the National Liberation Committee had called for widespread insurrection throughout Italy. Captain Huxley told her the Germans had started to withdraw from Genoa, Milan and Turin just as the 56th EVAC had become fully operational.

Over the next several days, she was surprised by how exceptionally light American casualties were. The tactical situation had been moving incredibly rapidly as forward elements crossed the Po River, and it was now Jerry who was bearing the brunt of the fighting.

Soon, enemy injured arrived in the hospital by the hundreds. Some days, scores of unguarded Wehrmacht ambulances drove up, disgorging their patients before turning themselves in at the motor pool. Carrie could hardly believe it. She and the others were working alongside captured German medical officers while caring for their sick and wounded. They called her and the other nurses *schwester*, meaning 'sister', and most of the soldiers were so young and dejected Carrie couldn't help feeling sorry for them.

On 28 April, the execution of Mussolini and his mistress coincided with the news Padua and Venice had been liberated. On the highway at the back of the hospital site, big 10-tonne trucks loaded with enemy POWs started moving southward in an endless stream. But Carrie was far from rejoicing. She hadn't heard from Vito since his scribbled note, which she kept under her pillow and read every night. She'd thought of trying to get out of the gate and see if he was still waiting, but common sense told her that he wouldn't be doing so. He knew she loved him, and he'd have discovered she was safe. Was he still in Bologna? If so, why hadn't he been in touch? No, he must have left the city. Where was he? She prayed and prayed so much she could scarcely focus on her job.

To make matters even worse, Max would hover in the periphery of her vision every waking moment of every day. He was watching her, making sure she didn't step out of line. Maybe even hoping she would do so and then he'd gleefully make good his threat. Well, she wouldn't give him the chance.

When the end of the fighting in Europe was finally declared on 8 May, she allowed herself to celebrate briefly with her friends. Everyone was concerned, however, that war still raged in the Pacific. God forbid they should be sent to serve out there!

A week later, on 17 May, Carrie was in the chow line with Louise.

'Wouldn't it be nice if we were shipped to a rest bivouac near one of the beautiful lakes in the north of Italy?' Louise pondered wistfully.

'I'd rather it be Montecatini near Florence,' Carrie said.

Louise nudged her. 'Of course. I wouldn't mind that either. Theo visited once and said it was great. Oh, speak of the devil.' She smiled as Theo came up.

'Hi, gals.' He kissed Louise on the cheek. 'Got some bad news, I'm afraid. We're relocating to Udine.'

'Oo-dee-nay?' Carrie repeated the word back at him. 'Where's that?'

'North of the city of Trieste, close to the border with Yugoslavia.'

'Oh, my God. Why are we being sent there?' Louise asked, her voice rising.

'Relations between Italy, the Allies, and Yugoslavia have become severely strained, apparently.' Theo creased his brow. 'Trieste and some other small towns nearby have been occupied by Yugoslav partisans claiming the territory as their own.'

'Jesus,' Carrie whispered. From what she could remember of Italian geography, Trieste was in the far north-east of the country. About as far from Florence as you could get.

'American troops are being rushed to the zone, and should fighting proceed, the 56th will serve as the EVAC hospital,' Theo said.

Louise's nostrils flared visibly. 'Why us? Haven't we done enough in this goddamned war?'

Theo shrugged. 'Hopefully, it won't come to much. I mean, how can a bunch of Yugoslav partisans take on the might of the Allies?'

'Ha,' Carrie said, on the verge of hysterical laughter. 'They're Resistance fighters. They believe themselves invincible.' She shook her head. 'I'm not hungry. I'm going back to our tent.'

Without another word, she spun on her heel and made her way across the stadium.

Lying on her cot, she curled herself into a miserable ball. When would she ever see Vito, Mimi and the Mancinis again? Tears spilled from her eyes and trickled down her cheeks.

Get a grip, girl, she told herself. But it was so darn difficult.

25

This could be Switzerland, Vito thought as he trained his binoculars on a chalet, nestled between fir trees on a grass slope. The jagged crags of the Schlern Massif, about twenty kilometres north-east of Bolzano near the Austrian border, towered above him. He exhaled a steamy breath in the cold alpine air and huddled into his coat. It had been over three weeks since he'd waited in vain for Carrie outside the stadium, three weeks of telling himself something or someone must have prevented her from meeting him. Maybe she hadn't even got his note? The disappointment he'd experienced when she hadn't shown up had almost crippled him. But, thankfully, he'd had other business with which to occupy himself – although she was never far from his mind.

Back at the Liberation Committee headquarters, Bianconini informed Vito and Ezio news had come through with respect to Mario Carità. According to informants, he'd been spotted hiding in the middle of a column of German troops heading for the Brenner Pass into Austria. The enemy was being held back in Bolzano. All Vito and Ezio needed to do was enlist the help of the local Liberation Committee to find Carità's whereabouts, then have him arrested.

'This needs to be done by the book,' Sarti, the hook-nosed official, said. 'He's a war criminal and must pay for his crimes. But only after a trial in a democratic court in front of a judge and jury. We're being criticised for our actions here in Bologna. I'm not happy some people are saying we're behaving like the fascists. The rule of law must be applied.'

Bianconini offered to go with Vito and Ezio. As a Garibaldi partisan commander, he reckoned he carried some clout.

'We'll need to move fast,' he said. 'The Americans are already in Verona and the Germans are on the run.'

'Will we make it to the Brenner in time?' Vito rubbed at his chin. 'I mean, before Carità escapes?'

'By my reckoning, it will take us about a week of cycling overnight, with rest stops in daylight hours. Not too arduous as we can keep to the flat-bottomed valleys. But we should definitely leave as soon as possible.'

'I'll give you an official letter,' Sarti said. 'Introducing you to the Bolzano Committee and asking for you to be helped.'

They thanked him and set off that very night. By dawn they were crossing the River Po at San Nicolo, sneaking across a pontoon bridge under cover of darkness. The road was littered with derelict Germany military vehicles, which had been bombed to bits and abandoned. Vito had expected danger, but there was nothing to fear. The entire area had been deserted by friend and foe alike.

He and his companions took shelter in the ruins of a farm-house where they slept for much of the next day. After two further nights' cycling, they'd bypassed Verona and had progressed up the Adige river valley as far as Rovereto, level with the head of Lake Garda. They'd arrived in the Operationszone

Alpenvorland, an administrative region whose control had been taken away from Mussolini's Social Republic after the 1943 armistice and had been governed directly by the Third Reich ever since. From what Vito could see by the light of the moon, Rovereto had been devastated by aerial bombardment. He, Ezio and Bianconini wheeled their bicycles off the road just in time as a convoy of German troops in trucks rumbled by.

Progress was slow from then on. They were in enemy territory and wouldn't be able to contact the Liberation Committee until they got to Bolzano. They cycled through several more nights, Bianconini consulting his maps and leading them off the main roads. The woodland tracks were dark and their headlamps ineffectual. But, in the early morning light, before they found somewhere to hide and sleep, Vito revelled in the beauty of the spectacular alpine scenery. They'd reached the foot of the Dolomites: a mountain range with peaks rising above 3,000 metres, dominated by vertical limestone walls, and sheer cliffs topped by rock pinnacles, spires and towers. Carrie would have loved it.

Cycling ever northwards, Vito and his friends kept to the narrow, deep, long valleys, where they foraged for food and hunted game. Green forests contrasted with the bare, pale-coloured crags above, and birds of prey soared high in the thermals. They kept an eye out for bears and wolves, hearing the grunts of wild boar in the thickets as they cycled past.

On a frosty morning at the beginning of May, later than originally planned, they made it to Bolzano's medieval main square. The Tyrolean architecture bore witness to the Austrian heritage of the region. The area appeared to be deserted, so they went straight to the Liberation Committee HQ in a porticoed street leading off the piazza. Bianconini presented the letter from Sarti to a janitor, who told them to wait. They sat on wooden benches in the entrance hall, before being ushered into a shuttered dining room, where a group of men and women were drinking ersatz coffee at a big oak table.

A bespectacled man in his mid-thirties, Signor Mair, introduced himself and told them to take seats.

'We were just discussing information that the gates to the Bolzano Concentration Camp have been opened,' he said as he poured Vito, Ezio and Bianconini steaming cups of the hot acorn drink and offering them a breakfast of bread and strawberry jam.

Vito remembered hearing about the barracks encircled by barbed wire on the outskirts of the city, from where prisoners were sent to concentration camps in Germany or made to work as local slave labour. One of the biggest Nazi *lager* on Italian soil, it held about 11,000 political opponents, Jews and Romani people.

'The SS are in the process of destroying all documentation relating to their heinous activities in the camp. Apparently, they've received orders to leave no trace behind when they retreat,' Signor Mair said.

'Bastards,' Bianconini growled. 'What's happening to the inmates?'

'We're looking after them. Fortunately, we have enough volunteers to take them in.'

After Vito and everyone else had finished their breakfast, he and his friends found themselves alone with Signor Mair. He requested a report from Bianconini on their journey from Bologna and wanted to know the real purpose of their visit to South Tyrol. Together, Vito and Ezio explained about their mission to find Mario Carità and have him arrested.

'Hmm.' Signor Mair took a packet of Nazionali cigarettes from his pocket and offered them all a smoke. 'There's a bottle-neck of German troops in and around the city. Your man could well be with them or he might have yet to arrive. We expect the Americans any day now and an armistice between German Armed Forces and the Allies before that. Maybe even today, God willing. Once the Americans get here, they'll register all the POWs and you should be able to search for Carità among them.'

'What if he manages to cross the border beforehand?' Vito asked, leaning in for a light of his cigarette.

'No one is getting across. The border is closed and there's an infantry division of Americans on the other side of the frontier in Austria.'

'Good.' Ezio smiled.

* * *

Vito woke from a deep sleep to find it was still early evening. He, Ezio and Bianconini had been shown to the ubiquitous mattresses placed on bare floorboards in an upstairs room. He lay there, listening to his comrades' snores while he thought about Carrie. Not for the first time, he wondered if she'd received his note. If she had, what had prevented her from meeting him? He hoped nothing had happened to her, that she was all right. The Allied front was moving so quickly, he doubted she'd be in Bologna for long. Wouldn't it be wonderful if the 56th EVAC were following the US forces soon to arrive in Bolzano? The war in Europe would be coming to an end soon. It would be too awful if she were subsequently sent to the Pacific, a cruel twist of fate indeed. He resolved to go and find her as soon as this business with Mario Carità had been settled rather than wait for her in Florence. He groaned to himself – his longing to be with her was tearing him apart.

A loud yawn came from Bianconini. 'Let's go find a bathroom then grab something to eat,' he said.

Ezio stirred on his mattress. 'I'm as hungry as a wolf.'

Down in the dining room, they all dived into plates of dumplings in chicken broth, served from a steaming soup pot by a black-aproned helper, accompanied by thick slices of home-made bread and goats' cheese.

'Where's Signor Mair?' Bianconini asked.

'Having a meeting next door.' The helper smiled. 'He'll be here soon.'

She was true to her word. Within minutes, Signor Mair had appeared, and was grinning from ear to ear.

'An armistice between the Allies and the German Armed Forces on the Italian front has just come into force.'

'*Ottimo!*' Bianconini exclaimed. Excellent.

Signor Mair went on to inform them that the Liberation Committee had divided Bolzano into sectors, and had instructed the partisans to peacefully occupy factories, warehouses, public offices, and institutional buildings, including the town hall and the police prefecture.

All that remained for Vito and his friends to do was to wait for the Americans. But, the next day, they were devastated to learn that the ceasefire wasn't holding up too well in Bolzano. At first, everything seemed to go according to plan. The city was practically deserted – the German residents keeping a low profile – and the strategy for the partisans to take up their assigned positions went off without incident. At around 9 a.m., they took possession of the police prefecture and unfurled the Italian tricolour from its flagstaff before communicating their success to the Allied headquarters via a radio operated by a secret agent.

But then, news came through that a group of trigger-happy partisans – contradicting orders – had fired on a German column from their location in the Lancia military vehicle factory. The enemy retaliated by lobbing hand grenades into the entrance of the main building, followed by bursts of heavy machine gun and howitzer fire. It was thought that the German units had recently arrived from the south and were probably Fallschirmjäger para-troopers. Part of the German column continued on its way to the Brenner, but the rest began to converge on the factory. The partisans gave as good as they got, but with the help of their armoured cars, the enemy managed to enter the internal courtyard, rounding up eighteen *partigiani* and marching them to the wall in front of the building.

Vito, Ezio and Bianconini growled with anger as Signor Mair explained. He went on to say that the Germans mowed down the partisans with bursts of machine gun fire. Ten died instantly or shortly afterwards and eight had survived, although mostly with extremely serious injuries.

'*Gesu Maria!*' Vito exclaimed. 'What's happening there now?'

'Thank God the Germans have been ordered to evacuate. News has come through that the Americans will be here tomorrow.' He gave a wan smile.

'Thank God.' Vito echoed the sentiment.

It would have been horrible if he and his comrades needed to be involved in another battle. They were here for the fascist Carità, not to fight Germans.

* * *

Vito shifted position in the chilly air as he kept his Tommy gun trained on the chalet topping the grassy slope. He was lying stretched out at the edge of the treeline with Ezio, Bianconini and two American soldiers who went by the names of Leroy and Wes. By coincidence, they were both Blue Devils from the same infantry division that had fought at Monte Battaglia.

Vito remembered the Americans arriving in Bolzano two

weeks ago, and how they'd had to deal with the Germans, whom they called 'Krauts'. The arrogant Nazis quartered in the city swaggered around armed to the teeth for ten whole days, even though the fighting in Italy had ended. A liaison commander from the Allied 15th Army Group told the Blue Devil officers they couldn't start 'ordering these people (the Germans) to move out, because we have a deal with them'. But finally, on 11 May, the velvet gloves were taken off and Colonel Fry was put in charge of the city as Military Governor.

A hard-chinned 'Kraut hater' from Idaho, his men had pinned the name 'Fearless Fosdick' on him the day he'd personally led a platoon to clean out a dug-in enemy stronghold. Once he'd arrived in Bolzano, he laid down the law. A German colonel tried to argue that he and his colleagues should keep their quarters.

'Colonel,' Fry snapped, 'where I come from, we shoot guys like you just to hear them drop.'

The German colonel – an old Prussian, Iron Cross in World War I, sporting a monocle, seeming to be straight out of a Hollywood movie – saluted, clicked his heels, bowed, and left. About three hours later, thousands of 'Krauts' began pouring out of the hills and their city accommodation into the designated transit camp.

Bianconini got on with Fry like a house on fire, as the British said. Using Vito to help translate, along with Fry's interpreter, Ray, they swapped stories about their war records, both obviously recognising their mutual integrity, which led to friendship and trust. It was thanks to this relationship that Fry gave Bianconini free rein to search for Carità. He led Vito and Ezio into the camp with a photo Ezio had brought with him from Florence. Dark-haired with small eyes set close together under bushy brows, Mario Carità was dressed in the grey-green uniform of a major in Mussolini's Republican Army, staring at the camera and smirking.

As the days went by and their search for the fascist torturer seemed more and more hopeless, Vito hit on the idea of spreading their net wider, to the towns and villages around Bolzano, where they let it be known that a substantial reward was on offer for any information about the fascist's whereabouts. Two days ago, news had come through to the Liberation Committee that a man fitting Carità's description was hiding in the chalet Vito and his companions currently had under observation. As soon as darkness fell, they would go inside.

The minutes ticked by and soon a magnificent sunset pinked the sky above the jagged mountain tops. It was truly beautiful, like something out of a children's storybook. Vito couldn't help wishing Carrie could see it – although not under these circumstances, of course.

'Time to head out,' Bianconini muttered when the time came.

Vito gripped his gun, knuckles white, and held it at the ready as he began to run across the moonlit field.

At the door, Leroy shouted, 'We're here to arrest Mario Carità. Open up.'

An ominous silence.

They kicked the door in. 'Search the place,' Wes commanded.

There was no one in the downstairs rooms, so they rushed upstairs, opening doors and pointing their guns.

Maybe he wasn't there, Vito couldn't help thinking.

Then all hell broke loose.

They found Carità sitting up in a double bed, a naked woman next to him.

'It's him,' Bianconini confirmed.

'Mario Carità. You are under arrest for murder,' Leroy said, his gun trained on him.

Without a word, Carità pulled a pistol from under his pillow and shot Leroy first, then fired two shots into Wes.

Bang! Bang! Bang!

Vito squeezed his finger on the trigger of his gun and let rip. So did Vito and Bianconini.

Their Stens roared.

Bullets flew.

The woman in the bed screamed loud enough to wake the dead.

Finally, Mario Carità toppled sideways onto the quilt, blood everywhere, his eyes staring sightlessly.

The woman cried out. 'You've killed him!'

A groaning sound came from Ezio.

Gesu Maria, he'd been hit.

Vito knelt next to him.

He lay slumped to the side, eyes closed, face ashen. Blood bloomed from a wound in his belly.

No! The word, at first a silent scream in Vito's head, escaped from his mouth.

He pulled off his coat, and clasped it to the bullet hole. *Must stem the flow.*

'I'll find a phone and call for an ambulance,' Bianconini said.

'What about the Americans?'

Bianconini shook his head.

'They didn't make it.' He went to the woman in the bed, pulled her to her feet, flung a blanket over her and said, 'Take me to the telephone.'

Vito bent to Ezio's ear and whispered, 'Hang in there, my friend.'

Ezio's eyes blinked open. 'Carità?'

'You got him.'

Ezio gave a sigh and his eyelids fluttered shut.

26

'Who is this Tito dude?' Carrie asked Captain Huxley as she helped him unbox supplies in the ward tent. They'd arrived at their new site yesterday, after a long and tiring 225-mile journey from Bologna. As they'd drawn closer to their destination – about three miles east of Udine – their convoy had needed to negotiate its way through crowds of Italian and Yugoslav partisans parading through the countryside, heavily armed.

'He's the leader of the Yugoslav Resistance. Communist. Unlike their Italian counterparts, the Yugoslavs developed into a unified fighting force that engaged in conventional warfare. Tito had Allied air support and assistance from the Red Army to rid his country of the Axis forces.'

Carrie tucked a curl of hair under her cap. 'Why is there still a problem with the Yugoslavs when the war in Europe is supposed to have ended?'

'Well, after Tito's army defeated the Wehrmacht, they took control of Rijeka and Istria provinces, which had been part of Italy before the war. Then they beat the Allies to Trieste by two days.' Captain Huxley sighed. 'Now the city is occupied by both the Yugoslavs and British Eighth Army New Zealand troops. The situation is very tense and there have been reports of armed clashes and artillery duels. We're here to prevent any further incursions.'

Carrie gave a sigh. 'I wonder how long we'll be staying...'

'It's anyone's guess. There are three US divisions in the vicinity going all out to convince Tito's government that the Allies mean business and that the Trieste incident should be settled peacefully.'

'Well, I sure hope they sort it out quickly.'

Captain Huxley sighed. 'Me too, but then we could always be redeployed to the Pacific. Although I might just have enough points to be sent home soon.'

'Lucky you, sir.' She smiled.

Everyone in the American Army was being awarded a number of points based on how long they had been overseas, how many decorations they'd received, the number of campaigns they'd taken part in, and also taking into account the number of children they had. All personnel in the 56th had been calculating their points, adding and re-adding, trying to reach the total that would take them home. The medical corpsmen needed eighty-five, but the nurses only required seventy-one. Carrie had worked out she was on sixty, so still had quite a way to go, but she imagined that Captain Huxley must be close. He had four kids back home, he'd once said and, at twelve points each, they'd have contributed massively to his overall score. And he'd been overseas since October 1942 as well.

At the end of her shift, Carrie headed to her bivouac. She crossed the spacious site to the nurses' accommodation area. The hospital had been situated on a lovely, gently rolling pasture covering approximately forty acres. Field poppies nodded their crimson heads in the breeze, and a stream gurgled its way towards the River Torre. To the north, on the distant horizon, the Carniche Alps formed a natural frontier between Italy and Austria. Carrie shaded her eyes, squinting in the bright sunshine. Some of the peaks were still white with snow.

In her tent, she took her writing case from her footlocker. The letter she was about to write was long overdue, but it would have been impossible to post it from Bologna and, even now, there was no guarantee Vito would receive it. She had to try, though. He might have gone back to Florence by now.

Dearest Vito

I'm so sorry I couldn't meet you in Bologna, but we were under strict orders not to leave the stadium. I tried to sneak out, but one of my superior officers stopped me. I really wish that had not been the case. I'm well but I miss you so much and can't wait to see you again.

As you'll see from the postmark, I'm in Udine. I don't know when this Tito business will be resolved. I expect we'll stay here until it is. No one has any idea about the next move. The current rumor is home, then on to the Pacific. That would mean you and I being even further apart. But of course I must do as I'm told. The thought of heading out there fills me with dread and my heart would break with longing for you.

I think about you all the time and pray you are safe and well. Also, Mimi and your family. How I long to be with you and them. I love you and will always love you, darling. Please write to me. If we can't be together in person, I hope we can keep in touch by post – although I'm not certain what is going on with the postal service in this part of Italy.

I'm enclosing a letter for Mimi. Please help her understand the English.

Sending you all my love

Yours forever
Carrie xxx

Dear Mimi

I hope you are well like I am. I miss you a lot and can't wait to see you as soon as I can. You can be sure I will come to you, for you will always be close to my heart. Please give Stella a hug and a kiss from me.

Your

Carrie xxx

* * *

Carrie posted her letter and the days passed while she waited to hear back. The Yugoslav partisans were quartered in locations all around the American camps and the two armies drilled in front of each other. Tito's men tried to impress local people with a show of strength; his soldiers and pictures of him were everywhere, and some place names were even changed from Italian to Slavic. The Allies were also trying to impress Tito with a show of *their* strength: planes above, tanks on the road, trucks all over. Some towns were pro-Italian, some pro-Yugoslavian. Geographically it made no sense. But there were strong feelings in the area; whole villages nearby had been sacked and burned by the opposite side in retribution for a killed partisan.

The Italians accused Tito's men of holding people up for cattle and food. Tito's men called the Italians ex-fascists and stuck posters on buildings claiming the area had been 'freed by Yugoslav blood and that blood alone'.

One evening, a drunken truckload of armed Yugoslav partisans went Italian-hunting. Roadblocks appeared, manned by both sides. More cows were taken without payment by Tito's men, with the individuals involved maintaining that their army had to eat.

The situation was as volatile as a powder keg. At the end of the month, things seemed to be reaching a climax when Tito ordered the American 91st Division to leave or be interned. Carrie and her friends waited for outright war. The 91st ignored the order, and nothing happened except for the Yugoslavs doing their usual demonstrations of parading their troops past Allied checkpoints.

It soon became clear that things were calming down and, since the patient load was not too heavy, hospital personnel were invited to take trips to various places of interest. Although quotas were limited, the lucky few managed trips to Lake Maggiore, the Riviera and even Austria.

Still hoping for news of Vito, Carrie couldn't resist the chance to visit Milan one day with Louise, Betty and Marge, travelling there and back in an ambulance. They visited the magnificent cathedral and went to see Leonardo da Vinci's *Last Supper*. It was in a church that had been badly damaged in an air raid, the windows blown out and the roof open to the sky. Carrie thought it to be more like a barn than a place for such a famous painting, which itself was in poor condition, although still impressive.

The 56th's commanding offer made provisions for daily transportation to Venice, and Carrie took advantage of the opportunity to travel there with her friends. On her return, she sat on her cot and once more took out her writing case.

Dear Mom, Daddy, and Helen

I'm back from a visit to Venice, a two-hour truck ride from here. It was wonderful, like something out of a fairy story. We drove on the causeway taking cars across the lagoon to a parking lot, and then rode on a gondola to Saint Mark's

Square. Everywhere are water-filled canals, and everyone goes about on boats. The buildings are all ancient, elaborately constructed in marble, the doorsteps going down into the sea. It's by far the most interesting place I've seen, incredibly beautiful, and it has been untouched by the war. Thank God, both sides agreed not to bomb it.

The heat of summer has arrived since I last wrote. I played some tennis the other day, the first time in years, and got thoroughly sweaty. It gets awfully hot here in this field, and there's no place to swim.

The hospital personnel are changing every day. Seven nurses with points over seventy have left and around sixty or so enlisted men with points in excess of eighty-five are also leaving. That takes away almost all our sergeants.

Carrie screwed up her face, thinking about what to recount next. She'd already decided she would write another letter to Vito and Mimi. They might not have gotten her first one. She glanced up as Louise rushed into their tent.

'Max is being transferred to a unit headed for the Philippines.' Her voice was shrill. 'I'm so scared Theo will be next.'

Carrie experienced a mixture of relief she would no longer need to fend off Max's advances – at every dance he still managed somehow to cut in on her – and worry that Louise and Theo might soon be separated. She got up from her cot and put her arm around her friend. 'How many points is he on?'

Louise chewed at her lip. 'About seventy-seven, I think.'

'He was in Morocco before, wasn't he?'

Louise nodded. 'Max arrived a lot later so has fewer points.'

Carrie gave her a hug. 'If the Pacific War drags on, Theo will have enough points to be sent home real soon. It would be a waste to send him to the Philippines.'

'I hadn't thought about that. Thanks, Tex.' Louise covered her mouth with a hand. 'Oh, my God, I almost forgot.' She reached into the pocket of her ward dress. 'This came for you.' She handed Carrie an envelope. 'Sorry, I should have given it to you first.'

Carrie squealed. 'It's from Vito.'

'I thought so.' Louise smiled. 'I'll leave you in peace.'

Carrie's fingers shook as she ripped open the envelope. Her eyes darted across the page as she started to read.

My dearest Carrie,

I just got your letter – it was forwarded by my parents. It's wonderful to know where you are, and that you are well. I'm sorry you were stopped from seeing me in Bologna. I thought something like that must have happened. You'll have seen from the postmark that I'm in South Tyrol. It's a long story, which I'll tell you in full when I see you again. Suffice it to say, Ezio and I came here with our partisan commander to get Mario Carità arrested. But, unfortunately, Ezio was seriously wounded in a shoot-out during which he killed Carità and was admitted to the hospital in Merano. They took a bullet out of his abdomen. He was in shock and had lost a lot of blood, but thankfully his vital organs were spared. The doctors have been brilliant. Ezio suffered peritonitis and nearly died. I've been with him night and day, and I'm relieved and happy that he's now on the mend. We should be able to get on a train to Florence next week. As soon as I know he's okay, I'll get on another train and make my way to Udine.

I long to see you, tesoro. News from home is good. Everyone is fine and Mimi keeps questioning about when you and I will return. They asked me to send you their love.

I'll give our little girl your letter when I see her.

Please write to me at my home address and let me know how you are. Post is taking ages to arrive and I just hope this letter gets through to you.

My darling Carrie, I love you and miss you so much. I can't wait for us to be reunited.

Yours forever,

Vito

Tears of happiness and relief spilled down Carrie's cheeks. Mario Carità would no longer pose a threat to Vito. Feeling a rush of sympathy for poor Ezio, and consequently Stella, she took a fresh piece of paper from her writing case and answered, telling Vito about her visits to Milan and Venice, saying how she would have loved to have gone there with him, and expressing her hope that she would see him soon. She also wrote that she'd send separate letters to Mimi and his parents, which she hoped he would translate when he was home. Finally, she asked him to pass on her regards to Ezio and her wish for him to get better as soon as possible.

After sealing the letters, she thought about Mimi. Vito had referred to her as 'our little girl'.

If only that could be true. That she and Vito could keep her with them. That they could form a family of three.

But how would that be possible?

Don't even think about it, Carrie told herself. It would be like 'pie in the sky'.

* * *

Max shipped out the next day, much to Carrie's relief. He left without Carrie saying goodbye. She'd deliberately made herself scarce when he'd been doing his final rounds.

He wasn't the only doctor from the unit on his way to the Philippines, though, and she hoped they wouldn't start sending nurses next.

A week later, Captain Huxley got his wish and was sent home. She would miss him; he'd been a father-figure to her. Then Betty and Marge, who'd both clocked up enough points, boarded a train for Naples from where they'd be shipped back to the States. This time, Carrie made sure she was around to bid them farewell. She hugged them with tears in her eyes; she loved them both like older sisters.

At the end of June, Carrie was in the lunch chow line, when she heard the news that the partisans on both sides had agreed to stand down. The 'volatile situation' had been defused. What would happen now?

She didn't need to wait long to find out. That evening, an announcement was made that all personnel were entitled to one month's leave. Applications should be made straight away and the furloughs would be allocated on a rotating basis.

Florence. She could go to Florence.

Her heart overflowing, Carrie ran to the admin tent and put her name down without hesitation.

27

The train rumbled and hissed as it pulled into Santa Maria Novella station. Carrie leapt up from her seat to get her suitcase down from the rack above, every nerve in her body tingling with excitement. How she'd longed for this moment.

Three days after she'd put her name down to go on leave, she'd been overjoyed to have received approval. Louise and Theo had also been successful in their furlough application but were heading to the Riviera instead. They wanted to spend their time swimming and lying under a beach umbrella watching the waves crash against the shore, apparently.

Carrie had travelled with them in an ambulance as far as Bologna, where Louise and Theo boarded a command car to proceed to Cannes. Carrie had almost envied them – the weather had gotten hot enough to fry eggs on the sidewalk – but she'd happily joined a group of GIs going to Florence, where the soldiers had signed up for courses at the University Study Centre, another option put forward by the Army for personnel waiting to be redeployed.

A gangly young private helped Carrie with her suitcase,

passing it to her and then saluting as she stepped off the train. Excitedly, she looked around for Vito. She'd sent a telegram to his family as soon as her leave had been approved, and just last week she'd received a reply saying he was back home.

'Carrie!' His voice echoed down the platform towards her.

And then she could see him, running towards her.

He swept her into his powerful arms and kissed her.

'God, Carrie. *Ti amo tanto.* I love you so much and I've missed you *tantissimo.*'

Her heart pounded, and she arched up on the tips of her toes to kiss him back. 'I love you and I've missed you too, Vito.'

They kissed again, more passionately, tongues dancing, lips sliding. Coming up for air, they gazed into each other's eyes, and smiled.

'We're together at last. All my wishes have come true,' Vito said as he picked up her suitcase with one hand and looped the other arm around her waist. 'Papà is waiting in his car with Mimi. We'll drop your luggage off at the hotel before going to my apartment if that's okay with you. Mamma has cooked *peposo* for dinner.'

'Sounds like a great plan.' She nestled into his side as they made their way to the station exit. 'I've been so worried about you, darlin'. And I'm really sorry for what happened to Ezio.'

'He's strong. And it was touch and go for a while. But he's home now, with his parents, and will make a full recovery.'

'Thank God.' She squeezed Vito's arm. 'How's Stella?'

'Relieved he's pulled through. You can imagine how scared she was. She's incredibly proud of him.'

'As I am of you.' She brushed a quick kiss to Vito's cheek, breathing in the sandalwood scent of his aftershave. He looked so handsome in his short-sleeved white shirt and beige linen slacks; she felt dowdy in her drab olive summer dress uniform in comparison. Her seersucker jacket had creased on the train ride, and it was so hot that sweat had pooled in her armpits. She couldn't wait to take it off.

'Carrie!' Mimi's high-pitched voice reverberated across the parking lot.

'Mimi!' Carrie lowered herself, held out her arms, and the little girl catapulted herself into them. 'My goodness, you've grown so much since I last saw you.' And she had. Mimi was growing up and she regretted every moment she spent apart from her.

They hugged and kissed and then Mimi said, 'When the war ended, I thought you'd come straight back.'

'I hoped so too, pumpkin. But the Army had other plans for me.'

'I wish you weren't in the Army any more.'

'And I wish it could be as simple as that.' Carrie gave a wry laugh and turned to Vito's dad. 'Thank you for coming to meet me, Jacopo.' She beamed a grateful smile.

'You're most welcome, Carrie.' He took her suitcase from Vito and stowed it in the trunk. '*Andiamo*.' Let's go.

They dropped off Carrie's luggage, as planned, and then they made their way back to the apartment, where Rita and Anna were waiting for them.

Jacopo popped the cork from a bottle of Asti Spumante sparkling white wine, and they all raised their glasses, and Mimi raised her own glass of orange juice. 'Let's drink a toast to peace,' Jacopo said. 'And no more wars.'

Carrie sighed. Suzuki, the Japanese Premier, had recently announced that his country would fight to the very end rather than accept unconditional surrender. How she feared she'd be sent to the Pacific and be separated from Vito again. She decided not to mention her worries, though. Now was not the moment. Now was a time for celebration, and happiness flooded through her at being back with Vito and Mimi.

* * *

After dinner, Carrie went with Mimi to tuck her into bed. After the little girl had brushed her teeth and changed into her pyjamas, Carrie listened to her say her night-time prayer.

'Blessed are You our God, who casts sleep upon my eyes and slumber upon my eyelids. May You lay me down to sleep in peace and raise me up in peace. Blessed are You who illuminates the entire world with Your Glory. Sh'ma Yisrael Adonai Eloheinu Adonai Echad.'

'You're so smart, Mimi, to have recalled it all,' Carrie said.

'Anna helped me remember the words.' Mimi smiled. 'She said Jews and Christians believe in the same God. My *mammina* taught me the prayer when I was four. Did you know her name was Noemi?'

'Yes, honey bunch. I did. And your *babbo* was Adamo.'

Mimi heaved a long sigh. 'My name is Noemi too. Mimi for short. I think I would like to be called Noemi when I'm grown up.'

'Your *mammina* would like that, I'm sure.'

Mimi's big, amber-coloured eyes met Carrie's. 'Can we go see my old house? I would like to show it to Stella while you are in Florence.'

'Of course, pumpkin. But I wouldn't want you to be too sad.'

An adorable smile dimpled Mimi's rounded cheeks. 'I won't. Now you are back, I won't be sad any more.'

Carrie's emotions swelled at her words. She kissed the top of Mimi's head. 'Sweet dreams, *tesoro*.'

Mimi cuddled her doll and Carrie's heart melted with love for the child.

'I used to have a babysitter called Stella,' Mimi said sleepily. 'I named my dolly after her.'

'That's nice,' Carrie said vaguely. 'Vito's friend Ezio's girlfriend is called Stella too.'

* * *

After Carrie had bid *arrivederci* to Anna, Rita and Jacopo, she accepted Vito's suggestion to go for a walk before he took her back to the hotel. The warm night air caressed her face as, hand in hand, they walked across the Piazza della Signoria. They stopped under the statue of David, and she feasted her eyes on the beauty of its male form. Once more, she was struck by how much Vito's features resembled David's and she said so to him.

Vito chuckled. 'Maybe one of my ancestors was a model for Michelangelo.'

He led her past the Uffizi Gallery buildings and along the Arno to arrive at the Ponte Vecchio. Arms around each other, they halted in the middle section to take in the view. 'It's good they're making such excellent progress rebuilding the bridges,' she said, relishing the feel of the cool breeze in her hair.

'Italy has been reduced to a pile of rubble like much of Europe. What a terrible war this has been.' Vito went on to tell her in detail about his mission in South Tyrol. 'You would love it up there, Carrie,' he said. 'The scenery is magnificent. Merano is such a pretty town and its hospital meant that it was spared from bombing. The doctors there saved Ezio's life...'

'I would like to visit one day, for sure.' She then shared with him her worry that she might be redeployed to the Pacific.

'We can only pray the Japanese will come to their senses and surrender,' he said. 'If you have to go, I'll wait for you, my darling. Although I hope it won't come to that.'

'Whatever happens, I'll need to return to the USA before I can be discharged from the Army.' Carrie paused to collect her thoughts. 'There's something known as "the GI Bill". It's an Act of Congress signed by President Roosevelt providing veterans with the funds for college education. I was thinking of going to medical school. I'd like to become a paediatrician. Caring for Mimi made me realise how much I love working with kids.'

Vito rubbed at his chin. 'Would this fund pay for you to study at the University of Florence?'

Carrie shook her head. 'I don't know. What are you asking?'

'I'd be truly honoured if you'd agree to marry me, Carrie. We could both be students. It's the perfect solution.'

'Solution?' The notion made her heart race.

'I couldn't figure out how I could afford to finish my studies in America after we were married. Your universities are much more expensive than ours and I would have living costs on top. I usually get part-time jobs to pay my way but doubt I could do that in your country.'

'So you'd like me to move here?' She looked him in the eye.

'My parents have a small apartment near Santa Croce they used to rent out before the war. They've offered it to me. We could live there for free until we are both working and can save up to buy our own place.'

She wrapped her arms around his waist. 'Looks like you've figured everything out perfectly. But it seems too good to be true. Let's just take things one day at a time. I'm done with making too many plans for the future. They have a way of backfiring on me.'

'This one won't.' He tilted her chin up and kissed her.

'You're always so confident, Vito. I like that about you.'

'Only like?'

She giggled. 'I mean love.'

He moved in for another kiss, deeper, hungrier this time. He cupped her buttocks with one hand and brushed her neck with his thumb. 'You taste so good, Carrie.'

She pressed herself against him, feeling his need.

'Maybe we should go to your hotel room.' The words rasped in his throat.

* * *

There were other American Army personnel staying in the hotel, but everyone appeared to have gone to bed by the time Carrie led Vito down the carpeted corridor to her room. She gave him the key to unlock the door, and they stepped inside.

'I wanna take a bath,' she said. 'I got so hot and sweaty on the train, I'm sure I must stink like a skunk.'

He laughed. 'Let me take one with you. I remember last time I was in this hotel I noticed how big the tub was.'

'Okay.' She smiled. 'That would be fun, I think.'

They undressed and, in the bathroom, she turned on the faucets before adding bath salts to the water. The aromatic scent of pine billowed around them. 'You get in first,' she said.

He did as she'd asked, and stretched out his legs so she could climb between them.

She leaned her back against his chest, and he lifted her hair from the nape of her neck and gave her a kiss. 'You're so beautiful, *amore.*'

'So are you, Vito.' And he was. She loved him, body and soul. Smiling to herself, she reached for the soap and handed it to him. 'You can wash me if you like.'

'I would like.' He laughed.

'Mmm. That feels so nice.' She sighed as he soaped her arms, her breasts and lower down.

'All part of the service.'

'And what great service it is,' she said, relaxing into the warmth of his gentle caresses. 'I could stay here forever.'

'Me too,' he said, dropping more kisses on her neck, 'but we have a comfortable bed to lie on.'

'Real beds are such a luxury. I can't wait to fall asleep in your arms.'

'Sleep can wait,' he said, rinsing the soap suds from her breasts.

'I guess I'm squeaky clean now.'

How her heart pounded. She'd waited so long for this moment.

She pulled the plug and got out of the bath. Then she dried herself while he did likewise, with such love burning in his eyes that she could barely breathe.

'Come,' he said, holding out his arms. He walked her to the bed, and they collapsed onto it.

She gasped as he took her nipple into his mouth and sucked hard, clamping his lips down, going from one nipple to the other, circling with his tongue.

'Please, Vito,' she moaned. 'Please make love to me.'

He filled her so completely she became a part of him. She arched her back and gripped his muscular shoulders while they rocked together. She raised her hips to meet him, matching his pace as his smouldering breath caressed her skin.

Her body tightened and she stared up at him, loving him so much it brought a tear to her eye.

Wave after wave of warm, tingling bliss.

He gave a muffled groan and rested his forehead against hers.

'You're everything to me, Carrie,' he said. He kissed her brow, her cheeks, her lips.

'And you're everything to me, Vito.'

'Goodnight, *amore*,' he whispered, turning them both on their sides. 'I'll stay with you until early morning.'

He spooned his body protectively around her back, and soon his regular breathing told her that he'd fallen asleep.

She played with his hand, wishing they could be like this every night, that the war in the Pacific had ended, that she didn't have to return to the States. She lay awake for what seemed like hours, her thoughts chasing each other. Would she really be able to study medicine in Florence? How she hoped that would be the case.

28

The next morning, Vito and Carrie made love again. Afterwards, while she rested in Vito's arms, a thought occurred to her.

'Yesterday, Mimi said she'd named her doll after her babysitter, Stella. If we could find that girl, she might be able to tell us more about Mimi's parents.'

Vito was momentarily silent. And then, he said, 'It's a long shot. But Ezio's fiancée used to earn pocket money babysitting for different families before the Germans came. I'm due to visit him this morning. He spends the day at Stella's place. I'll ask them.'

'Wow! Wouldn't it be amazing if she was the same Stella?'

'As you said a while ago, there are many girls with that name in Florence. But it's definitely worth asking.'

Vito kissed Carrie deeply, arranged to meet her for lunch at the Gilli, and then took his leave.

She spent the morning on tenterhooks, hoping against hope. It would be a big coincidence, but life was full of coincidences and Mimi deserved the dice to roll in her favour, for once. Carrie was convinced that only when she knew the truth about her parents would Mimi be able to move on. Maybe not straight away, but in the years ahead the knowledge would help her to heal from the loss.

My little girl never asks about them any more. It's not healthy.

At midday, Carrie made her way to the *caffè*.

Vito was already there, sitting at an outside table. He got to his feet as she approached, smiling like the cat that had got the cream.

'You're not going to believe this,' he said as he pulled out a chair for her.

'Don't tell me Ezio's Stella is also Mimi's?' Glee made Carrie's voice sing.

Vito nodded. 'Stella would like to meet you, so she can tell you all about them.'

'What about Mimi?'

'Stella would prefer you to come on your own. She's worried her disfigurement might scare the child.'

'I get it. I'm so sorry for what happened to Stella. But I can't wait to meet her and hear what she has to say about Noemi and Adamo.'

'From what Ezio told me, she doesn't know if they are still alive. We *gappisti* acted independently of each other and no one knew what others did in case they were caught and revealed information under duress.'

Carrie's breath hitched with disappointment. *Disappointment and regret.* 'So we're no closer to learning the truth.'

'All is not lost.' Vito took her hand. 'There's something she'd like to lend you that might help us in our search.'

'Oh? What could that be?'

'A photograph of Noemi and Adamo with Mimi.'

Carrie's heart soared. 'That's so kind of her. A photo is something we can show people who could have known them under different names. Did you find out when I can meet Stella?'

'This afternoon.' Vito smiled. 'But before we go, let's have something to eat.'

* * *

'Stella lives in the San Marco neighbourhood.' Vito took Carrie's arm as they left the *caffè* after he'd eaten not only his panino but most of hers. 'Her family's apartment is about a ten-minute walk from here.'

When they reached the San Marco square, Vito pointed out the ochre-coloured arcaded low-rise buildings of his university.

'That's where we both will be studying,' he said.

His certainty tempted fate, in her opinion. But she kept her superstitious thoughts to herself.

Before too long, they'd arrived at a terrace of tall buildings with slatted window shutters. Vito pressed the bell and a dark-haired girl stuck her head out of the window.

'It's on the second floor,' she said, lowering a basket tied to a rope. 'You'll find the key inside this.'

Vito explained that this was a common way of letting visitors into apartments.

Carrie steeled herself not to gasp at the sight of Stella's poor face when they met her on the landing. Her long dark brown hair was worn loose and partly covered her pockmarked cheeks. She had a walking stick in one hand and held out the other.

'*Ciao*, Carrie. I am pleased to meet you,' she said in Italian.

Carrie shook her proffered hand. '*Piacere*.' It's a pleasure.

'My parents are both out at work. Ezio is in the living room,' she said.

Carrie went to where Ezio was sitting in an armchair. 'Please, don't get up.' She shook his hand. 'How are you feeling?'

'A lot better, thanks.'

Stella cleared her throat. 'I'll go and make us a coffee.'

'Let me help you,' Carrie offered.

In the small kitchen, Stella spooned ground coffee into a moka pot, filled it with water and set it on the stove. 'I'm interested in knowing your story, Carrie.' She looked her in the eye. 'I presume Vito has already told you mine.'

'I'm in awe of your bravery. I'm not half as brave as you.' She went on to recount some of her past, leaving out the horrors of Anzio and Bill. Stella didn't need reminding of the tragedies of war.

After Carrie had finished telling her about her life, Stella reached for an envelope in a kitchen drawer.

'I hope this helps,' she said as she handed it to her.

Fingers shaking, Carrie extracted the small black and white photo. The image of a toddler Mimi standing between her parents in what was obviously the garden of their home brought a lump of sadness to her throat. Adamo was smiling as he stared at the camera, his handsome face framed by the same dark, curly hair as his daughter. Noemi, on the other hand, was only shown in profile as she was gazing down at Mimi. Her hair was fairer, straighter, and pinned back from her face in a bun. Both Bettinellis looked to be in their late twenties or early thirties.

Carrie prayed she would find out what had happened to them, though she dreaded learning what was almost certain to be a devastating truth.

'Thank you,' she said to Stella. 'I will take good care of this and pray it will help us find some answers.'

'How is Mimi? Ezio told me she'd been injured. I'm glad Vito's family is looking after her.'

'She's made a good recovery and has truly endeared herself to us.'

'She's an endearing child.' Stella smiled. 'I used to love babysitting her.'

'When you are feeling up to it, it would be nice if she could see you again.'

'Yes, well. Maybe.' Stella chewed at her lip, and Carrie guessed she was torn between wanting to see the child and concern about her appearance.

A hissing sound came from the stove and the delicious aroma of freshly brewed coffee infused the air. Stella filled the four small cups she'd set on a tray, then added a bowl of sugar.

Back in the living room, they found Vito and Ezio smoking and playing a game of cards.

Everyone drank their coffees except for Carrie. She still couldn't stomach the bitter taste, and hope no one would notice.

Stella suggested that perhaps it was time for Ezio to have a rest.

'Let us know if you find out anything,' he said before Stella showed Carrie and Vito to the door.

Out on the street, Vito linked Carrie's arm with his again. 'I'm under strict orders to take you back to the apartment now. Mimi's orders, that is,' he chuckled.

Carrie chuckled with him.

How she loved the little girl.

The next morning, Carrie made her own way to the Mancinis'. Last night, Vito's dad had said he knew someone who was a member of the National Liberation Committee, so now they had a photo of Adamo and Noemi, she and Vito had thought they should show it to him on the chance he might recognise them.

Jacopo had said he'd phone him straight after breakfast to

arrange a meeting. Carrie hoped he would be able to see them today; she'd go out of her mind if she had to wait any longer.

Mimi ran towards her as Vito let her into the apartment. '*Buongiorno*, Carrie.'

'*Buongiorno*, pumpkin.'

'Nonna is going to take me to see my friend, Olivia,' Mimi announced. 'Remember she was at my birthday party?'

'That's nice,' Carrie said. 'I hope you have fun.'

'Papà will take us to meet his contact as soon as Mimi has left with Mamma,' Vito whispered to Carrie.

There wasn't time for a coffee – they would grab one later – and within minutes Carrie was heading along the narrow sidewalk of Cavour Street. Her chest fluttered with nerves. If this led to another dead end, she'd be so disappointed.

The Committee offices were housed in an austere-looking three-storey building clad in blocks of stone. Iron bars covered the ground-floor windows; round arches framed the upper ones.

'This was the palace of Cosimo Medici the Elder,' Jacopo said as he led Vito and Carrie through the heavy iron entrance door to a paved inner courtyard boasting big terracotta plant pots – empty, perhaps because of the war – and a marble statue of a muscular youth with a dog on the plinth by his side.

Carrie's eyes popped as they went up the wide marble staircase to the second-floor offices of the Committee. The walls of the reception area were decorated with colourful frescoes depicting a procession of people dressed in Renaissance clothing, some on horseback and others on foot, winding their way along a road leading through green hills and rocky cliffs topped by a turreted castle under a cerulean-blue sky.

Jacopo explained to the receptionist they had an appointment with Signor Piero Bertocchi, and soon they were being led through to a small room at the side. After introductions had been made, the middle-aged man got to his feet, kissed Jacopo on both cheeks, and shook Carrie and Vito's hands.

'Can you show me the picture?' he asked. 'Jacopo has already told me about it.'

Eagerly, Carrie retrieved the envelope from her purse and extracted the photo.

Piero Bertocchi took it from her and peered down at it. 'I don't recognise the young woman, but the man looks familiar. I think I've seen him before, but I can't be sure.'

Carrie's spirits sank. 'Do you know anyone who might have known his partisan name?'

Piero Bertocchi tapped his chin. 'Bianca Manfredi. If he's who I think he is, she'll be able to tell you all about him. I could do it myself, but if I've mistaken him for someone else, it would be wrong of me.'

'Who is Bianca Manfredi?' Jacopo asked.

'One of our bravest Resistance fighters. She was captured and tortured by Mario Carità, but she managed to escape and hide until Florence was liberated.' Signor Bertocchi handed the photo back to Carrie. 'I'll phone Bianca now and find out if she's willing to talk to you.'

Without waiting for an answer, he lifted the receiver on his desk and put through the call.

Carrie shifted her weight from one foot to the other, listening to rapid-fire Italian she couldn't understand.

'Bianca has agreed to see you right away.' Piero Bertocchi picked up a piece of paper from his desk and wrote on it. 'Here's her address. She will expect you as soon as you can get there.'

'*Grazie.*' Carrie smiled. 'I'm so grateful to you.'

'It's the least I can do. Good luck with your quest.'

* * *

After waving goodbye to Jacopo, who needed to get to his office, Carrie once again linked arms with Vito and crossed the Arno on the Bailey bridge like they'd done before. Bianca lived in an apartment in the Porta Romana neighbourhood, a twenty-minute walk from the river.

They came to a big oak entrance at street level, next to a venue selling cooked tripe – a Florentine speciality Carrie prayed she'd never be offered – and after Vito had pressed the bell, they stood in the cold until Bianca came to open the door herself.

A petite woman who looked to be in her mid-thirties, with light brown hair and wearing thick eyeglasses, Bianca showed them up to her apartment on the second floor. Inside, they sat by an open fireplace without a fire.

'I can't get any firewood,' Bianca explained. 'So best keep your coats on.'

They did as she suggested. Bianca offered them a coffee, for which they thanked her but declined.

'I hear you have a photograph to show me.'

Carrie's fingers trembled as she handed it over.

'Yes, that's Achille.' Bianca released a sigh. 'I didn't know he had a daughter.'

Vito shuffled forward in his seat. 'She's called Mimi and she was hidden in a convent with other Jewish children. They've all gone back to their parents, but Achille and his wife – Adamo and Noemi Bettinelli – have disappeared off the face of the earth. Their house was requisitioned by the Nazi-fascists and is now derelict.' Vito shook his head. 'We're afraid something has happened to them.'

Bianca nodded. 'There's no good way of saying this, so I'll come right out with it. Achille sacrificed his life for our freedom.'

'Oh, no!' Carrie put a hand to her mouth. Her deepest fear had been confirmed. 'Can you tell us what happened to him?'

'I can, for his story is closely linked to my own. Do you understand Italian, my dear?' Bianca addressed the question to Carrie.

'More or less. If there's something I don't get, I'll ask Vito to translate for me,' she said, holding back her tears.

She needed to be strong for Mimi's sake.

'What do you know about Radio Co-Ra?' Bianca asked Vito.

'Radio Co-Ra?' He drew his brows together. 'Sorry, but I've never heard of it.'

'It was top secret. I'll start at the beginning of my story.'

A sad smile played across her thin lips.

'I began working as secretary and bookkeeper for a lawyer, Enrico Bocci, in 1931. I loved my job and was made a part of the Bocci family, who were good people and anti-fascist like I was. After the Armistice, in September 1943, when the Germans occupied Florence, the leaders of the Action Party decided to establish a clandestine radio communications service under the initials Co-Ra, abbreviation of Radio Commission, so as to provide the city's budding Resistance organisation with news and military intelligence. One of the organisers was an ex-air force captain, Italo Piccagli, who'd joined the Resistance and had become one of the key figures. His personal network of contacts in the military field allowed him to set up an efficient information service. Also on the Co-Ra committee was the physicist, Carlo Ballario, who oversaw technical matters.

'At the end of January, through his anti-fascist contacts, my boss was put in touch with the head of an Allied mission, who went by the name of Nick. He was an Italian agent enlisted in the British Eighth Army and had arrived in Florence with a transceiver and the ciphers needed to create a radio link between the Florentine Resistance and the Allied Command.

'My boss contacted Piccagli and Ballario and so the group was born. I'll never forget the first transmission, a conventional message, "The Arno flows to Florence", which was sent to the Allied radio centre in Bari-Monopoli. As proof of contact, the phrase was then retransmitted unencrypted by the Allies on the Radio Bari frequency.'

'Was Adamo – I mean Achille – a part of the network?' Vito asked.

'He was a brilliant engineer, an associate of Ballario, who recruited him. Achille worked tirelessly on the transceiver. He transmitted communications requesting Allied intervention in support operations for the partisan bands, as well as asking for armaments and supplies by air drops. He also transmitted information about the enemy's Apennine defensive lines, their garrisons and depots, traffic of goods directed to Germany, railway movements and the movement of troops. This information either came from the Action Party's intelligence network or was collected through various channels by spies.

'I used to take Nick – the head of the Allied mission, who at that time was hiding at my boss's house – the information to be turned into code as he was the only one who had the cipher. Afterwards, I would deliver the notes to where the radio had been set up for the day. In addition to always being brief, so as not to give time to the German radio direction finders to intercept the source, we never used the same place twice in succession.'

'How amazing,' Carrie said after Vito had translated for her; Bianca's Italian was too fast and the subject matter too complicated for her to understand. 'Mimi's dad sure was brave. And you too, Bianca. I'm in awe of you.'

'*Grazie.* Your praise means a lot. I wish I didn't have to tell you what happened next, but you did ask for the truth.'

Carrie leaned across the space between them. 'I need to know, for Adamo's and Noemi's daughter's sake.'

'Well, at the beginning of May last year, we moved the set-up to a large furnished apartment in Piazza d'Azeglio, rented for us by a third party. There were servants' quarters in the attic above, where the transmissions could be carried out in relative safety. The war front was moving towards Tuscany at that time, so broadcasts increased in length and frequency.' Bianca's expression turned grave. 'Rome was liberated on 4 June and the Allied landings took place in Normandy on the 6th. An important meeting of the Co-Ra members was convened for the 7th in our new headquarters. The Allied Command had requested information about the German forces and the extent of our partisan formations. I was taking notes to give the answers to an encrypted questionnaire that Nick had decoded.' Bianca twisted her hands in her lap. 'At around dinner time, three armed men in civilian clothes showed up at the door. We refused to open for them, but they shot the locks and broke in, together with a group of about ten SS troops and fascist militiamen.'

'Oh, my God.' Carrie's voice trembled.

'Before we could react, they grabbed us and made us line up with our backs to the wall, hands raised. Achille was still transmitting from the room in the attic. He must have heard the commotion. After sneaking downstairs, he succeeded in grabbing a gun one of the Germans had distractedly placed on a table. Achille shot and killed the man but was then gunned down by a burst of machine gun fire from one of the other soldiers.'

Carrie gasped and Vito put his arm around her. 'Did Adamo die straight away?' he asked.

'He was carried to the hospital in Giusti Street, where he passed away a couple of days later.'

Vito leaned forward. 'What about you, Bianca? Piero Bertocchi told us of your capture and torture by Mario Carità.'

'We were taken to the Villa Triste. Myself, my boss, and three others. Captain Piccagli handed himself in and, together with my boss, assumed responsibility for the entire operation. I was horribly tortured. They shone a bright spotlight into my eyes for hours on end, partially blinding me, and they beat me repeatedly, but I managed not to reveal anything. Eventually, I was transported to the railway station. Before they could put me on a train to deport me to a concentration camp in Germany, a scuffle broke out. I took advantage of the resulting confusion and fled. I hid in a safe house until Florence was liberated.' Bianca's words came out choked. 'My boss, Enrico Bocci, was cruelly tortured as well, I subsequently learned. By all accounts he was murdered by Carità, but his body has never been found. Captain Piccagli, four paratroopers sent by the Eighth Army to assist with our work, and an unknown Czechoslovakian partisan were shot in the woods of Cercina north of Florence on 12 June last year.'

'How dreadful.' Carrie's voice caught on a sob. She was glad Vito had kept his comforting arm around her. 'I'm so sorry this happened to you.'

Bianca glanced at the photo again. 'Now I must tell you about Achille's wife. We knew her by the name of Libertà. She was a *stafetta*.' A courier.

'What happened to her?' Carrie asked, her heart in her mouth. It hadn't occurred to her until now that Bianca would also know of Noemi's fate.

'She managed to visit Achille in the hospital, to hold his hand while he lay dying. He never regained consciousness.' Bianca sighed. 'She was distraught, of course. But she was determined to fight back and threw herself into the battle for the liberation of Florence. I discovered that she relayed messages between command posts and the Action Party.'

'So brave of her,' Vito said. 'I remember how perilous our lives were at that time.'

'Indeed. She was captured by a patrol of *tedeschi*.' Germans.

'They took her to Villa Cisterna, Colonel Fuchs's headquarters, and marched her to a room where they planned to interrogate her, I believe. Left alone, she managed to escape.' Bianca's shoulders drooped. 'I found out that she was killed by a burst of machine gun fire as she tried to climb over the perimeter fence. Apparently, she was buried in the gardens of the villa.'

Tears streamed down Carrie's face. How her soul hurt for Noemi and Adamo. But it ached for Mimi even more, left an orphan by this horrible war.

'Thank you for telling us all of this, Bianca. It's so incredibly sad.'

Bianca rubbed at her poor, injured eyes. 'Thank God peace has come. I pray that the evil perpetrators of these horrific deeds will be brought to justice without delay.'

Vito leant forward. 'Mario Carità is dead. He was in a shoot-out with some Americans in the Tyrol. I saw him killed before my eyes.'

A big smile spread across Bianca's face. 'Good riddance.' She spat into the empty fireplace. 'May he burn in hell.'

'Amen to that,' Carrie said with a heavy heart. 'Well, I guess I should be heading back to my hotel.'

Vito helped her to her feet, then turned to Bianca. '*Grazie. Sei stata molto gentile.*' You've been very kind.

Bianca embraced them warmly before taking them to the door of her apartment. 'I live alone now,' she said sadly. 'My parents passed away, and my brothers were taken to Germany. They'll come home soon, I feel it in my bones. We can only hope for better days to come, eh?'

Vito took her hand. 'The future will be brighter. With people like you in it, how can it not be?'

'I agree,' Carrie said. 'You are truly an inspiration.'

29

The afternoon sun slanted through a gap in the shutters, painting a triangle of light on the sitting room floor as Carrie and Vito sat Mimi down to tell her about her parents. They'd talked it over beforehand and had agreed they would approach the topic in the same way that they had when they'd told her Noemi and Adamo were missing.

'Sit here, sweetie.' Carrie lifted the little girl onto her lap. 'Remember when we told you that we couldn't find your *mammina* and *babbo*? I'm afraid we have some very sad news...'

Mimi burrowed her head into Carrie's shoulder. 'They've died, haven't they?' Her voice choked with sobs. 'I dreamt that had happened to them...'

'I'm afraid so, *tesoro*.' Vito wrapped his arms around Carrie and Mimi. 'Your parents... they were incredibly brave.'

'Did the Germans kill them?' Mimi asked plaintively.

Carrie smoothed the hair back from her face. 'They did, pumpkin.' She pressed a kiss to her forehead. 'I'm so sorry.'

Mimi hiccoughed on another sob.

'You don't need to worry.' Vito hugged her. 'We'll take good care of you.'

'*Grazie.*' Mimi's sobs eased. 'How did you find out about my *mammina* and *babbo*?'

'Your babysitter, Stella, pointed us in the right direction.' Carrie kept the fact of the photo to herself. It might upset Mimi too much to see it.

'Stella is my best friend Ezio's sweetheart,' Vito clarified. 'We only thought to ask her when you told us you'd named your doll after her.'

Mimi leant back and fixed them both with a pleading look. 'Can we go and visit her?'

Carrie shook her head slowly. 'We can't promise you that, pumpkin. But we'll phone and ask if she'd like to see you.'

'Of course she'll see me. She loves me and I love her,' Mimi said adamantly.

Vito took her hand. 'Both Stella and Ezio have been wounded. We might have to wait until they're better.'

'I've been injured too,' Mimi said. 'And my parents are dead. You must tell Stella. When she knows that, I'm sure she'll want to give me a hug.'

The precocious wisdom of Mimi's words went straight to Carrie's heart. 'I'll contact her as soon as I can.'

* * *

A week later, Carrie and Vito held Mimi's hands as she skipped along the narrow sidewalk between them. Florence baked in the July heat. Sweat prickled under Carrie's officer's cap. She wished she could have put on a cool summer dress and left her hair uncovered, but that was not to be.

They were making their way to Stella Fabbri's apartment. At

the entrance to the palazzo, Vito pressed the bell and Stella lowered down the front door key in a basket tied to a rope like she'd done before.

She was waiting for them upstairs. 'Welcome,' she said. 'Mimi, *carissima*.' She hugged the child. 'I'm so pleased to see you again. And I'm so sorry about your parents.'

'*Grazie*.' Mimi touched her fingers to Stella's pockmarked cheeks. 'Vito told me what that horrible man did to you. I'm so sorry.' She lifted her bangs and pointed to the scar on her forehead. 'Look what happened to me.'

With tears in her eyes, Stella kissed Mimi's scar. 'Ezio was wounded too, *tesoro*. He's in the living room and would like to meet you.' She smiled at Vito and Carrie. '*Entriamo*.'

Ezio was in the armchair like last time. He held his hand to Mimi. '*Ciao, bambina*. My condolences for the loss of your parents.'

She shook his hand, thanked him, and then asked, 'Can I see your scar?'

Ezio chuckled at her directness. 'Are you sure? It's nasty.'

'Not as nasty as mine, I bet.'

Cautiously, he untucked his shirt and showed her the round bullet wound.

'*Guarda!*' Look!

'You're right. It's nasty.' Mimi lifted her bangs. 'But mine is even more nasty, I think.'

He chuckled again. '*Va bene. Hai vinto*.' Okay, you win. 'We've both been lucky, *bambina*. And now we can enjoy the freedom of our lives in a free Italy.'

'Alleluia to that,' Vito said.

Carrie went through to the kitchen with Stella while she made the ubiquitous coffee.

'*Grazie* for bringing Mimi to see us,' she said. 'And for

returning the photo.'

Carrie had sent it back with Vito a couple of days ago. 'Thanks for lending it to me. It helped us find out what happened to Noemi and Adamo.'

'Ezio told me. Such a sad story.'

'It is. One among far too many. Thank God the war in Europe is over.'

'We can look forward to the future now. Ezio and I will be married next month. I hope you can come to our wedding.'

'Thank you. I'd love to, but I might be redeployed to the Pacific.'

Stella gave a gasp. 'I hadn't thought of that...'

'I'm praying it won't happen.' Carrie sighed. 'In the meantime, it's impossible for Vito and me to make plans.'

'He loves you a lot. Anyone can see that.'

Carrie felt not only her cheeks warming but also her heart.

'And I love him too,' she said, amazed at how she yearned for him, even though he was only in the next room.

She heard his chuckle echo through the walls, followed by the sound of Mimi's high-pitched voice.

'*Amore vero*,' Stella said, breaking her thoughts. True love.

Carrie gave herself a shake.

True love. Two words, so simple, yet here she was and there they were.

'You've gone quiet,' Stella said.

'I'm thinking good thoughts. How about you and Ezio? Have you made plans, Stella?'

'Oh, yes. Ezio and I will be going back to the university in October to finish our studies. When we are married, he'll move in with me here as there's more space in this apartment, so it makes sense.'

'It sure does.' Carrie envied Stella the straightforwardness of her situation, although not how much she'd suffered. 'You've both been so brave. And Vito.'

When the coffee had brewed, Carrie carried the tray back to the sitting room. There, she drank down the bitter espresso. If she was fixin' to move to Italy, she'd better start learning to like the stuff.

Stella handed a glass of milk to Mimi, which she accepted gladly. 'I've missed you so much,' the little girl said, sitting next to her on the sofa. 'But I'm too big for a babysitter now.'

'You are, indeed. But we can still be friends, can't we?'

'I'd like that,' Mimi said solemnly. 'I miss my *mammina* and *babbo* so much.'

'We've been encouraging Mimi to talk about them as much as possible, haven't we, pumpkin?' Carrie chipped in. 'It helps with the grieving process.'

'In that case.' Stella smiled. 'I have something for you, Mimi.' She reached into the pocket of her dress and pulled out the photograph. 'You can keep it,' she said.

Mimi took the picture from her, tears streaming down her face. '*Grazie.* Now I won't ever forget what they looked like.'

'You can be so proud of them,' Stella said. 'They were heroes. And they loved you so very much.'

'Do you think they are in heaven?'

'I'm sure they are.' A sad smile skimmed across Stella's lips. 'They will be with you forever, Mimi. Keeping watch over you for the rest of your life.'

* * *

Carrie spent the remainder of her leave in Florence almost entirely in Vito's company. They talked for hours on end, sharing everything about themselves and falling ever more deeply in love. They enjoyed walks along the Lungarno by the jade-green river at sunset, while the dipping sun bathed the Ponte Vecchio with glorious golden hues. They huddled on the steps of Piazzale Michelangelo, the city below them embraced by the mellow light and surrounding hills, and likewise Carrie embraced Vito. They climbed ancient stairs past the ruins of stone statues in the grounds of Villa Bardini, set on the side of a slope above the Arno, to enjoy the dilapidated flowery pergolas and verdant walkways, stealing kisses along the way. In the cool of the early mornings, they took Mimi for cycle rides in the exclusive Florentine suburb of Fiesole, situated on twin hills where, before the war, English and American expatriates had bought and restored Renaissance villas, equipping them with magnificent landscaped gardens where they'd sit and enjoy the Tuscan sun. Carrie relished the breathtakingly stunning view from the sloping olive groves ahead. Behind stretched vineyards and cypresses and holly tree woods.

Vito had been warned beforehand that certain areas still needed to be cleared of the mines laid by the Germans, so he took care to lead Carrie and Mimi only down safe paths past the wild narcissi and anemones and carmine-coloured tulips, their petals ending in long graceful points. Sounds from the valley drifted up: the songs of the *contadini* peasant farmers working the land, the rag collector drawing out the mournful cry '*Cen-ciaio!*' and bells from the campanile church towers in Florence below. Carrie breathed it all in. Life was truly magical in Vito and Mimi's company. How would she bear it when she had to leave them again?

On Carrie's last afternoon before she had to return to Udine, she and Vito took Mimi to see the Bettinellis' house. They walked slowly across the centre of town – it was too hot to quicken their pace – and, when they arrived, Mimi burst into tears at the sight of the overgrown yard, the boarded-up front door and windows, and the property's derelict state.

'I don't like it here any more,' she said. 'Let's go somewhere else.'

Carrie picked the sobbing girl up and hugged her tight. She wiped her tears with her thumb.

'I understand, sweetie. Shall we go for *gelati*?'

'Please,' she managed between sobs.

So they went for an ice cream in Piazza Santa Croce.

After they'd given their order to the waiter, Mimi climbed onto Carrie's lap. 'I wish you and Vito could be my new mamma and papà,' she said.

Carrie's gaze met Vito's over the little girl's head as she burrowed into her shoulder. 'Let's talk about this later,' she mouthed the words.

'*Va bene,*' okay, he whispered in reply.

Thankfully, their ice creams arrived at that moment, and Mimi's attention was distracted by a big chocolate and strawberry cone.

After dropping her back at the apartment, Carrie bid a tearful farewell to the family, promising to try to see them again before she left Italy. 'I don't know when that will be. If I'll be posted to the Pacific or sent back home to the States,' she added.

Vito took Carrie out for dinner in the Palazzo Antinori wine cellars. The eatery specialised in Tuscan dishes, but she'd lost her appetite and toyed with the idea of suggesting they give it a miss. She dreaded leaving the next morning and her stomach felt hard as stone.

Vito took her hand while they walked along Del Giglio street, and before too long they'd arrived at the restaurant. A waiter showed them to a table for two at the side of the long, vaulted room. He left them to peruse the menu, and Carrie inhaled the enticing aroma of meat grilling. She realised she was hungry after all.

They ordered a bottle of Chianti and Florentine T-bone steak. Their wine arrived first, and they clinked glasses.

'Let's drink to the war in the Pacific ending soon,' Vito said.

'I'll second that.' Carrie sipped the fruity red *vino*. 'But I have a horrible feeling our unit will be redeployed out there real soon.'

'I hope not. Haven't the Allies started bombing raids on the Japanese home islands? That should make them surrender...'

But Carrie did not want to think any more on the matter, so she changed the subject. 'I was so sad for Mimi this afternoon. Seeing her old home in such a state must have broken her little heart.'

Jacopo had already told her that the house had belonged to Mimi's grandparents. Unfortunately, they were part of the group of Jews rounded up in November 1943 and sent to Auschwitz. Mimi had no surviving relatives so, theoretically, the property should be hers. Jacopo was making sure her rights would be protected.

Vito took Carrie's hand, lifted it to his lips, then made direct eye contact with her. 'What do you think about Mimi's wish that we could be her new parents?'

A warm glow spread through Carrie. 'I would like nothing better, honey. But how would that be possible?'

'I'll look into it. Papà is a lawyer, he'll help us, I'm sure.'

Carrie squeezed Vito's fingers. 'That would be great. In the meantime, I'm glad she has a loving, stable home.'

'And I'm glad I've got you,' he said.

After Vito had eaten the lion's share of a massive T-bone steak, he paid the check – he insisted – and walked Carrie back to her hotel.

They kissed for a long time on the bed before making love. True love, Carrie thought as they were locked together. They fell asleep in each other's arms and, in the morning, made love again.

Saying goodbye at the train station tore at Carrie's heart.

'I'll see you soon,' Vito said. 'Take care, *amore mio*.'

A kiss on the lips. A tight hug.

She sat by the window in the train compartment she was sharing with a group of GIs and waved until she could no longer see Vito waving back at her. It took all her self-control not to break down in tears. She was a lieutenant in the Army, she reminded herself, and needed to behave accordingly.

But damn her aching heart.

30

Two weeks later, much to Carrie's surprise, she and the unit were back in Tuscany.

'I so wish we'd been shipped back to the States,' Louise said, when the hospital convoy arrived in Montecatini.

'Yeah, me too,' Carrie replied dejectedly.

Eight days after returning to Udine from Florence, she'd learnt that the 56th would become a Pacific Theatre reserve unit and they'd been ordered to leave for the Montecatini Redeployment and Training Area. Carrie's only consolation was that the spa town was situated about twenty miles north-west of Florence. Maybe she'd be able to apply for a pass and visit Vito, Mimi and his parents while she was here? After a short period of training covering aspects of Pacific and jungle warfare, the unit was to prepare for departure, though, so she doubted that would be possible. She'd probably end up having to say goodbye over the telephone. The prospect filled her with sadness.

Her ten days at Montecatini flew by. There were lectures, physical tests, and educational films on how to treat tropical diseases like lymphatic filariasis and dengue fever. She barely had a minute to herself. At least she was quartered in a good hotel. It was nice to have electricity, running water, and fully equipped toilets and bathrooms rather than be living in a field. From what she could see, the town had been mainly untouched by the war. Shame there wasn't time to enjoy the luxurious bathing establishments, parks and gardens. Even worse, no passes were being issued to anyone.

Then, suddenly, everything changed. It was announced that the United States had dropped atomic bombs on the Japanese cities of Hiroshima and Nagasaki. Two days later, Emperor Hirohito submitted a declaration of surrender to the Allies, and President Truman relayed the news to the American people.

Carrie and Louise hugged each other with joy. The invasion would not, after all, take place. American soldiers would not be obliged to run up the beaches near Tokyo, assault-firing while being mortared and shelled. They wouldn't need doctors and nurses to take care of them when they were injured or even dying. Many young men would have the future they wouldn't otherwise have had. As for the victims of the atomic bombs – which, by all accounts, had been massive in number – Carrie felt devastated for them, of course she did, and she hoped that such awful weapons would never need to be used ever again. War was horrific and it was always innocent civilians who suffered most. Of that she was 100 per cent sure.

She and her friends waited for official confirmation that the 56th wouldn't be redeployed to the Pacific. It didn't take long to arrive; they could enjoy the facilities of Montecatini while they waited to be sent home.

Nightly dances were organised. Movies and plays were put on daily in the four theatres. The American Red Cross Club provided a tailoring shop, as well as reading and game rooms, and a bar. Hospital personnel enjoyed the relaxing sulphur baths in Montecatini Terme's famous establishments, and passes were issued to the Tuscan seaside resort of Forte Dei Marmi, but all Carrie wanted to do was apply for another period of leave in Florence. She'd missed the chance to attend Ezio and Stella's wedding, which had taken place the week before and had coincided with her birthday. She didn't want to miss anything else.

She was going back to the States soon, she knew she was, but she felt a burning need to spend as much time with Vito and Mimi as she could beforehand. At least her departure wouldn't be forever. She would return, she was determined. Much as she loved her parents and sister, her life in Dallas was in the past. A new future beckoned, hopefully as Mimi's new mom, she prayed, and then as a fully qualified doctor. Was it too much to ask for? She sure hoped not.

* * *

In mid-September, Carrie was on leave in Florence and was making the most of her last few days. Orders finally came through for the nurses to depart from Naples on the SS *Vulcania*, a former Italian luxury liner, the following week. They would sail to New York and from there go to a staging camp in Boston.

It was Vito's twenty-first birthday – a big family celebration would be held in the evening – and she walked with him and Mimi to the little girl's elementary school in the city centre. It was her first day; she'd been too young to attend before she'd left Florence to go into hiding with the nuns. She looked so cute in her blue *grembiule* with wide white collar and red bows – a smock worn by all Italian schoolkids to protect their clothes.

'I can go in by myself,' Mimi insisted confidently when they were outside the gated entrance to a tall building.

Carrie bent to kiss her on the cheek. 'I'm so proud of you,

pumpkin,' she said, eyeing the courtyard inside, where there was a playground for the kids.

Mimi's attention had been distracted by the sight of Olivia, her friend from the convent.

'*Ciao*, Carrie and Vito,' Mimi said before running off. 'I'll see you later.'

'*Ciao*, Mimi.' Carrie smiled.

Jacopo had found out that she and Vito should have no trouble adopting Mimi once they were married. Carrie couldn't wait.

'Let's go grab a coffee,' Vito suggested, taking her hand. 'Then there's somewhere I'd like to show you.'

'Oh?' She inclined her head towards him.

'It's a surprise.'

They went to the Gilli and sat at an outside table under an awning. 'I'll sure miss this place...'

'You won't be gone for long,' Vito said.

They'd discussed what would happen so many times Carrie's head had spun. 'First, discharge from the Army.' She ticked off the list on her fingers. 'Next, I'll need to drop the bombshell on my family that I'll be moving to Italy if I get my funding.'

'You'll get it, Carrie, I'm sure.'

She leaned in for a kiss. 'Even if I don't, I'll be back.'

It was their backup plan. She'd work as a nurse in Florence until Vito graduated. Then he would support her while she studied medicine. Whatever happened, they'd tie the knot and then apply to the courts to adopt Mimi. It seemed too good to be true.

They drank down their coffees, paid the check, then Vito took Carrie's hand.

'Where are we going?' she asked.

'To see our future home.' A smile lit his eyes. 'I didn't take you before because it needed a fresh coat of paint.'

It only took about ten minutes for them to walk to Piazza Santa Croce. Behind the Basilica, Vito led her up a dark little street, under the high walls of centuries-old buildings with iron grilles over their ground-floor windows. The sidewalk was so narrow, Carrie feared she'd topple sideways, or fall into one of the basement workshops, whose doors – the only apparent source of air – seemed to be permanently open. She clung onto Vito's arm, and he tucked her into his side.

He took a gigantic brass key from his pocket and unlocked the entrance door to a four-storey palazzo. 'The apartment is at the top,' he said, as they started to climb the stone staircase that led off a pleasant patio filled with potted red geraniums, aromatic lavender and rosemary plants.

It was a good thing she was physically fit, Carrie thought as they reached the final landing. She stood catching her breath.

Vito produced another key and they stepped inside.

'Oh, my goodness!' Carrie gasped. 'It's beautiful.'

And it was. The door opened onto a big, bright living area with high ceilings. She rushed across the hardwood floor to gaze at the view from one of the two windows flooding light into the lovely room. Across the terracotta rooftops, Giotto's tower rose above the cathedral next to the octagonal shape of Brunelleschi's dome.

'I love it,' she said.

'There's more.' Vito's smile reflected his pride.

A small kitchen also boasted fabulous views towards the distant Apennines. 'Come,' Vito said, taking her hand again.

He led her into a single bedroom, as luminous as the rest of the apartment, with a shower room just next to it. 'For Mimi,' he said, smiling.

'It's perfect for her.' Carrie gazed through the window at Santa Croce below. 'And she'll be able to ride her bike down there in the square every day.'

They went into the master bedroom. Carrie took in the view of the Arno and the Ponte Vecchio. 'Wow!'

'There's a big bath as well.' He winked.

She laughed and he laughed with her, and it occurred to her that she was no longer worried about the future. Her heart beat with confidence. She could make her plans and feel positive those plans would work out.

'Oh, Vito,' she said, 'this is just wonderful.'

'Not quite wonderful yet, but I'd like to make it so.'

'What do you mean?'

He dropped to his knee.

'I want to propose properly,' he said, taking a diamond solitaire ring from his pocket. 'Will you marry me, darling Carrie? I promise I'll love you to the end of my days.'

In a heartbeat, she was on her knees before him, kissing him, tears of joy streaming down her cheeks. 'Of course I'll marry you, darling Vito.'

'You've made this the best birthday of my life.' He slid the ring onto her finger and kissed her passionately.

She returned his passion, giving him her heart, her soul, her everything.

'I love you so much, Vito. I'll never stop loving you for as long as I live.'

EPILOGUE
MIMI, SPRING 1946

I'm standing at the entrance of the Santa Croce Basilica next to Nonno, Nonna and Anna. I run a hand down the white silk of my bridesmaid dress and clutch a posy of pink roses with the other. Vito is already inside the building, waiting by the altar with Ezio. Carrie is due to arrive any minute now and I'm so excited I'm like a bottle of fizzy orange about to pop.

A silver car pulls up and Nonno rushes to open the back door. Carrie is sitting next to her daddy, who has come all the way from Dallas with her mamma and her sister, Helen. They are in the car behind and Helen will be what Carrie calls her 'maid of honour'.

Carrie is helped out of the car by her daddy, who will 'give her away'. It seems strange to me that she's being 'given' to Vito. But life is strange, Carrie once said to me, and I know that to be true. When I found out that I'd inherited Mammina and Babbo's house, I said I didn't want it. But Nonno told me the law was that I had to accept it, and now it will be sold and the money held in trust for me for when I'm grown up. It might be useful as I'd like to be an artist like Mammina, and artists don't earn a lot of money until they become famous. Which I will be one day, I hope.

Carrie comes towards me on her daddy's arm and she looks so beautiful with her trailing white veil that a big lump forms in my throat. I swallow it down and go to stand behind her. I missed her so much when she had to go back to America with the Army. She didn't return to Florence until after the New Year, and she has been improving her Italian like crazy ever since – with my help – so she can go to the university and study medicine. I think she'll be a fantastic doctor – she took such good care of me when I was wounded.

Inside the church we all make a procession down the aisle, Carrie and her daddy in front, Helen and me behind. An organ is playing nice music, and I smile at the congregation as we pass. There's Stella and Signor Bianconini with his wife. I give them a wave. Also Carrie's friends, Louise and Theo, who have come specially from America. They were married at the end of last year, and Carrie whispered to me that Louise is expecting a baby in the autumn. I don't know how she knows that a stork will bring one then, but Carrie is so smart I guess she has a way of finding out.

We get to the altar, where the scent of incense fills the air. Carrie gives me her bouquet of white roses, and I go to sit with Nonno, Nonna and Anna in the front pew. This is the first time I've been to a wedding, and I wonder if a Jewish one would be so very different. Anna once asked me if I wanted to carry on being brought up in the faith I was born into, and I said that I wanted to learn about it and also learn about what she believed. For her to become a nun she must really love God. I'm still too young to make up my mind one way or the other, even though I've turned seven. For now, I'm happy I don't have nightmares any more about what happened to Mammina and Babbo. It took me a long time to tell anyone about my bad dreams – I didn't want them to worry – but one night I screamed so loud Carrie and Vito rushed into my bedroom to find out what was wrong. They took me to see a special doctor after that and it helped to talk about my worries.

I sit and listen to readings and prayers and then Vito and Carrie are exchanging rings in front of the priest, and then they kiss and it's as though I can feel their happiness. I decide that I like weddings. I like them very much.

Carrie and Vito start to walk down the aisle. I follow behind alongside Helen and we step out into bright sunshine. The rest of the guests come out of the church and start throwing rice at the newlyweds. Nonna hands me a packet and I join in, laughing. We stand on the steps of the Basilica while photos are taken, and a sudden feeling washes over me. I realise that it's love. Love for Carrie and Vito, love for Nonno, Nonna and Anna, love for my friends. I sense Mammina and Babbo are here with us, somehow, giving us their blessing. What happened to them was a tragedy, everyone says. War is a tragedy. But all I can think about is how glad I am to be looking forward to the future. Not to be an orphan any more.

Now that Carrie and Vito are married, they will adopt me. I'll call them Mamma and Papi, we decided together. I've already moved into their apartment and I'm so happy there.

With a huge smile on my face, I scoop up a handful of rice from the ground and throw it up into the air.

AUTHOR'S NOTE

I was inspired to write *The Tuscan Orphan* when a friend told me about how his parents met for the first time in Italy when his mother was with the American Army Nurse Corps.

Carrie and Vito, however, are entirely fictional characters as well as Ezio, although the events they experienced all took place. My two partisans and their comrades are inspired by the brave men and women of Florence who fought to free their city from oppression. I read *La Resistenza a Firenze* by Carlo Francovich for research into this tragic period of history.

Mimi is also fictional, as are Anna and the San Ruffillo convent. Likewise, Vito's parents.

I placed Carrie with the 56th Evacuation Hospital after reading the fascinating memoir *Remembering World War II* by Lieutenant Elizabeth Janet Sutheit – who was an officer with the 56th during the Allied Italian campaign – and *They Called Them Angels, American Military Nurses of World War II* by Kathi Jackson. I also read *GI Nightingales: The Army Nurse Corps in World War II*, by Barbara Brooks Tomblin.

Bill is loosely inspired by Paul A. Kennedy, the author of

Battlefield Surgeon: Life and Death on the Front Lines of World War II.

Noemi is inspired by the Florentine Resistance fighter, Tina Lorenzoni. Adamo is loosely based on Luigi Morandi, a Radio Co-Ra operator. Bianca is inspired by Gilda Larocca, Enrico Bocci's bookkeeper who became a *stafetta* and took messages between the Radio Co-Ra operators and the Allied mission. Stella is based on Tosca Bucarelli, who carried out the failed operation in the Paskowski Bar and was subsequently cruelly tortured by Mario Carità. The infamous torturer himself is a person in the public domain, a war criminal who died as described in my story, although I've used artistic licence to include Vito and Ezio in his demise.

This is entirely a work of fiction and a romance. Any errors or inventions will be mine.

Florence is a place I know and love. I was privileged to have spent part of my gap year there on an Italian language course and loved to stroll through the city while absorbing its unique atmosphere. I made Florentine friends whom I shall never forget and have been back several times over the years to reacquaint myself with the Ponte Vecchio, the museums and the breathtaking views. Tuscany is such a beautiful part of Italy, rich in history and art, and I plan to set my next novel there as well.

ACKNOWLEDGMENTS

I would like to thank the entire team at Boldwood Books for their help and encouragement in the publication of *The Tuscan Orphan*, in particular my lovely editor Emily Yau, whose advice has made this a better book, I'm sure.

Thank you, Allison Buck, for help with Americanisms and American Army background.

Thank you, Joy Wood and Nico Maeckelberghe, for beta reading the book as I wrote it and for giving me pointers on nursing details.

Special thanks to JH, for his input.

Last, but not least, I'd like to thank my husband, Victor, for his love and support as I write my novels.

ABOUT THE AUTHOR

Siobhan Daiko writes powerful and sweeping historical fiction set in Italy during the second World War, with strong women at its heart. She now lives near Venice, having been a teacher in Wales for many years.

Sign up to Siobhan Daiko's mailing list for news, competitions and updates on future books.

Visit Siobhan's website: www.siobhandaiko.org

Follow Siobhan on social media here:

facebook.com/siobhan.daiko.author
twitter.com/siobhandaiko
instagram.com/siobhandaiko_books

Letters from
the past

Discover page-turning
historical novels from
your favourite authors
and be transported
back in time

Join our book club
Facebook group

https://bit.ly/SixpenceGroup

Sign up to our
newsletter

https://bit.ly/LettersFrom
PastNews

Boldwood

Boldwood Books is an award-winning fiction publishing company seeking out the best stories from around the world.

Find out more at www.boldwoodbooks.com

Join our reader community for brilliant books, competitions and offers!

Follow us
@BoldwoodBooks
@TheBoldBookClub

Sign up to our weekly deals newsletter

https://bit.ly/BoldwoodBNewsletter